What they're saying about Robert Gandt's books. . .

More thrilling than a back-to-back showing of Top Gun *and* Iron Eagle, *this red-hot piece of military fiction is certain to keep readers riveted. . . some of the most suspenseful battle scenes in recent military fiction.*
—PUBLISHERS WEEKLY

Robert Gandt is a former Pan Am pilot who also happens to have the pen of a poet.
—CHRISTIAN SCIENCE MONITOR

Gandt is a rare treasure, a Navy jet jock with the rare gift of being able to tell a compelling story in a believable and exciting manner that leaves the reader exhausted at the end.
—PACIFIC FLYER

Written in a wonderful bold style, with pathos, humor, tragedy, and gripping suspense . . .
—STEPHEN COONTS

Gandt has a way with words that will send the reader soaring.
—NEWS CHIEF

Former navy pilot and military historian Gandt is a first-rate storyteller.
—PUBLISHERS WEEKLY

THE
PRESIDENT'S
PILOT

A Novel

Robert Gandt

THE PRESIDENT'S PILOT

Robert Gandt

Black Star Press
ISBN-13: 978-0615995434
ISBN-10: 0615995438

For Annie,

again and always

Also by Robert Gandt

Nonfiction

SEASON OF STORMS
The Siege of Hongkong, 1941

CHINA CLIPPER
The Age of the Great Flying Boats

SKYGODS
The Fall of Pan Am

BOGEYS AND BANDITS
The Making of a Fighter Pilot

FLY LOW, FLY FAST
Inside the Reno Air Races

INTREPID
The Epic Story of America's Most Famous Warship

THE TWILIGHT WARRIORS
*The Deadliest Naval Battle of WWII and the Men Who Fought
It*

Fiction

WITH HOSTILE INTENT

ACTS OF VENGEANCE

BLACK STAR

SHADOWS OF WAR

THE KILLING SKY

BLACK STAR RISING

Anyone who is capable of getting themselves made President should on no account be allowed to do the job.
— HENRY CLAY

Patriotism is the willingness to kill and be killed for trivial reasons.
— BERTRAND RUSSELL

CHAPTER ONE

Lyle T. Bethune, Vice President of the United States, swore under his breath. His orders couldn't have been more explicit. Under no circumstances—*none whatsoever*—was he to be disturbed here at the guest cottage.

It was Sunday morning. Bethune was tilted back in his padded leather recliner, halfway through a second Bloody Mary. A three-log fire crackled in the fireplace. The mellow sax of Sonny Rollins wafted from the wall speakers. Bethune was alone, with the exception of his executive administrative assistant, Ms. Sally Abruzzo, who was at his feet on the Tabriz carpet. Sally was in the process of unzipping Bethune's Calvin Klein relax-fit jeans.

And the goddamn phone was ringing.

Bethune shook his head. He couldn't believe this shit. It was the yellow phone on the corner of his desk, the secure, satellite-linked device which had no other function than to receive calls from the President of the United States.

Bethune listened to the phone ring. He would ignore it. He was indisposed. Taking a shower. Gone to church. Hell, it was Sunday.

Sally had his zipper undone. The phone continued to ring.

Bethune tried to think. It was almost ten o'clock in Washington, which made it—it took him a few seconds—five in the afternoon in Tehran. *Damn*. He knew why the phone was ringing.

He let it ring twice more. Abruptly he reached over Sally's head and punched the speaker button. "Good morning, Madame President. I was hoping you'd call."

He heard a muffled laugh from Sally.

The voice of President Libby Paulsen swelled from the speaker, crisp and clear, brimming with vitality. The same voice, Bethune remembered, that dazzled the delegates on the critical third night of the convention and clinched her nomination. *Their* nomination.

The President was calling to update Bethune on the summit meeting in Tehran. It was going well even though Iranian president Sadeq Hosseini, beady-eyed dissembler that he was, was playing games. He'd just called a recess to confer with his ministers.

"What's to confer about?" said Bethune. "All he's got to do is sign the agreement and start cashing in."

"Not this guy," said the President. "It's some kind of honor thing. He has to impress his ministers by haggling over every detail."

Bethune wasn't surprised. The President had gone to Tehran with the most generous proposal ever offered to the Islamic Republic of Iran. The most generous part would be the lifting of the long-standing trade sanctions against Iran. All the Iranians had to do in exchange was formally renounce its support for Islamic Jihad and the Taliban and, while they were at it, acknowledge the right of Israel to exist as a nation. That was all. No requirement to forswear nuclear weapons development. No agreement to turn over their stash of weapons-grade enriched uranium. Like the treaty recently negotiated with North Korea, the Iranian accord was based on little more than trust.

And as Bethune had predicted, the conservative media in the U.S. were going crazy. "Selling Out to the Devil" screamed the headline in yesterday's *New York Post*. Libby Paulsen was being reviled on Fox and every conservative talk show. Her approval rating had dived five more points, deeper than G.W. Bush's worst numbers.

The President asked if Bethune had caught Senator Stroud's comments on "Meet the Press."

Bethune didn't have an immediate answer. Sally Abruzzo had gone fishing inside his Jockey shorts.

"Stroud?" Bethune's voice was cracking. "Oh, him. Don't worry. When the Iranian accord is a done deal, Stroud will just look like another reactionary windbag."

Which sounded good, but Bethune didn't believe it. Senator Kent Stroud was the chairman of the Senate Committee on Foreign Relations. The deal with Iran was guaranteed to send Stroud and the neo-nut coalition into a teeth-gnashing frenzy.

The President was saying something about getting the Iranian agreement ratified by the Senate. Bethune had to force himself to listen. He was looking at the top of Sally's head. The breeze from the overhead fan was playing with her blonde hair. Bethune caught the scent of her perfume, a subtle, musky fragrance.

He met Sally three weeks after the inauguration. It was a staff party, and there was no mistaking that look in her eye. She was fun and sexy, not the brightest bulb on the tree, but smart enough to be discreet. Bethune knew that she lived in Georgetown, had a husband who did something over at Treasury, no kids. He didn't want to know more.

Bethune made frequent use of the guest cottage. It was inside the perimeter of the Naval Observatory and was patrolled by uniformed Secret Service agents. A team of plainclothes agents stayed just outside the door. If they were curious about what Bethune and his executive administrative assistant did here on Sunday mornings, it never showed in their unchanging expressions.

"Lyle?" It was the President's voice on the speakerphone. "Are you still there?"

He was, barely. Sally was applying herself with new energy. "Oh, sure, I'm still here."

This was a game with Sally. She liked to do it while he was on the line with someone—cabinet secretary, ambassador, Congressman. Even the President. *Especially* the President. Bethune thought it was a little kinky, but what the hell. It got his mind off the problems this administration confronted.

Problems like Iran. Like North Korea. Or problems like Senator Stroud and the right wingers who were trying to bring the

President down. One of them, a media mogul named Casper Reckson, was running daily op-eds calling for the removal of the President. Not impeachment or resignation. Removal. No one seemed to care that the reckless bastard was talking sedition.

Bethune tried to follow what the President was saying. Something about the Iranians coming back from the recess. Bethune wished they would hurry the hell up. Sally had him aroused to an explosive state.

Something caught his eye. A movement in his peripheral vision. Bethune peered over his left shoulder. Against the dark-paneled wall of the study, he glimpsed a blurry object that didn't belong.

The object looked very much like a pistol. It was in the hand of someone he vaguely recognized. In his erotic stupor, Bethune struggled to understand what it meant. It took him exactly one-and-one-half seconds.

"No, don't!" he said, but it was too late.

<>

"Lyle?"

No answer.

"Lyle?"

Nothing. A low hiss from the handset. Then a click.

Libby Paulsen stared at the silent telephone. The mobile secure phone—the communications specialists called it the SatMaster—was a new gadget they'd brought on this trip. It was a portable device that piggy-backed off the communications array aboard Air Force One.

Libby frowned. Something wasn't right. She could still hear Bethune's voice. *No, don't.* He had sounded agitated. Not at all the laid back Lyle Bethune whose Kansas-twangy preacher's voice could restore order to a bar brawl.

Then something else. A dull popping sound, and another, like wine bottles being uncorked. Or like . . .

Couldn't be. She told herself not to jump to conclusions. There was an explanation. Lyle often sounded distracted during their phone conversations, and she had a good idea why. The same old Bethune distraction. How many times had she heard those guttural sounds while he was on the phone? She knew he was getting it on in the middle of a phone conversation.

But that was Lyle Bethune. She had known about Bethune's proclivities before they were paired up on the national ticket. At the convention, Bethune had promised that if he and Libby were nominated he would forswear the temptations of the flesh, which Libby took to mean that he would be careful not to get caught.

Lyle Bethune had been the choice of the national committee for the number two spot. While the inexperienced Libby Paulsen had star power, the ticket needed balancing with an old Senate hand like Bethune. Bethune had the connections to get things done in Washington. He would be Libby's advisor, mentor, and behind-the-scenes big brother. Bethune's presence would reassure voters that the country wasn't being run off the rails by an uncredentialed novice.

More important, it reassured Libby Paulsen. Lyle Bethune was her anchor.

Libby glanced around. She was in a thickly carpeted anteroom adjoining the main conference chamber in Hosseini's presidential palace. At the far end of the room, the White House communications team had set up their consoles. A team of six Air Force technicians monitored links to the White House, the Pentagon, and to the glistening blue-and-white Boeing 747-200B parked six miles away at the old Mehrabad airport. Any security alert or national emergency would be flashed directly to the console here in the palace.

Standing by the door of the chamber was Jill Maitlin, senior White House advisor. Maitlin was talking to her Iranian counterpart, a glum-looking man named Al-Bashir, over whom she towered by nearly a foot.

Jill detached herself from the Iranian and walked over to Libby.

"What did you say to that guy?" said Libby. "He looks like he swallowed a roach."

"I asked him when his guys were going to stop dicking around and come back to the meeting."

"And he said?"

"Very soon."

"That's what he said half an hour ago."

"It's his job to say that. What he means is that Hosseini is clueless about how to deal with the infidel American woman."

"How much longer will he be clueless?"

"Five minutes. Ten at the most."

She was wrong. In the next moment the door to the conference chamber swung open. Standing in the doorway was President Hosseini, surrounded by his six ministers. They were all smiling.

Libby smiled back. *Here we go.* For better or worse, she was about to make a deal with the devil.

<>

Nothing was making sense.

They were dragging him along a path, steering him by his elbows. He could hear the crunching of their shoes on the loose gravel. He was blindfolded, mouth sealed with duct tape, wrists tie-wrapped behind him. His heart was beating wildly.

Why had they grabbed him?

Because somebody made a huge fucking mistake, that's why. They'd grabbed him on the dirt path in Rock Creek park. He was four miles into his Sunday run, making a good eight minute mile pace, Black Eyed Peas rocking on his iPod. He barely noticed the runner coming the other way. As they passed, the guy slammed into him, knocking him into the bushes. Before he could yell or fight back or ask what the sonofabitch was doing, it was too late. There were two more. Within seconds they had him gagged and trussed like a chicken.

He'd gotten a glimpse of their faces. They could have been cops. Short hair, grim expressions, impenetrable shades. But no badges, no Miranda speech, no questions.

Now they were taking him somewhere.

They had the wrong guy, and he would tell them as soon as they took the tape off his mouth. There was no reason he'd be on anyone's hit list. He had no enemies and few friends. Except for jogging against red lights, he was a law-abiding conformist. He was so boring his wife had begun calling him Mister Bland. And she didn't mean it as a compliment.

They stuffed him into some kind of van. The ride took about twenty minutes. They made him sit on the floor, legs in a lotus position. He heard the faint crackle of voices on a radio. With the blindfold wrapped over his ears, he couldn't make out what was being said.

They unloaded him from the van and herded him along the path. The toe of one of his Reeboks caught in the loose gravel and he stumbled. The two men at his elbows kept him upright, yanking him along like a tethered animal.

They stepped onto a hard surface, maybe a tiled porch or patio. They shoved him forward. He sensed that he was crossing a doorway, entering an enclosed room.

He possessed an acute sense of smell—one of the perks of being a clean-living runner. There was something familiar in the room, a fragrance he recognized. And something else. Something unpleasant. His mind was still processing these sensory inputs when they snatched away the blindfold.

"Take a look around, Tom."

Oh, shit. They knew his name. They hadn't grabbed the wrong guy.

His eyes were adjusting to the artificial light. For the first time he got a good look at the men who brought him here. Two wore dark slacks and white oxford shirts with loosened neckties. The other was in a running outfit with a stripe down the trousers. The guy who'd slammed into him in the park.

He was in a dark-paneled room. His eyes scanned one wall, saw shelves of books, a couple of pewter sculptures, a compact hi-fi.

The adjoining wall had a curtained window and a framed painting that looked like the skeleton of a chicken. The familiar scent was still in his nostrils, faint but recognizable.

It was coming to him where he'd last smelled that fragrance. At home, this morning. It was lingering over his wife's dresser after she'd left for her Sunday outing with the girls from the office. It was called L'Embrace. Sally's favorite fragrance.

Take a look around, Tom.

He saw her. She lay face down, but he knew the shape of that derriere. He'd seen it a thousand times in his own bedroom. He knew the long legs, the blonde hair that was splayed like corn silk against the carpet. A dark pool of blood spread beneath her.

There was a man in the chair facing her. His face was familiar to everyone in America. His knees were apart. His trousers were undone, and he was exposed. He was dead, judging by the glazed-over eyes and the purplish hole in his forehead.

A wave of revulsion swept over Tom Abruzzo. He whirled to the men who had brought him here. He tried to yell but nothing came out. The tape was still over his mouth.

"Sorry about that, Tom."

The men in oxford shirts were holding semiautomatic pistols. Each wore the same unpitying expression. Tom Abruzzo heard the *ploom* at the same instant the bullet struck his chest.

CHAPTER TWO

"What's he doing now?" said Morganti.

Lt. Col. Lou Batchelder peered down from the left side window of the Boeing cockpit. On the ramp below he could see a man in a blue U.S. Air Force uniform. He was talking to an Iranian military officer. Half a dozen more uniformed Iranians, all wearing battle dress utilities, were clustered behind the officer. The officer was waving his arms, pointing to the large metal hangar at the far end of the ramp. The American was shaking his head negatively.

"Looks like he's arguing with the Iranian officer," said Batchelder.

"Figures. Pete Brand would argue with Mother Theresa."

"That guy doesn't look like Mother Theresa. He looks like Godzilla in a uniform."

"Brand is making waves. We'll be lucky if the Iranians don't kick us out of here."

Batchelder kept his silence. In the U.S. Air Force, badmouthing your boss when he was out of the cockpit was a bad idea. It was an especially bad idea in the Presidential Airlift Squadron. It was a fast track to early retirement.

But Morganti had a point. Brand was definitely making waves. The Iranian general was red-faced, railing at Brand, stomping the concrete with his black boots. Brand kept shaking his head.

Batchelder turned to Morganti, sitting in the right seat of the Boeing. "What's between you and Brand? Why are you so down on the guy?"

"He's trouble. Always has been. You tell me, how the hell did someone like Brand get to be the Presidential Pilot?"

Batchelder didn't have an answer to that one. But he had a

good idea why Morganti didn't have a warm feeling about Pete Brand. Everyone had assumed that Col. Joe Morganti would be the next Presidential Pilot when Al Crawford, the outgoing boss, got his general's star and left for a Pentagon job. That was the way the system worked. A senior pilot in the Presidential Airlift Squadron moved up to the job of squadron commander, which carried with it the title of Presidential Pilot. Morganti had been in the unit nearly four years and was next in line. He had more time in Air Force One than any pilot in the squadron.

It didn't happen. To everyone's astonishment, the job went to an outsider. Pete Brand came from the Special Ops branch of the Air Force. Spec Ops units flew to places like Mogadishu and Bagram and Baghdad. They were as removed from the sanitized opulence of Air Force One as Somalia was from Washington.

How did a guy like that get to be the Presidential Pilot? Good question, thought Batchelder. Someday he'd ask Brand himself.

He looked outside again. The Iranians were stalking away. Brand was no longer in sight.

"What's happening now?" said Morganti.

"The Iranian is getting into his vehicle. He looks pissed."

"Good. He'll complain to his boss, who will pass it on to the President. Maybe she'll be smart enough to get rid of Brand."

Batchelder said nothing.

A minute later, he saw Col. Pete Brand's wiry frame entering the aft compartment of the cockpit. Brand removed his uniform coat and loosened his tie. He settled into the jump seat behind Batchelder.

Morganti said, "Who was that guy you were arguing with?"

"The base commander."

"What did you do to piss him off?"

Batchelder watched Brand's reaction. Morganti was pushing the limit of disrespect. Copilots didn't use that tone with the aircraft commander, even if the two were the same rank.

Brand didn't seem to notice. He said, "He was ordering us to move the aircraft into the hangar."

"And why did you not agree?"

"I had a hunch."

"A hunch?" Morganti made a show of rolling his eyeballs. "About what?"

"A hunch that something might happen. I want to stay out here on the ramp, just in case."

"In case of what?

"In case we have to leave in a hurry."

Morganti shook his head. "I can't believe this. The President comes to make peace with Iran, and you try to start a war because of . . . a hunch."

Brand removed the sunglasses. For a long moment he locked gazes with Morganti. "The only thing you need to believe, Colonel Morganti, is that I'm the Presidential Pilot. You're the second-in-command. It's my call, not yours."

A silence fell over the cockpit. *Here it comes,* thought Batchelder. It had been building for two days. These guys were going to have it out right here in the cockpit.

But they didn't. In the next moment, a Secret Service agent appeared in the back of the cockpit. He was wearing a gray suit with a coiled wire from inside his jacket to his earbud.

"Colonel Brand? We just got a Code Yellow from our command post. Something happened that you need to know about."

<>

President Libby Paulsen took a sip of the thick Iranian coffee and winced. *Ugghh.* Ghastly stuff, strong enough to peel paint.

They were seated at the long mahogany conference table, Libby and her team on one side, Hosseini flanked by his ministers on the other. He had just finished a rambling discourse in Farsi. Now the interpreter was speaking. The people of Iran were willing to forgive the United States' long and shameful record of oppressing the Islamic Republic of Iran. A new page in history was about to be turned.

Libby kept her expression neutral. *A new page in history.* Amazing. A new page in history could be turned with just a few billion oil dollars.

Libby met Hosseini's gaze across the table. He smiled. She smiled back. *Like old friends.* The right wingers back home already hated her. After today, they'd be burning her in effigy.

She felt a nudge at her elbow. She looked up to see Gus Gritti, her National Security Advisor. Gritti was a Marine four-star and a Middle East specialist.

"What is it, Gus? We're in the middle of—"

"A Code Yellow," said Gritti. He leaned over and whispered in her ear. "The Vice President."

Libby stared at him. It took a moment, then she remembered. The popping wine corks on the telephone. The hissing silence, then the click.

"Something has happened to Lyle."

Gritti nodded. "The Secret Service detail at the Naval Observatory is reporting that he's been shot to death, along with one of his staff."

Libby felt her heart hammering in her chest. Her suspicion had been correct. She could hear Bethune's voice on the phone. *No, don't.* She had been an aural witness to an assassination.

She looked across the table. The interpreter had finished speaking. Hosseini was watching her, a quizzical look on his face.

She turned to Gritti. "Who did it?"

"A man named Abruzzo. The Secret Service agents killed him just after the assassination. They think he's the husband of the woman who was with the Vice President."

Libby closed her eyes. *Oh, bloody hell.* She didn't want to think about how this was going to play in the press. Even worse, she didn't want to think about doing this job without Lyle Bethune. Without her anchor.

She looked around the table again. They were close to a deal. There were still details to work out, most having to do with the lifting of sanctions. It was going to be controversial. It would be worth it if it brought an end to state-sponsored terrorism. Other countries would follow Iran's example.

"I have to go on with the conference," said Libby.

"Madame President, I strongly advise you to forget the conference."

"We almost have an agreement."

"We don't know the extent of the crisis. Another country could be involved. Maybe Iran. The Code Yellow indicates that we should execute Angel Swoop."

Libby stared at Gritti. Angel Swoop was the presidential emergency egress plan. In the event of a threat to the executive branch of government, the President was supposed to be whisked to safety aboard Air Force One. No President had been extracted in an Angel Swoop operation since 11 September, 2001.

For several seconds she considered. Hosseini and his ministers were watching her. Libby wrestled with her feelings. *What should I do? What would Lyle Bethune do?* They were so close. Was the killing of the Vice President sufficient reason to walk away from an accord that would change history?

Gritti thought so. Whoever sent the Code Yellow thought so. There was too much that they didn't know. *Damn, damn, damn.*

She glanced at Jill Maitlin, sitting at her right. She caught Jill's nod.

"Okay," Libby said to Gritti. "We're leaving."

<>

General Vance McDivott was cool, but it had nothing to do with the temperature. The thermostat in the Joint Chiefs situation room was pegged at sixty-eight Fahrenheit. McDivott's reputation for coolness dated back to his stints as a squadron commander in the first Gulf War, a wing commander in Iraq, and an Expeditionary Force Commander in Afghanistan. McDivott's cool demeanor had carried him all the way to the second-highest slot in the U.S. military. He was the Vice Chairman of the Joint Chiefs.

McDivott was scanning the array of six-foot high plasma screens that covered one wall of the windowless room. With him was Jim Ripley, an Air Force two-star and a Deputy Vice Chief of Staff. Unlike McDivott, Ripley was perspiring. He kept mopping at his brow with a handkerchief.

"Where's Bouncer?" McDivott asked.

Ripley pointed to a green dot on one of the screens. "There. His chopper is just cranking up to leave VMI. He wants to talk to you."

McDivott squinted at the screen. Bouncer was the call sign of Chuck Greeley, Army general and Chairman of the Joint Chiefs. Greeley was an alumnus of the Virginia Military Institute. He'd flown to the campus at Lexington, Virginia to address a military weapons symposium.

"Tell him I'll get back to him," said McDivott.

"I've already told him. Twice. You know Greeley."

"I know Greeley."

"He's asking why you executed Angel Swoop and DefCon Two without going through him. Or the Secretary of Defense. Or anyone else."

"He'll find out."

DefCon Two—Defense Condition Two—was the second-highest readiness status of the U.S. military. Following the assassination of the Vice President, every unit and installation had been placed on a ready-for-war posture. The concentric rings of air defense missile batteries around Washington were on high alert.

McDivott wasn't ready to explain to the Chairman why he'd given the orders. Not yet. In McDivott's opinion, Greeley belonged to a class of general officers who would embrace the politics of *any* administration—even one as loathsome and liberal as the Paulsen crowd—if it preserved their careers. Greeley was a poster boy for the President's touchy-feely, panty-hosed new military.

McDivott saw Ripley mopping at his brow again. He hoped Ripley wasn't cracking. Jim Ripley had seemed to be the ideal candidate when McDivott had inducted him into Capella. Now

McDivott wasn't so sure. He'd have to keep an eye on Ripley.

McDivott swung his gaze over to the opposite wall, to the framed portrait mounted over the console. *What would old Iron Pants do?* It was the question McDivott often asked himself at moments like this. The jowly visage of Gen. Curtis LeMay—Old Iron Pants—gazed back at him. LeMay was the cigar-chomping warrior who had presided over the aerial devastation of Japan. It was LeMay who built the Strategic Air Command into an overwhelming nuclear force. It was LeMay, then the Air Force chief of staff in the early 1960's, who clashed with the inexperienced President, John F. Kennedy, over the Cuban missile crisis. LeMay wanted to launch the Strategic Air Command against the Soviet-built missile sites. Kennedy rejected LeMay's counsel. He opted for a naval blockade of Cuba. The result was a compromise with the Soviet Union over the removal of the missiles. The communist regime of Cuba remained in place, ninety miles from the U. S.

LeMay swore that such a treasonable act would never be repeated. He began recruiting like-minded patriots to a secret society he called Capella. By the time LeMay was shoved into retirement in 1965, Capella included not only senior officers in every branch of the service but over thirty members of Congress, dozens of highly placed officials in the CIA, FBI, and Defense Department, and a cadre of spokesmen in the news media.

LeMay was Capella's guiding spirit until his death in 1990. The mantle was silently passed to another senior military officer. Then another, and another. The succession continued. The responsibility for carrying out LeMay's mission now rested with Gen. Vance McDivott.

McDivott turned back to the large screen in the center of the array. It was a scrollable map, zoomed in to the Middle East. A pulsing red dot lay over the airport in Tehran, Iran.

"Do they have the flight plan?"

"Not yet," said Ripley. "They'll get it half an hour out of Tehran.

We don't want to be going back and forth over details of the order."

McDivott watched the pulsing red dot that represented the President's jet. A thought kept nagging at his subconscious.

"Are we sure about the aircraft commander? It's Brand?"

"It's confirmed," said Ripley. "His first trip in command. Do you know him?"

McDivott nodded. He knew the sonofabitch, all right. "Brand worked for me during the U.N. relief operation in Sudan. He was the on-site airlift commander. On his own, without going through channels, he arrested a United Nations field commander."

"What the hell for?"

"He accused him of selling relief supplies to the rebels."

"Was he right?"

"It didn't matter. The commander was a French general. The U.N. responded by kicking all the U.S. forces out of the theatre. The whole goddamn airlift was canceled, and our ambassador had to make a formal apology to the frogs."

Ripley shook his head. "A maverick. How did a guy like that get to be the Presidential Pilot?"

"Good question," said McDivott. "We're going to find out."

CHAPTER THREE

Brand gazed out at the Mehrabad ramp. Heat waves were shimmering off the sections of concrete. Tufts of grass jutted through the relief cracks in the aging tarmac. In the backdrop Brand could see the white-capped Alborz mountain range, north of Tehran.

Brand's first hunch had been correct. Something did happen. A Code Yellow. The Vice President. But he knew there was more. Brand's inner voice was still talking to him. As he sat peering out at the Mehrabad ramp, he glanced at the digital clock on the instrument panel. He knew what was going to happen next.

It took four-and-a-half more minutes. The Secret Service agent was back in the cockpit. Same guy, same coiled wire to his earbud. He handed the printout to Brand.

Brand scanned the message. "Angel Swoop? That means we're out of here."

"Yes, sir. In a hurry." The agent's name was Evans. His usual station was at one of the communications consoles in the upper deck behind the cockpit. "Just in over the Purple net, and it's been authenticated."

"Where's Yankee?"

"On her way." Evans peered for a second at the tablet computer in his hand. "The motorcade will be here in five minutes."

Yankee was the call sign for the President. Brand looked at the printout again. He noticed the name at the bottom.

"Why does this have General McDivott's signature?"

Evans shrugged. "Sunday morning in D.C. McDivott's probably the senior service chief on duty. According to the playbook, the Angel Swoop order is supposed to come from the Vice President, but that's obviously not an option. Looks like McDivott's just cutting some red tape."

Brand nodded. The report about Bethune's assassination had arrived several minutes ago. No surprise that they were leaving Tehran ahead of schedule.

He handed the message to Morganti in the right seat. "They have us going to Mildenhall. Go ahead and load the flight plan." Mildenhall was an RAF base in southern England.

"Don't believe it," said Morganti. "Mildenhall's a bogus destination."

"How do you know?"

"I've been around long enough to know. They won't transmit the real destination until we're wheels up."

"Fine. Load the flight plan anyway. At least the FMS will have something on the screen."

Morganti scowled and turned his attention to the FMS—the flight management system console. He began inserting the waypoints of the new flight plan.

For the next few minutes the cockpit was quiet. At the flight engineer station behind the copilot, Chief Master Sergeant Roy Switzer was setting up his panel for engine start. Lt. Col. Lou Batchelder, the third pilot, was in the jump seat behind Brand. Switzer's relief flight engineer, Chief Master Sergeant Bruce DeWitt, had gone down to the electronics bay in the lower nose compartment to check out a bad UHF radio.

Brand gazed around the airport ramp. The two C-17 support aircraft were parked a hundred yards from Air Force One. The four-engine transports hauled the President's limo, four Humvees, and a company of U.S. Army Rangers.

Tehran had been a security nightmare. The Iranian military was responsible for clearing the streets along the route from the airport to the presidential palace. Secret Service agents and Army Rangers were deployed on rooftops along the route, but they depended on the Iranians to screen for hidden explosive devices. Or suicide bombers concealed in doorways. Or snipers peering through slatted windows.

Brand could hear the clicking of Morganti's fingers on the FMS keyboard. Morganti was right, he thought. They weren't going to Mildenhall. But England was as far west as they could fly with the fuel on board. Taking on more fuel in Tehran was out of the question. Jet fuel was like food and water. Too easy to contaminate.

But Air Force One's range was not limited by its fuel load. Unlike all the civilian versions, this Boeing 747 could refuel in flight. Air Force One could rendezvous with tanker aircraft and stay airborne indefinitely.

He wondered again about Morganti. The copilot was still hunched over the FMS console, inserting the flight plan. Morganti was like a hundred such officers Brand had known in the Air Force. Good airmen. They were competent, by-the-book, hardnosed, and risk-averse. Protective of their turf. The kind the Air Force selected for squadron and air wing command. The kind that resented outsiders like Pete Brand taking their jobs.

Which was sufficient reason for a guy like Morganti to have hard feelings about Brand. But Morganti's attitude went beyond hard feelings. The man had a monumental chip on his shoulder. It was a problem that Brand knew he would have to confront. A personality clash in the cockpit was a calamity waiting to happen.

"Here they come," said Batchelder.

Brand turned to peer out the side window. The President's motorcade was coming through the outer security perimeter, turning onto the tarmac. In the lead was an unmarked Humvee. No flags, no insignia. Then a black panel truck, which Brand knew contained a dozen Secret Service agents with communications gear and weapons. The truck was followed by two Russian-built Iranian military vehicles bristling with machine guns. Then came the President's black, armored limousine. It was trailed by another Humvee and four more Iranian vehicles.

The motorcade sped through the protective ring of Iranian

armored vehicles that encircled Air Force One. A dozen Rangers spilled from the Humvees to form a cordon at the foot of the mobile stairs. The President's limo pulled to a stop. A pair of Secret Service agents positioned themselves at either side of the passenger door. One opened the door.

Evans had already briefed Brand on the departure protocol. It was going to be a get-out-of-Dodge operation. No ceremony, no farewell speech, no banter with the media. Most of the reporters who accompanied the President would be left at the palace after her abrupt exit. They would be pissed.

The President stepped onto the tarmac. She paused, blinking in the harsh sunlight. She was wearing a loose-fitting, gray pant suit, purposely tailored, Brand assumed, not to offend Islamic sensibilities. Her trademark leather satchel hung over her shoulder.

She stood gazing around the ramp. The two Secret Service agents flanking her didn't look happy. Their heads were swiveling, faces showing their tenseness. She removed her sunglasses and peered up at the cockpit. For a long moment she met Brand's gaze. She looked worried, Brand thought. Abruptly she wheeled and headed for the boarding ladder. She moved with long, purposeful strides, one hand clutching the leather satchel.

Brand watched until she was gone from his view. *She hasn't changed.* Still a good looking woman, even in the frumpy outfit. Same long-legged, flouncy stride. The walk of a woman always in a hurry to get somewhere. He recognized that intent, gray-eyed gaze. He'd seen it before.

<>

That goddamned McDivott.

General Chuck Greeley gnawed on his unlit cigar and glowered down at the Virginia countryside. What was McDivott up to? Nearly an hour had passed since the assassination of the Vice President. Every attempt Greeley made to contact McDivott, who was supposed to be his deputy in the Pentagon command center, received the same reply. He'll get back to you.

Then McDivott issued the Angel Swoop order—and DefCon Two—without clearing it with anyone. The sonofabitch had overstepped his authority by a country mile. There was going to be a rearrangement of chairs in the Joint Chiefs this week. Greeley would see to it.

"What the hell?" said Tom Zuckerman, the Army colonel who served as Greeley's aide. Like most armored cavalry officers, Zuckerman distrusted helicopters. Even choppers as plush as this UH-60 Black Hawk, which was the Chairman's personal mount.

"Now what?" said Greeley. The way things were going this morning, nothing surprised him.

"The Purple net," said Zuckerman. "It's off line." Zuckerman was sitting at the communications console. The Black Hawk carried a comm package nearly as sophisticated as the array in Greeley's Pentagon office. Seated next to Zuckerman was a communications specialist who could access every wireless and satellite link in the U.S. military spectrum.

But it wasn't working. Zuckerman and the specialist kept poking at their keyboards, staring at the blank screens before them. "I can't believe this shit," said Zuckerman. "Nothing."

"Use the cell phone."

"I did. No one's picking up."

Greeley shook his head in frustration. This was what happened when you put your faith in all this high tech crap. One little electronic spasm and the commander was out of the loop. Well, he'd be back in the loop in—he did a quick calculation—fifteen minutes. That was when he'd get some straight answers from McDivott.

It had been an error in judgment naming McDivott to the Vice Chairman's job. It went against all Greeley's instincts. He'd yielded to pressure from Stroud, the senator who could make or break Greeley's own career. Greeley caved in and submitted McDivott's name to the President, who was not a McDivott fan either but wanted to placate the right wingers in the Senate.

Big mistake.

Despite being the same rank, Greeley and McDivott were so dissimilar they might have come from opposite planets. At Congressional appearances Greeley came off looking like a rumpled uncle in uniform. McDivott, by contrast, had sleek gray hair and the chiseled features of a film star. Greeley was famous for his mangled syntax and convoluted sentences. McDivott could mesmerize an audience with his messianic voice and his warnings about America's invisible enemies. Vance McDivott, insiders liked to joke, had you spellbound or had you scared shitless.

Well, Greeley wasn't scared shitless of McDivott. Firing the sonofabitch would take only a brief word with the President, with whom Greeley had a good rapport. McDivott would be history.

Or maybe he wouldn't. Greeley had a feeling that Vance McDivott wouldn't leave the stage quietly. Greeley had heard rumors. McDivott was connected with an extreme right wing movement called Capella. Capella was reputed to have members in every branch of government and in each military service. It was Greeley, not McDivott, who was the outsider.

Through the cabin insulation Greeley could feel the metallic whine of the Black Hawk's turbine engines. The chopper was rocking in the heat waves from the farmland below. Greeley guessed they were at about three thousand feet.

He shifted the cigar to the corner of his mouth. During his last physical at Walter Reed, the surgeon told him he got more nicotine from gnawing than when he smoked. Screw the surgeon. Greeley was the senior officer in the entire goddamn U.S. military. He'd gnaw anything he wanted.

The patchwork of farmland was yielding to a suburban sprawl. Somewhere down there were the air defense rings that surrounded Washington. The outer ring had a thirty mile radius, the inner five. No aircraft could cross the outer ring without air traffic control clearance. Now that they'd gone to DefCon Two, no one could penetrate the inner ring without specific authorization from the Pentagon. Greeley wondered if the pilots were having the same communications troubles that—

What was that?

Something on the ground. Something that didn't belong .

Greeley had been a soldier for thirty-four years. He'd seen it before. A few times in Iraq, once in Afghanistan, but those were combat zones. This was the Commonwealth of Virginia in the United States of America. He wasn't supposed to see such a thing here.

He blinked. It was still there. It was no longer on the ground. Greeley knew exactly what he was seeing now.

So did the pilot of the Black Hawk. Greeley felt the helicopter bank hard to the left, descending with a stomach-heaving lurch. He had to cling to the sides of his seat to keep from being flung across the cabin.

Greeley kept his eyes on the object. It was climbing, zigzagging like a crazed bat, trailing a plume of fire.

Chuck Greeley's life condensed into a single flashpoint in time. He stared at the object. What he saw was a Hawk surface-to-air missile. Swelling in size. No longer zigzagging.

The helicopter lurched hard back to the right. Greeley lost sight of the missile. He saw an arc of chaff and flares spewing in the helicopter's wake. It was their last—and only—defense against a supersonic air defense missile. Greeley tried to remember whether the Hawk was an infrared or radar-guided weapon. It didn't matter. He had seen enough live firepower demonstrations to know what would happen next.

When the impact came, it was above him, in the power plant section of the aircraft. The engines absorbed the shuddering explosion of the warhead.

He glimpsed Zuckerman's face across the cabin. The former tank commander wore an expression of pure disbelief. He'd been correct in his distrust of helicopters.

Time slowed to a crawl. The destruction of the Black Hawk seemed to be playing out in slow motion. Greeley felt the dull *whump* of the fuel tanks detonating.

Damn it, he thought. He was supposed to die from cholesterol and cigars. Not this. It was his last thought before the world dissolved in an orange blur.

<>

They closed the main cabin door.

In her office in the forward cabin, Libby Paulsen heard the first engine starting. The low whine resonated through the airframe. Then the second engine. While the third was still spinning up, she felt the jet begin to roll across the ramp. The crew wasn't wasting time. Fewer than five minutes had elapsed since she arrived with the motorcade. She had changed from the ugly business costume to the tailored blue jump suit she preferred when she was aboard Air Force One.

"How are the Iranians?" Libby asked.

"They're cool," said Jill Maitlin. She was in the settee facing Libby's desk. "They raised hell about being wanded and frisked by the Secret Service, but when they saw that everyone was getting the same treatment, they calmed down."

Libby nodded. Inviting the Iranian foreign minister, Mahmoud Said, and Hosseini's chief of staff, Kamil Al-Bashir, to fly back to Washington on Air Force One had been Jill Maitlin's idea. The idea met a storm of resistance from Gus Gritti, and even more flak from Mike Grossman, the chief of the Secret Service detail. They didn't have any data on the Iranians. There wasn't time to run checks on them. For all anyone knew, they could be planted terrorists. Grossman said he would assign an agent in the cabin to watch the two Iranians. Just in case.

Libby didn't care. This was too good an opportunity to pass up. The Iranians were authorized by Hosseini himself to continue the negotiations. With luck, they might even have a deal by the time Air Force One landed in Washington. Libby was already thinking about the press conference where she and the Iranians would stand together, treaty in hand. It would be a single item of good news in an unbelievably horrific day.

"It may seem a little early," said Jill, "but have you given any thought to nominating a new Vice President?"

Libby stared at her. "*New* Vice President? I still have to figure out how I'm going to eulogize the old one."

"No problem. He gets a state funeral. Flag-draped casket, dirge music, horse-drawn caisson. Lots of pomp and ceremony."

"That's the easy part. I have to give a speech. What do I say about him?"

"The usual stuff. What a great American Lyle Bethune was. What a terrible loss to the nation this has been. And, oh, yeah, what lousy luck it was to get shot while getting a blow job."

Libby groaned. "The Christian Coalition will go crazy."

"They're already crazy."

"Good point. You write the speech."

"Sure thing. What's a senior advisor for?"

Libby shook her head. That was Jill Maitlin. Nothing fazed her, not even an assassination.

Jill Maitlin had been with Libby since her first year in Congress. Jill kept a placard on her desk that read *Take No Shit*. It was her motto and her style. Jill had come up in the rough and tumble arena of Washington politics. She'd worked as a staffer in Speaker Fred Atwater's office before moving across the river to the national party office. She was still there on the national staff when she spotted the newly-elected Representative Libby Paulsen as a rising star. Jill Maitlin signed on as one of the early members of the Paulsen team.

It was a successful mix of talents. Libby brought brains and charm to the office, Jill the toughness. When Libby needed backing up, as she often did, she turned to Jill Maitlin. As a team they had gone on to the Senate, then the White House.

Number four engine was whining to life. Libby leaned back and peered out the cabin window. She saw the Iranian armored vehicles escorting them to the runway. For a moment she felt the anxiety build up in her. Were the Iranians crazy enough to attack Air Force One on the ground in Iran? She pushed the thought away. They might be crazy, but they weren't stupid. They understood the utter devastation that would rain down on them if anything happened to the U.S. President in their country.

Air Force One reached the end of the taxiway. Without stopping it trundled onto the runway. Libby was reaching for her coffee cup when a man's voice came over the bulkhead-mounted speaker. "Good evening from the cockpit."

Libby knew the voice. A soft baritone with a Midwestern flatness.

"This is your pilot, Colonel Pete Brand. On behalf of the President of the United States, welcome aboard Air Force One. We have been cleared for takeoff from the Mehrabad International Airport. Would you please check that your seat belts are fastened."

Libby could see the face that went with the voice. Long, straight nose, chin that jutted like the prow of a boat. Intensely blue eyes that could fix on you like lasers. Not a movie star face, but certifiably handsome.

She was checking her seat belt, just as the man said—and then caught herself. Damn it, she was President of the United States. She commanded entire armies and navies and air forces. She didn't have to take orders from that sonofabitch Pete Brand.

CHAPTER FOUR

"Iranians?" asked McDivott.

Ripley nodded. Air Force One's passenger manifest was displayed on his computer screen. "Al-Bashir and Said. They weren't on the inbound manifest. Probably officials from Hosseini's government."

"Why are they on Air Force One?"

"You know Paulsen. Sucking up to the ragheads."

McDivott shook his head. He knew Paulsen. Sucking up to the ragheads was the essence of her foreign policy. He turned back to the sixty-inch plasma screen on the wall. In the middle of the North Atlantic display the two pulsing yellow symbols were nearly joined. The in-flight refueling would be finished in fifteen minutes.

Ripley had been opposed to using the static fuel. Removing the President was one thing. Downing an Air Force airplane with everyone aboard was another. If the world ever learned that they'd ordered the transfer of the CAFEM-301 to the President's airplane, they could all be tried as assassins.

McDivott dismissed Ripley's objections. Even if they later found traces of the CAFEM-301, it wouldn't prove anything. The substance was carried in small amounts on most Air Force aircraft. It was a catalytically altered jet fuel that was so inert you couldn't light it with a blow torch. It was supposed to be injected into the *empty* tanks of combat aircraft so they wouldn't explode if they took a hit. The chemists who invented CAFEM-301 hadn't anticipated that it might be fed to the engines of Air Force One one night over the North Atlantic.

McDivott continued to stare at the symbols on the situational display. In the pulsing pattern of the symbols, he saw something emerging. An opportunity. He stared at the display another full minute. And it came to him.

McDivott almost laughed. There it was, like a gift. A gift from Allah.

He turned back to Ripley's computer screen. Ripley still had the names highlighted: *Al-Bashir* and *Said.*

McDivott pointed at the names. "They're the ones."

Ripley looked up. "Excuse me?"

"The Iranians on Air Force One."

Ripley stared, still not getting it. "I don't follow what you—"

"Terrorists, General Ripley. The ones responsible for the death of the President."

<>

"Visual on the tanker," called out Morganti.

Brand looked up from the display panel. Through the windshield he saw the navigation lights and the gray shape of the KC-135 refueling ship. It was a militarized version of the old Boeing 707. The tanker was barely visible against the darkness of the western sky.

One of the rules of Angel Swoop was that the in-flight refueling of Air Force One would be conducted in radio silence. The only communication between tanker and receiver would be with light signals.

"Autopilot coming off." Brand pressed the red disconnect button on the yoke.

They were sliding up behind the tanker. Brand could see the refueling boom extending like a stinger from the tanker's tail cone. Near the end of the boom were the two vanes which the boom operator moved to steer the boom to the receptacle in Air Force One's nose.

This was the tricky part. Brand had to place the 747 directly behind and beneath the tanker. He would maintain that position— no wobbling or oscillating—until the refueling was complete.

The long swept wings of the KC-135 filled up the windscreen. Brand saw the boom inching toward them, swaying slightly in the slipstream, seeking the opened refueling receptacle in the nose of the 747. The boom wobbled once, then went rigid. In the cockpit, they heard a *clunk*.

"Contact," said Morganti.

A few seconds passed. From the flight engineer's station Sergeant Switzer said, "Good connection. We have fuel transfer."

< >

Chief Master Sergeant Bruce DeWitt emerged from the lower avionics bay. He took the stairway to the second level—the main cabin area—then continued to the upper deck, which housed the cockpit and the communications compartment. DeWitt nodded to the Secret Service agent stationed in the passageway outside the cockpit, then he opened the door with his key.

The cockpit was dark, barely illuminated by dim red lighting. All eyes—those of the three pilots and Switzer, the senior flight engineer—were riveted on the object in the windshield. The gray mass of the KC-135 tanker.

Switzer glanced at DeWitt. "Did you find the problem?"

"I reset the UHF module. If that doesn't fix it, then we'll have to do without it."

Switzer shrugged and returned his attention to the refueling operation. The matter of one inoperative UHF—ultra high frequency—radio was insignificant. Air Force One had four of them, plus half a dozen radios of different wave lengths.

DeWitt knew that Switzer, being senior and an asshole, would have questions. He'd want to know why it took DeWitt fifteen minutes to reset the module, a procedure that required one button push. DeWitt had answers. He didn't care whether Switzer believed them or not. What happened next would be blamed on static electricity. Any evidence to the contrary would be covered up by a Capella team after they landed.

Or so they had promised.

It was taking all DeWitt's self control to hide his anxiety. As a Capella member he was duty bound to carry out this mission. But another side of him—the flight engineer whose unblemished twenty-four-year career had been rewarded with the assignment to the Presidential Airlift Squadron—was repulsed by what he was doing. Sabotaging the airplane you were trusted to protect was a violation of everything he believed.

I'm a patriot, DeWitt reminded himself. *I'll do what I have to do to remove the traitor from the White House.*

Still, he didn't like it. He would be glad when it was over.

"How much longer with the tanking?" Brand asked from the left seat.

"Almost there," answered Switzer. "Another twelve-thousand pounds."

DeWitt was surprised to see that Brand was doing the flying. A new aircraft commander usually turned over the refueling to an experienced pilot like Morganti. Especially a night operation. DeWitt could see Brand's hands making tiny movements with the yoke and throttles. He was keeping the 747 in precise position behind the tanker. The guy acted as if he knew what he was doing. Even Morganti seemed impressed. He kept glancing at Brand as if he was seeing something he hadn't noticed before.

Two minutes ticked past. "That's it," Switzer announced. "Eighty-eight thousand pounds, flow stopped."

"Signal the boomer to disengage," said Brand.

Morganti toggled the signal light. Seconds later, they heard the clunk of the mechanical toggles releasing the boom nozzle. The refueling boom retracted from its receptacle in the 747's nose.

And then it happened.

First a buzzing sound—*zzzzzttttttt*—rising in intensity like a gathering storm. Then a flash, followed by a *crack*. A blackness as dark as the night sky engulfed Air Force One.

<>

"What the hell happened?"

It was Morganti's voice. Brand couldn't see him in the darkness. Not even the flight instrument display was visible. He was blind, no outside reference.

"I don't know," said Brand. "Maybe a static discharge when we separated from the tanker."

He didn't believe it. There were too many safeguards against static discharge.

In the next moment, a beam of light fixed on the cluster of standby flight instruments on Brand's panel. It was coming from Switzer's flashlight behind him at the flight engineer's station.

"I see the flight instruments," said Brand. "Get the power restored."

"I'm working on it," said Switzer. Brand could hear him resetting circuit breakers, throwing switches on the electrical control panel.

Seconds later, the emergency cockpit lights flicked on. They provided just enough light to see the instrument panels.

"Look at this," said Morganti. He was punching the keyboard on his display screen. "The data link is gone, both sides. So are the GPS navigation displays. Hey, wait a minute—" He selected a radio on the audio panel, then keyed the transmitter. Then another. "The radios are out. Every damned one of them, dead as a stone."

"Can't be," said Switzer. He ran his hand over the circuit breaker panels. "Nothing is tripped back here."

Brand's mind was racing. With no radios and no satellite navigation, they were in trouble. *The tanker*, he thought. They had to stay joined with the tanker. The tanker was like a mother ship. All they had to do was stay in formation and the tanker could guide them to a safe base.

The tanker was gone.

Brand peered into the darkness ahead. He saw only the empty night sky.

Morganti was looking too. "Where's the tanker?"

Brand didn't answer. There was no way a big, lumbering KC-135 could move out of visual range in the space of two minutes. He couldn't be further than a mile or two away. His lights ought to be standing out like beacons in the sky.

Brand was hearing an inner warning. It was ringing in his subconscious like an alarm bell. The KC-135 was invisible because its lights were extinguished. There was only one reason for that. They didn't *want* to be visible.

Why?

Brand pushed the question to a corner of his mind. Forget the tanker. They had to get themselves out of this mess.

He glanced back at the flight engineer station. Switzer was still at his panel. DeWitt was behind him, wearing a frozen expression. "Sergeant DeWitt, get down to the avionics bay. See if you can get our radios back."

DeWitt stared as if he hadn't heard. Finally he mumbled, "I really don't think it'll . . ."

"Just fucking do it," snapped Switzer.

DeWitt blinked. He turned and opened the cockpit door. Then he lurched back into the cockpit as if he'd seen an apparition.

<>

Libby Paulsen stared at the sergeant.

He was staring back, eyes wide as Frisbees. The Commander-in-Chief was obviously the last thing he expected to see when he opened the cockpit door.

The sergeant called to the front of the cockpit, "Ah, sir . . . we have a visitor. It's the, uh. . ."

"President of the United States," Libby announced and brushed past the sergeant as she entered the cockpit.

She knew it was a breach of protocol. By tradition the President didn't visit the cockpit of Air Force One without being invited. But something was going on with the airplane. Something that was scaring her to death. She needed to hear it from Brand.

Brand didn't seem surprised. He was watching her from the left seat. "Come on in, Madame President." He motioned for her to take the jump seat that Batchelder had just evacuated as if he'd been ejected. Batchelder was quivering at attention behind

Morganti's seat. Morganti was flying the airplane.

Libby gripped the back of the jump seat. "What's going on, Colonel Brand? Do we have a problem?"

"Yes, ma'am. We've experienced an. . . electrical failure."

"What does that mean? Like a power outage?"

Brand nodded. "Something like that. We've restored the lights and essential electrical supply, but we've lost all our communications capability."

"I don't need a technical explanation. Are we in trouble or not?"

Libby saw the other men in the cockpit watching them. Their eyes flicked between her and Brand.

Brand said, "We'll have to divert. Go to an airport where we can get maintenance and re-establish communications." A moment's pause, then, "With your concurrence, of course."

Libby recognized the inflection in his voice. *With your concurrence, of course.* She guessed that was for the benefit of the others in the cockpit.

"Which airport?"

The crewmembers' eyes swung to Brand.

"I suggest Goose Bay." Brand held up a navigation chart. "It's here, on the northeast coast of Labrador."

"Hey, wait a minute," said Morganti. "You didn't ask me about that."

Libby kept her eyes on Brand. "Why Labrador?"

"The weather forecast is clear. And because there's a U.S. Air Force facility at Goose Bay."

She gave it a moment. "You're the pilot. You're sure that's our best option?"

Brand nodded. "I'm sure."

She saw Morganti's face harden. She could feel the hostility between him and Brand. What was that about? She'd find out later.

Libby turned to Brand. "What caused this electrical failure?"

Another moment's pause. The ice blue eyes were boring into

her. "We don't know yet."

Libby gnawed on her lip for a moment. This was one of those moments when she was supposed to remind everyone that she was the Commander-in-Chief and she expected a straight answer. But she didn't. She recognized the look in Brand's eyes. Something *was* going on. Libby felt another jolt of fear stab at her. First the news about Lyle Bethune. Then, after they left Tehran, the report that General Greeley was dead, killed in his helicopter. *What next?*

In the next three seconds she found out.

"Hey!" said Switzer. He was staring at the engine instruments on the forward panel. "Number one just flamed out."

Brand and Morganti swung back to the panel. "Igniters on," said Brand. "Run the check list."

Libby watched, holding her breath. *Why would an engine flame out?* Nothing was making sense.

"This is crazy," said Switzer. "Now we're losing number two."

Libby felt the airplane decelerating. The nose was yawing to the left. She had to grab the back of the jump seat to keep from falling. "What's going on?" she blurted. It came out like the cry of a frightened child.

No one answered. Brand took control of the airplane from Morganti. He was busy trying to straighten the jet's sickening sideways yaw. Switzer was throwing switches on his panel. DeWitt was standing behind him, an expression of disbelief frozen on his face.

The nose was slanting downward. Libby knew without being told that they were losing altitude. They had to, with half their engines no longer running. How far would they descend? Would they have to—

"Number three flaming out," said Brand. His voice was flat, without emotion.

A wave of raw fear surged through Libby's veins. Her fingers gouged the fabric of the jump seat. She felt her heart thumping like a jackhammer. As if in a dream, she heard the pilots reciting the check list. They sounded businesslike, talking in matter-of-fact voices. She knew it was an act. They were trained to speak that way, even when things were going to hell. She wanted to shout at them: *Do something, damn it. Get the engines restarted.*

The engines weren't restarting. Over Brand's shoulder she could see the digital altitude indicator. The numbers were ticking downward too fast for her to read. Red and amber lights were flashing on the center instrument panel. Some kind of aural warning was going off, warbling like a sick parrot.

A sense of inevitability swept over Libby. They were down to one engine. She had a sure sense of what was coming next.

It took ten more seconds.

"There goes number four," she heard Brand say in the same emotionless voice. "We've lost all four engines."

Libby felt the nose of Air Force One tilt further downward. Through the windshield she could see the black void of the Atlantic Ocean.

Libby didn't want to see any more. She stepped backwards, walking uphill on the tilted cockpit deck, past the flight engineer station, until she'd reached the aft bulkhead of the cabin. She sensed the presence of someone else. In the darkness she could make out the profile of the sergeant—the one named DeWitt—whom she'd encountered when she first entered the cockpit. He was breathing rapidly, muttering to himself. "The bastards," Libby heard him say. "They didn't tell me they'd do this."

Libby gripped his arm. "What are you talking about? Who didn't tell you? Tell you what?"

Suddenly aware of her presence, the sergeant stared at her in shock. He snapped out of his trance. And said nothing.

CHAPTER FIVE

*S*ilence.

In his years of flying, Brand had never heard this sound. No whine of turbines, no assuring engine rumble resonating through the airframe. Only the eerie whoosh of air flowing over the bulbous nose section of the Boeing 747. The magnificent four-engine transport had become a six-hundred-thousand-pound glider. Air Force One was in a death plunge to the ocean.

Brand glanced over at Morganti. The sour expression on the copilot's face was gone, replaced by a look of bewilderment. Behind them Switzer was still reading off the items of the engine restart checklist.

The digital altimeter was counting down. They were descending through 11,000 feet. Brand said to Morganti, "Tell the cabin to prepare for ditching." It was futile, he knew. Ditching Air Force One on a tossing sea in the blackness of night had a survivability chance of nearly zero.

"The interphone's not working," said Morganti. "The P. A.'s not working. Nothing's working on the audio panel."

Brand turned in his seat. He saw Sergeant DeWitt in the back of the cockpit looking bewildered. Standing next to him was the President of the United States, looking just as bewildered. "Sergeant DeWitt," Brand yelled, "the PA's not working. Get back and tell the cabin crew to prepare for ditching."

DeWitt didn't move. He stared back at Brand, his face etched with confusion.

"Go!" Brand ordered. "Get the passengers ready for ditching."

DeWitt blinked once, then a look of comprehension came over him. He whirled and left the cockpit.

Brand swung his attention back to the instrument panel. Through the windshield he saw only blackness. The relentless scrolling of the digital altimeter showed that the surface of the

Atlantic lay less than 10,000 feet away. Fewer than four minutes to impact.

"What the hell's going on?" said Switzer. He had the checklist in his hand. "What did we miss? Let's do the check list over again."

"Forget the check list," said Brand. Checklists were for standard, logical scenarios. There was nothing standard about this problem.

Brand switched his gaze to the blackness beyond the windshield. He forced himself to shut out the stream of check list items and procedures. *Think. What are we missing?* He let his mind drift. Sift through the possibilities.

What could cause all four engines to fail, one after the other? What was common to all the engines?

From somewhere deep in his subconscious, a thought was making its way to the surface. It came to him in a flash.

Fuel. The engines were okay until we took on the fuel from the tanker.

Brand snapped his attention back to the cockpit. *Why would fuel from the tanker be contaminated?* Another answer flashed into his mind. Just as quickly he shoved it aside. He had to deal with this problem first if he wanted to save the airplane.

Brand turned to Switzer. "Feed all engines from the center wing tank."

"Center wing tank?" said Switzer. "That doesn't make sense. Why would—"

"We didn't take any fuel from the tanker into the center tank, right?"

"Ah, yeah . . ."

"So the center tank fuel wouldn't have been contaminated."

"Contaminated?" Switzer's eyes widened as his brain processed this new possibility. "Oh, sweet Jesus . . ." The sergeant's hands went to the fuel control panel, opening valves, closing others. "Okay, all engines feeding from the center. Holy shit, this is getting crazy."

They waited. Each pair of eyes was glued to the standby analog engine data monitor. Seconds ticked past.

Nothing was happening. The exhaust gas temperature gauges, the first indication of an engine restarting, hadn't changed."

"It's not working," said Morganti. "So much for your great idea."

Brand said nothing. If his theory were correct, the fuel controllers would be receiving fuel from a fresh source. The engines *had* to relight. In theory.

They weren't relighting. Morganti was right. So much for his great idea.

"Three thousand feet," called out Morganti in a raspy voice. "This is it. We're going in the water."

Brand adjusted himself in the seat and fastened his shoulder harness. He had to switch his focus. Forget the non-starting engines and get ready to do what no one had ever done before. Ditch a loaded jumbo jet at night on the high seas.

Through the windshield Brand saw flecks of white. *Whitecaps.* They were close. Less than two minutes from the surface of the ocean. The radio altimeter, which would give them a precise height above the surface, was blanked out. Another casualty of the electrical outage. They had only the barometric altimeter, which Brand knew wasn't accurate enough to gauge their exact altitude. He could fly straight into the blackened ocean without leveling off. Or he might flare the Boeing a hundred feet too high, which would cause them to stall and plunge straight down. Either scenario was fatal. Even if he somehow timed it right and flared just above the tossing ocean, the airplane would shatter like an egg carton when it hit the water.

He heard something. From somewhere below, a low whine. Steadily increasing in pitch.

"Number one!" blurted Switzer. "I think . . . yeah, no shit, we're getting a relight on number one."

Brand was already easing back on the yoke, reducing airspeed to configure for ditching. Even with one engine running, they wouldn't be able to remain airborne for long. They had to have—

"Number two," called out Switzer. "Number two's spinning up."

Brand could feel it now, the soft rumble of the big fanjet engines accelerating. As number one spun to idle power he slid the throttle forward. With all the thrust coming from the left side, he had to step on the left rudder pedal to keep the jet straight

"Number three," said Switzer, and then a few seconds later, "and here comes four. We're getting them back."

As each engine came up to idle speed, Brand brought the respective throttle forward. He glanced at the altimeter. *Three hundred feet.* The whitecaps were clearly visible against the black surface of the Atlantic. The Boeing's descent had stopped. With all four throttles advanced, Brand nudged the yoke back. The jet's nose tilted upward.

Climbing. The whitecaps slipped from view in the windshield. Brand could make out the blue-black horizon line between the sea and the sky and, above, the twinkle of stars.

For nearly a minute the cockpit was quiet. All four engines were running. Brand didn't know for how long.

It was Morganti who broke the silence. "Does anyone know what the hell's going on?"

<>

Libby knew.

The knowledge had been growing inside her since they were on the ground in Tehran. Since she heard about the deaths of the vice president and the chairman of the joint chiefs. At first she attributed her suspicions to simple paranoia. She was overreacting to a sequence of untimely accidents. Then the engines of Air Force One failed, one after the other like cheap light bulbs. Libby knew.

But she didn't dare speak it. Not yet.

Paralyzed with fear, she had watched the drama in the cockpit as if she were a detached witness. She'd been right about Brand.

She knew nothing about the technical details of Air Force One, but she knew that Brand had somehow saved them from crashing into the ocean.

For now. Things were happening in a bewildering sequence. What was next?

Fresh in Libby's mind was the behavior of DeWitt, the flight engineer, when the engines flamed out. *The bastards. They didn't tell me they'd do this.* Libby didn't have a chance to press the sergeant about what he meant before Brand sent him to the cabin. She would tell Brand about it later.

If there *was* a later. Libby knew they were still in great danger. Brand was busy flying the airplane. In the dim light, she saw Switzer with a manual opened on his engineer's desk, his finger tracing a schematic drawing of one of the aircraft's systems. Switzer had managed to restore enough electrical power to illuminate a few emergency lights. Batchelder was in the jump seat directly behind Brand. Morganti, in the right seat, was wearing his same sour look.

Libby positioned herself behind the pilots' seats. "We're still in serious trouble, aren't we?" She could hear the querulousness in her voice.

Brand nodded. "Yes, we are."

"What are we going to do?"

"Land. Soon. We can only use the fuel that's in the center tank. Sergeant Switzer has just calculated that it will last for about an hour of flying time. Maybe a few minutes more. Maybe less."

"An hour? But we're over the middle of the Atlantic."

"The *North* Atlantic. Greenland is three hundred miles to the northwest. We'll land at a field at the southern tip of the island, a place called Narsarsuaq."

Land. For the first time since the emergency began, Libby let herself think about what could happen after they were on the ground. "And then what? After we land, what do you think we should—"

The cockpit door opened behind her. The bulky shape of Sergeant DeWitt entered the cockpit. He slid past her to take his station next to Switzer. The sergeant avoided eye contact with Libby.

"I have to talk with my staff," said Libby. "When you can spare a minute, Colonel Brand, I'd like you to meet us in the office."

Brand nodded. She caught the quizzical look on his face as she turned to exit the cockpit.

<>

The presidential suite was a conical-shaped compartment that filled the entire front nose section of the 747 below the cockpit deck. The suite had a bedroom, shower, lavatory, and, on the right side, an office with an angular desk and facing seats. On the right wall were windows. Libby liked the office aboard Air Force One. She found it cozy and efficient, without the ostentatious trappings of the Oval Office or the Cabinet Room in the White House.

The office was illuminated with only a thin row of receded emergency lights. Libby gazed across her desk at the people in her office. Jill Maitlin was perched on the arm of a chair, smoking a Dunhill. In the dim light, the glow of the cigarette reflected from her glasses. Jill never asked permission to smoke. Nor did she care whether anyone objected.

Seated in the chair facing Libby's desk was Gen. Gus Gritti, wearing a polo shirt and slacks. The chief of the Secret Service detail aboard Air Force One, Mike Grossman, stood in the corner next to Pete Brand.

"So what do we do after we arrive in Greenland?" Libby said. "What are our options?"

Jill Maitlin didn't wait for anyone else to speak. "When we're safely on the ground, we communicate with Washington. Then we wait for transportation back to the U. S."

Brand shook his head. "Sorry, but that happens to be the worst thing we can do. Once they know we're still alive, they'll do whatever they can to eliminate the President."

"They?" said Jill. "Who do you mean?"

"I mean whoever made two very sophisticated attempts to destroy Air Force One. You already have confirmation of the murders of the vice president and the chairman of the joint chiefs. Doesn't it seem likely that someone is trying to remove the President?"

Jill exhaled a cloud of smoke. "Are you suggesting some kind of conspiracy?"

Before Brand could answer, Gritti spoke up. "Colonel Brand may be right." The Marine general waved his hand to disperse the cigarette smoke. "This whole scenario has the feel of a coup attempt."

Libby nodded grimly. It was the same dark suspicion that had been swelling in her mind. "Put a name to it, General. You're the National Security Advisor. If you had to speculate, who do you think would be behind such a thing?"

Gritti ran his hand through his close-cropped gray hair. "There have always been rumors. For years I've heard about a secret, ultra-conservative clique within the military. They're supposedly patriots who have sworn to defend the U. S. against traitors within the government. Until today, I never considered such a thing to be a threat. Now I'm not so sure."

"We don't have any choice," said Jill. "Air Force One is damaged. We can't fly back on our own."

"Not necessarily," said Brand. "We're crippled, but still operational. On the ground we may be able to purge the main tanks, then take on uncontaminated fuel. Sergeant Switzer thinks he can restore enough electrical power to regain some of our basic flight instruments and systems controls. As far as communications, it may be best that we *not* emit any radio signals. Not until we're someplace safe and understand what's going on."

"What about the airport in Greenland?" said Grossman, the Secret Service team leader. "What's to keep the tower operators from sending the report that we've landed there?"

"There isn't any tower. Just a runway and a small contingent of workers to service transient airplanes. The field won't be manned unless they're expecting an inbound, which isn't likely this time of night. If you can deploy your security people as soon as we land to secure the radio facility, no messages will go out about our arrival. We can immobilize the radio facility, do the refueling, and be airborne again. If we're lucky, it won't take more than an hour."

"And then what?" asked Libby.

"We fly to North American airspace. We find out what's going on. You resume being president."

At this, Jill Maitlin stabbed a finger at Brand. "Resume? She never *ceased* to be president. Thank you for your opinion, Colonel, but national security matters are beyond your sphere of responsibility."

Gritti cleared his throat. "For the record, I think Colonel Brand may be right. Even if our suspicions are unfounded, we'd be doing the right thing by being prudent."

Grossman spoke up for the first time. "I concur. We don't know the extent of the danger. If we're wrong, we can apologize later."

Jill Maitlin crushed out her cigarette. She leaned over Libby's desk. "Madame President, sneaking back to the U. S. like that is just going to make you look like a weak and frightened chief executive, which is exactly what your enemies want."

Libby gnawed on her lower lip, saying nothing. What Jill didn't say was that it would make Libby look *even more* like a weak and frightened chief executive. Libby could feel the eyes of everyone in the room on her. Waiting for her to make a decision. That was the trouble with advisors. When they offered conflicting advice, what was she supposed to do?

She knew. *Decide.* Wasn't that why they elected her President? To make the hard call. She hated it.

She looked at Jill. Her arms were crossed in front of her. She looked exasperated. Both Grossman and Gritti were frowning.

Libby glanced at Brand. The blue eyes gazed back at her, telling her nothing.

Libby let out a long breath. "We'll do as Colonel Brand suggests." She turned to Gritti and Grossman. "Gentlemen, I'll count on you to make sure everyone aboard understands the game plan." Both men gave her a curt nod.

"Libby," said Jill, slipping into the familiar form they normally used only in private, "are you sure you about this?"

"I'm sure," Libby said, not feeling sure at all. She saw Brand heading for the door. "Oh, Colonel Brand, there's something else I wanted you to know."

Libby followed him to the doorway. In a low voice, so the others couldn't hear, Libby described the strange outburst of Sergeant DeWitt.

Brand's expression didn't change. "Did you ask him what he meant?"

"Yes. He wouldn't say."

"How did he behave?"

"Shocked. As if he were in a daze."

Brand showed no reaction. He nodded and headed for the stairway that led to the cockpit.

Libby stepped back into the office. Grossman and Gritti were gone. Jill was lighting another cigarette. Jill said, "Do you remember my telling you that appointing Brand was a bad idea?"

Libby had heard this before. "Does it matter that he just saved all our lives?"

"That's his job. Any of the dozen or so better qualified candidates you could have appointed would have done the same thing. Brand is trouble. You shouldn't be listening to him."

"Even if he's right?"

"He's not right. We should stay on the ground where we can be protected by the military."

"The same military that's been trying to kill us?"

"We don't know that for sure. This could just be the work of a few discontented Air Force officers."

Libby said nothing. She didn't believe it. But she knew something about Jill Maitlin. For all Jill's legendary toughness, she had a secret fear. She was afraid of flying. Jill abhorred airplanes and, by extension, people who flew them. People like Pete Brand. And that was her reason for wanting to remain on the ground.

Libby flopped back into her chair. Jill was right about Brand. He *was* trouble. But she was wrong about one thing. Libby hadn't appointed Brand to the post, at least not overtly. The candidates for Presidential Pilot were selected by a panel of senior Air Force officers, and the President merely gave her approval. Never would an officer like Pete Brand have made the list. Not without pressure from someone in high office.

Why Brand? Libby had her reasons. She would never share them with Jill Maitlin or anyone else. Libby closed her eyes, feeling the dull thrum of the jet engines resonating through her padded chair. She let her mind drift. To another place. Another time.

CHAPTER SIX

Republic of Guinea-Bissau

The explosions are coming closer. It has to be a bad dream, Libby thinks. No earthly way can this be happening. She wants to close her ears to the sounds.

Representative Libby Paulsen is still in her first term in Congress. She is part of a fact-finding mission to West Africa. And something has gone badly wrong. She is hunched in the corner of a Quonset hut with her arms wrapped around her knees.

"Are they dropping bombs?" Libby hears her voice quavering. She sounds like a spooked kid.

"Mortars, I think," says Jill Maitlin. She extracts another Dunhill and lights it, gushing a stream of smoke into the fetid air inside the hut. "We seem to be at ground zero in this little war."

Between explosions Libby hears staccato bursts from automatic weapons. The gunfire is coming closer too. Libby gazes around the hut. A single light bulb dangles from the ceiling, powered by the generator clattering outside the hut. With the exception of Jill Maitlin, the other members of the Congressional mission look just as terrified as she is. The U. S. Ambassador to Guinea-Bissau, the Honorable Herman J. Barkley, looks like a man who wants nothing so much as to get the hell back to New Jersey. It is no secret that Barkley, a wealthy African-American who made his fortune developing low-income housing in Newark, was a generous contributor to the President's campaign.

Huddled on the far side of the hut are the two State Department envoys assigned to the mission. Each is thirty-something, bespectacled, dressed in the same sweat-splotched safari outfits. They are trying to make calls on their cell phones. The phones aren't working.

It happened so suddenly. The trip to West Africa was supposed to be a good will visit to a little-visited part of the world. The six Congressional representatives and their aides have split up in Dakar. Each is headed off to visit a different republic on Africa's western shore. Libby had drawn the Republic of Guinea-Bissau.

A U. S. Air Force C-40B transport—the militarized version of the Boeing 737— has dropped them at the Osvaldo Vieira airport in Bissau where they are joined by Ambassador Barkley. After their tour of Guinea-Bissau, they are supposed to return to the embassy in the afternoon for briefings and a photo op, followed by a cocktail reception.

As they pile into the vans at the airport, Libby observes the Kalashnikov-carrying security troops climbing into their own van. They are wearing sneakers, ill-fitting fatigues, red berets. "Did I miss something?" she says to the ambassador. "Is there some reason we need those guards?"

"It's for show," Barkley says. "This is West Africa. They love the military stuff, the uniforms and guns." Barkley laughs in his deep baritone voice. "Trust me, this place is safer than Newark."

The tour is uneventful for the first three hours. They stop at an open market, then tour a rubber plantation. Libby is feeling the effects of jet lag, hoping the day would pass and they could return to Dakar.

The last stop is in the village of Bissora, in the northwest of the republic. They are watching a tribal group perform a native dance when the first explosion comes. In the space of a few seconds the dancers and musicians have vanished.

More blasts, seconds apart. The frame building across the unpaved road erupts in a mushroom of dirt and smoke.

Libby stares at the destroyed structure. Pieces are still raining down from the swirling dirt cloud. It has to be some kind of demonstration. Didn't Barkley say this place was safe?

Then she sees the ambassador's face. Barkley looks like he's been walloped with a mallet. "I don't understand," Barkley mutters. "This can't be happening."

Libby looks around her. A few seconds ago there were performers, smiling natives, vendors selling trinkets. Now they are alone. "Where are the security troops?" she asks.

In the next second her question is answered. A plume of dust erupts behind one of the Toyota vans. Stuffed with soldiers with red berets and Kalashnikovs, the van swerves onto the dirt road and rumbles out of sight.

From the nearby forest comes a long rattle of gunfire. Libby spots a dark-skinned figure running toward their remaining van. He looks familiar. "Hey!" yells Jill Maitlin. "That's our driver."

Libby and Jill run after him. He is a slender young man. His eyes are wide with fear. When he sees the women coming after him he puts on a fresh burst of speed.

They nearly catch him. The Toyota's wheels kick dirt in their faces as the van lurches onto the road back to Bissau.

"Asshole!" Jill Maitlin yells after the departing vehicle.

They hear the chatter of gunfire from the nearby forest. Then another explosion. Libby feels a ripple of fear pass through her. They are trapped in a war zone. And they are on their own.

<>

Two hours have passed. This damned Quonset hut is the best refuge they could find. The mortars are concentrating on the frame buildings along the unpaved street in the middle of Bissora.

Huddled inside the hut, Libby and Jill try their own cell phones. They don't work.

"Towers are shut down," says Libby.

"Or blown up," says Jill Maitlin.

Barkley keeps punching buttons on the GPS/transceiver they'd been issued back in Dakar. "This thing is a piece of crap. It's supposed to keep us in touch with the Air Force crew at the airport no matter where we are in the country. Guess what? Nobody's answering."

"Somebody has to know where we are," says Libby.

"They don't know anything," says Barkley. "All they were told was that we'd be somewhere in the northwest sector of the country this afternoon. We were supposed to keep them informed by cell phone."

Another explosion rattles the tin walls. The dangling light bulb sways and flickers, casting an undulating glow over the inside of the hut. It is just a matter of time, Libby thinks. Whoever wins this battle will come calling.

In the next instant, she hears it. A hammering on the door of the hut.

No one speaks. They stare at the metal door as if it were a portal to hell.

More hammering. Libby looks at her companions. They are hunkered against the far wall. Barkley's face is a frozen mask. The two State Department officers look like kids caught out after curfew. Only Jill Maitlin looks unafraid, but Libby knows it is a facade. Jill Maitlin's long, plain face seldom changes expression.

Then a voice. "Ms. Paulsen. Ambassador Barkley. Are you there?"

Libby rushes to the door, then stops. The voice sounded American, but she's learned that accents here in Africa are deceptive. What if . . .

She yanks the door open.

The image of the man in the doorway will remain seared into her memory for years to come. Olive green flight suit, blue Air Force service cap. Cold blue eyes, silver oak leaves on his shoulders. A holstered pistol. Ten feet behind him stands a mud-splattered truck.

"Please say you're going to get us out of here," says Libby.

The officer flashes a smile. "I'm going to try, Ma'am." Libby sees the eyes making a quick scan of the interior of the Quonset hut. "I'm Lt. Col. Brand. I'm the aircraft commander of the jet that is supposed to fly you back to Dakar."

"How many of you are there?"

"Two. Sergeant Rosak, my crew chief, is in the truck."

"How were you able you find us?"

"Your Mark 12 transceiver. It's been transmitting your GPS position. When you hadn't moved for an hour and we didn't hear from you, we knew you were in trouble."

Barkley is on his feet. The terrified expression is gone from his face. "Why did it take so long to get someone out here? We've been stuck out here for over two hours in the middle of a war."

Brand's eyes fix on the ambassador. "No one has heard from you since the cell phone towers went down. You haven't been transmitting or receiving on your satellite radio as you were expected to do." Brand spotted the Mark 12 transceiver lying on the dirt floor. He picked up the radio and examined it. "The transmit-receive key is still locked. Lucky for you, it sent your GPS position automatically. That's the only way we knew where you were."

Barkley glowers at the radio. "No one told me about a damned switch lock. We could have been killed because of that thing."

"You're not out of the woods," says Brand. "The rebels have the Bissau airport sealed off, and they're putting up roadblocks." He checks his watch. "Everyone needs to board the truck now."

While they climb into the truck, Libby takes another long glance at Brand. There is something about him. The curt manner with the officious ambassador. The way he directs them to board the truck. Definitely not one of the courteous, protocol-observing officers the Air Force usually assigns to Congressional missions.

Brand takes the wheel. The burly crew chief, Sergeant Rosak, climbs into the right seat. Libby and Barkley take the rear seats while the others clamber into the tarp-covered truck bed.

"Where'd this vehicle come from?" says Barkley. "This isn't one of the vans we hired for this trip."

"The vans you hired are gone," Brand says over his shoulder. "Along with the drivers. This truck belongs to the rebel commander who just took over the airport."

"He let you have it?" says Libby.

"Not exactly."

"You wanna know where the truck came from?" says Sergeant Rosak from the front seat. "Col. Brand swiped it right from under their nose. Don't be surprised if the rebel commander isn't real happy when we get to the airport."

Libby feels her fear returning. Through the windshield she can see long shadows playing over the red clay road as dusk settles over the country. The thick forest on either side of them conceals invisible danger.

As they come out of a turn beneath a canopy of overhanging trees, the danger becomes visible.

"Oh, shit," mutters Rosak.

There are four of them. One holds a Kalashnikov, the others machetes. They look like the troops assigned to guard them this morning, but these are even more ragtag. They wear tennis shoes and baseball caps. They have the road blocked with tree limbs and a piece of corrugated tin.

"Now what?" says Rosak.

"Keep your heads down," Brand orders over his shoulder. He keeps the truck rolling toward the blockade.

The soldier with the Kalashnikov stands in the middle of the road. He motions for the truck to stop. Brand waves as he slows the truck nearly to a stop. The soldier gets a look at the two flight-suited men in the front. A scowl spreads over his face.

"Americans!" he yells to the others. Brandishing the machetes, the soldiers converge on the stopped truck.

The soldier in charge is reaching for the truck door handle on the driver's side when Brand pops the clutch and stomps on the accelerator. The truck lurches, stalls, then lunges ahead. They crash into the roadblock. Tree limbs wrap around the front of the truck. Rosak ducks just in time to miss a spiked branch that punches through the windshield. The corrugated tin smacks the hood, then scrapes over the top of the cabin.

The truck is howling like a banshee, still in low gear. Branches are flapping like appendages from the front bumper and the hood. They roar down the red clay road. "Stay down!" yells Brand.

They hear the first burst from the Kalashnikov at the same instant the rounds zip through the truck cab. They pass over Brand and Rosak's ducked heads, blowing out what's left of the windshield. A second later the next burst smacks into the back of the truck.

Libby hears someone yell. It's one of the Foreign Service officers. "Oh my god, I've been shot!"

More rounds ping into the steel tailgate. She feels the truck swerve. She guesses that one of the tires had been hit. Brand keeps the truck on the road, shifting through the gears, opening up their distance from the shooter. They hear one last three-round burst, which misses them.

Libby leans over the back of the cabin. The State Department officer, the one named Fitzpatrick, is moaning and clutching his leg. Jill Maitlin had his trouser leg pulled up and is probing the wound. "He's okay, I think," she says. "The bullet was mostly spent after it came through the tailgate." A few seconds later she holds up the warped lead bullet, still blood-stained. She hands it to Fitzpatrick. "There's a trophy for you. Hell, in this administration that'll get you a promotion."

Libby feels an ominous whap-whap coming from beneath the rear of the truck.

"Uh, Colonel, I think we've got a flat tire."

"I'm a lieutenant colonel."

"I think it's the left rear."

"Call me Pete."

"Pete. What about the tire?"

"Not a good place to change tires. We'll just press on with the three good ones."

Which they do. The shredded rubber continues slapping against the fender for another couple miles before it departs the wheel. Sparks are flying from the tireless rim as they pull up to the Bissau airport. It is just after sundown.

The entrance is guarded by a dozen rebel soldiers. This time Brand stops. The soldiers are just as ragtag as the ones they encountered at the roadblock. Same tennis shoes, baseball caps, ragged fatigues. They seem to recognize Brand. They make a show of checking the IDs of each occupant. They search under the seats and beneath the chassis. While they are still checking the truck, a camo-painted Land Rover wheels up. A heavy-set, gray-headed African man in fatigues dismounts and storms over to Brand.

"That's the guy," says Rosak. "The rebel commander who took over the airport. This is his truck we swiped. He's gonna be pissed."

Rosak is right. The commander is pissed. He is yelling at Brand, pointing at the damaged vehicle, slapping his holstered pistol menacingly. Brand keeps shaking his head no.

The commander is still ranting when Libby comes around the front of the truck. "Excuse me, sir. I would like to thank you."

The commander turns to glower at her. His hand remains over the pistol. "Who are you?"

"I'm Congresswoman Libby Paulsen." She extends her hand. "And you, sir?"

His cheeks puff out. Tentatively, he takes her hand. "Colonel Raimundo Tchonga of the Guinea-Bissau Peoples Resistance." He nods toward Brand. "This man has committed a crime against—"

"On behalf of the President of the United States, I am here to thank you for offering the use of this truck."

"I did not offer—"

"By your actions you have saved the lives of a United States ambassador and a United States Congresswoman."

"The United States is not our friend."

"Oh, but it is." Libby isn't releasing the colonel's hand. She is giving him what she hopes is her most sincere expression. "When your people are in control of Guinea-Bissau, you can count on us for our support."

"What can you do?"

"I will speak to the President. He'll be pleased to hear what you've done for us here."

The colonel seems to ponder this. He looks at Brand, then the bullet-holed truck, then back at Libby. The almond eyes soften. He nods and makes a sweeping gesture in the direction of the airport ramp.

Minutes later, flanked by a squad of armed rebels, Libby and her fellow passengers are clambering up the boarding ladder of the blue-and-white Boeing jet with "United States of America" emblazoned on the fuselage. The cabin door clunks shut behind them. From her padded seat in the front of the cabin, Libby hears the comforting whine of the engines spinning to life. Not until she feels the nose tilting upward, lifting from the concrete runway, does Libby allow herself to relax.

The flight to Dakar takes twenty-five minutes. Enough time to reflect on what happened. A hell of a day. She was nearly killed. She shared the company of an inept ambassador, two State Department twits, and her tough-as-nails legislative aide.

And a maverick officer named Pete Brand.

Libby knows that she should be exhausted. Jet lag, the adrenaline surges of the afternoon, the tiresome chatter of Barkley and the State Department twits have left her feeling drained. By the time they land in Dakar and return to the hotel, she wants only to sleep.

But she doesn't. In the quiet of her hotel room, something is nagging at her. She has been saved from a terrible calamity in the village of Bissora. She should thank the person responsible for saving her.

Yes, that's the least she can do. With that thought, she picks up the phone to call Brand's room.

CHAPTER SEVEN

L ibby opened her eyes. She was alone in the Presidential office. Being alone was a rare condition in her life. Jill was gone, probably back to the cabin to brief the passengers on the Greenland landing. Libby thought that maybe she should go back too. Show them that she was in good spirits. Show them she was still in charge.

She didn't. Libby remained in the leather office chair. She closed her eyes again and let her mind return to Africa. With perfect clarity she could recall the events of that evening in Dakar. She could see the sun setting over the South Atlantic, the soft pink afterglow clinging to the horizon. She could still see Brand seated at the end of the hotel's beachside bar as she walked in.

He rises, flashing the same smile she'd seen back at the Quonset hut. For the first time she notices that Brand is a good-looking man. Out of uniform he seems taller, more slender. He's wearing a loose polo shirt, cargo shorts, andals. The military sternness has slipped from his face.

They order drinks. Vodka tonic for her, a local beer called La Gazelle for him. Libby feels the tension of the day slipping away from her. She touches her glass to Brand's. She says what she came here to say. "Thank you."

"Nothing to thank me for."

"You got us through the blockade."

"You got us past the rebel commander at the airport. That was impressive."

"I was terrified."

"Not that anyone could tell."

"In a previous life I was an actress," she says. "It's my single qualification to serve in Congress."

They order more drinks. They talk about politics, the Middle East, Congress, the Air Force. About themselves.

Brand is divorced, she learns. His wife hated Air Force life, the constant change of duty stations, subordinating her academic career to her husband's. Instead of accompanying Brand on a transfer to Germany, she accepted a professorship in the school of communication at Tufts. The divorce came a few months later. An amicable split. No kids, no recriminations.

Libby delivers the fairy tale version of her marriage. It's the version her office passes out to the media. Ken Paulsen, her husband, is a lawyer and lobbyist. Married twelve years, no children. They enjoy skiing and biking, take vacations in the Rockies. The magazine writers love them. They're a power couple in the Washington social scene.

She leaves out the rest. A House representative, at least one who wants to be reelected, never mentions that hers is a marriage in name only. Nor does she discuss her husband's multiple infidelities.

Clustered around a table at the other end of the thatched-roof bar are half a dozen members of the Congressional mission. Ambassador Barkley is holding forth about his role in their escape from Guinea-Bissau. The civil war has already sputtered to a stalemate. Each side is claiming to be in control of the country. Libby wonders whether the rebel colonel will invoke her name if the resistance movement takes over the country.

Standing at the bar are the two State Department envoys, clad in nearly identical shorts and tropical shirts. They're chatting up a pair of sunburned British girls. The one named Fitzpatrick is showing the girls his bullet wound from the afternoon's adventure.

Libby senses Jill Maitlin watching her from the group at Barkley's table. Libby recognizes that bird-like gaze. It conveys either intense interest or utter disapproval. With Jill it's hard to tell. Since joining Libby's staff as legislative aide, Jill Maitlin has assumed the roles of advisor, mother confessor, and chaperone.

Libby is surprised that she and Brand have so little—and yet so much—in common.   Her political orientation is to the left of Brand's, but not by as much as she expected. He is cut from a different mold than the conservative military officer corps she knows in Washington. He seems to have little interest in politics. Or else he's being diplomatic. Brand doesn't seem the diplomatic type.

She tells herself that she should leave. She's fulfilled her obligation. She's joined her rescuer for a drink, thanked him for his meritorious service, done her duty as a member of the House of Representatives. It's late and she's tired. The Congressional mission departs early in the morning on a commercial flight to the U. S. Time to leave.

She doesn't move. Instead, she hears herself say, "Another drink?"

"Sure," says Brand.

Libby sees the group at Barkley's table rising and heading for the dining room. As they file past the bar the ambassador gives her a wave. Libby waves back. She pretends not to notice the baleful glance from Jill Maitlin as the gangly woman follows the group out of the bar.

A four-man Senegalese band is playing at the far end of the bar. The State Department envoys are on the dance floor with the two giggling tourists.

Brand says, "That woman, the tall one—"

"Jill Maitlin. She's our legislative office chief of staff."

"She looks displeased."

"Jill thinks it's her job to protect me."

"Do you need protecting?"

"I don't know. Do I?"

He smiles. "No."

Libby almost came down in the slacks-and-shirt combo that Jill counseled her to wear on trips like this. "Don't show too much flesh," was Jill's advice. "I know these third world politicos. They think you've come here to entertain them."

As she was about to leave the room, Libby decided to hell with the advice. She changed into the sleeveless red-and-blue print dress, flats, no hose. The kind of outfit she'd wear on a summer evening in Georgetown. The thin fabric reveals just enough figure—and bare legs—without crossing the line of flashiness.

She likes the way Brand looks at her. Not ogling her legs or figure, but definitely noticing. He has a way of fixing those blue eyes on her when she speaks. She is accustomed to men trying to impress her with titles or money or connections. It's an unwritten rule that Washington bureaucrats and military officers have to chat up attractive Congresswomen. It's a requirement. Just enough suggestive patter to establish their alpha maleness.

Brand isn't doing any of that. He's polite, but not deferential. They are sitting on adjoining lounge chairs, his knee a few inches from hers. But he isn't making a play. Still, there's something about him. The way he nods when she talks about the tedium of Congressional committees. The way he smiles, saying nothing, when she tells him how shit-scared she'd been when they plowed through the roadblock.

A thought strikes Libby. For the first time since leaving Washington she feels relaxed. Too relaxed. Careful, girl. She knows it's the vodka and the jet lag and, most of all, the buzz from their close call in Bissora. Isn't it a cliché that rescued women feel an attraction to their rescuers?

She's done most of the talking, which is different. Congresswoman Libby Paulsen has the reputation of being a good listener. Her job, as she sees it, is to listen respectfully to her constituents, cantankerous and long-winded as some of them are. She's good at it. Too good sometimes. Jill Maitlin has to wade into crowds to extract Libby from her fans.

So why is she running her mouth like an adrenalized parrot? Because she trusts him? Because he makes her feel comfortable?

Or something else? Never mind, she tells herself. Jill Maitlin isn't there to shoot warning glances at her.

She asks questions. How long did Brand's marriage last?

"Five years, three months and a week. Give or take a day."

"Longer than mine."

"I thought you were married."

"I'm in a marriage. It looks better at election time."

He nods, not prying, swirling the beer in his glass. "Why did you run for congress?"

She doesn't answer right away. It's the same question she gets at talk shows and mag interviews. She usually answers, "I wanted to make a difference." *Or* "I thought I could do a better job than the incumbent." *When she was really laying it on she would say something like,* "I wanted to give something back to this great country."

"The truth?" *she says.*

"Any version you want."

"Power. The same reason all politicians run. Congress is a pure power trip. Isn't it the same in the military? You get to command a squadron or an air wing?"

"If you're a good politician."

"Are you a good politician?"

He laughs, and she notices again how the eyes crinkle and the dimple appears in his right cheek. "Zero political skills. Unelectable, unpromotable."

"I find that hard to believe after what I saw today."

"Stealing trucks doesn't get you promoted to general."

"Even if it saves the life of a congresswoman?"

"Only in the movies. Not in the real Air Force."

"What would you do if you weren't in the real Air Force?"

He pretends to think about it. "Something to match my skill sets. A truck driver maybe?" *He sips at his beer.* "And you? What would you do if you weren't in congress?"

"You mean when I'm not in congress. Voters get a chance to

fire me every two years. Then I go on to my next life."

He clinks his glass against hers. *"To our next lives."*

It has a strange resonance. Our next lives. *It makes no sense here on the shore of Africa, three thousand miles from home in a thatched-roof bar with a stranger to whom she owed her life. But she likes the sound of it.*

For a moment, Libby's imagination wanders. *As she often does, she fantasizes about being free. Not being in congress. Not living in a place like Washington. Not married to someone like Ken Paulsen.*

The bar has emptied. *The band is still playing, but the pair of State Department officers and the sunburned British girls have disappeared.* The white-jacketed Senegalese bartender is watching them expectantly.

Her drink is finished. *Brand empties his glass and sets it on the bar.*

"Thank you again," she says. *"Not just for saving my life. I had a nice evening."*

"Me too. Going to dinner?"

She shakes her head. *"It's been a long day."* She rises from the lounge chair. *"See me home?"*

They walk in silence through the lounge, past the entrance to the dining room, out to the lamp-lighted pathway that led to the upper tier rooms. *A watchful porter is stationed at the landing at the top of the path.* Libby leads, feeling self-conscious in the clinging summer dress, hearing the soft fall of Brand's footsteps behind her.

She stops at the door to her room. *As she fumbles with the key, it occurs to her that for someone with the reputation of being cool and poised, she's a klutz.* "Well, I'll say good night. Thank you again."

"You were a trooper."

Libby leans forward, gives his cheek a light kiss, then turns to fumble some more with the key. *She manages to get the door open and steps inside. When she turns, she sees that he is still there. As she'd hoped.*

Libby takes Brand's sleeve and draws him inside.

CHAPTER EIGHT

The cockpit was still dark. The only illumination came from the standby lights that Switzer had managed to restore. Brand entered, then quietly closed the door behind him. Batchelder was in the left seat assisting Morganti, who was navigating the 747 to their destination on the coast of Greenland. Switzer sat at the engineer's station with the aircraft systems manual spread out before him. With a flashlight he was studying a schematic of the failed electrical systems.

Sergeant DeWitt was standing behind Switzer. He glanced up at Brand, then returned his attention to Switzer's manuals.

Brand opened the storage bay on the aft bulkhead of the cockpit. He pulled out a leather flight bag. It bore the gold lettering *Aircraft Commander*. Shielding the bag with his body, he withdrew an object and tucked it into his belt. For a minute he stood in the darkened back of the cockpit sizing up DeWitt.

The sergeant was a couple inches taller than Brand, maybe thirty pounds heavier, but he looked soft. DeWitt had the thick waist and the jowly features of a man unaccustomed to exercise. Not the physique of a fighter.

Too late, DeWitt sensed danger. Brand seized the sergeant's lapel, yanking him off balance. Brand hauled DeWitt across the cockpit deck and slammed him into the back bulkhead. DeWitt was trying to wriggle free when Brand slammed his right fist into the sergeant's jaw.

Morganti heard the commotion. He whirled in his seat. "Hey! What the hell are you doing?"

Brand ignored him. He had DeWitt pinned against the bulkhead with his left arm. He gave the sergeant a backhand, then a straight-armed jab to the face. Brand felt the gristle snap in DeWitt's nose. Blood spurted from the sergeant's nose. Switzer was staring at them from the engineer's seat. Batchelder was watching the scene with a look of disbelief on his face.

"Talk to me, Sergeant," Brand said to DeWitt. "Who told you to sabotage this airplane?"

DeWitt's eyes bulged. His knees gave way and he slid toward the floor. Brand snatched him upright. He shoved him back against the bulkhead.

"I know what you did, DeWitt. As the aircraft commander I have a duty to protect this airplane. If I don't get answers—" Brand snatched the Beretta from his belt and shoved the muzzle into the sergeant's face— "I'm going to put a bullet right through your head."

"Hold on!" Morganti yelled. "Stop that! Are you crazy?"

Brand paid no attention. He knew as well as Morganti that striking an enlisted man was a court martial offense. So was killing one, for that matter. Brand jammed the muzzle of the Beretta harder into DeWitt's forehead. The only thing that mattered was that DeWitt believed he'd do it.

DeWitt believed it. His eyes widened with fear. Blood was gushing from both nostrils.

"Talk, Sergeant," Brand said. For emphasis he gave DeWitt a wallop with the barrel of the Beretta. He shoved the muzzle under DeWitt's chin. "Who told you to do this?"

A shudder passed over DeWitt's body. He slumped in Brand's grasp. "Okay, okay, goddamnit. Put the fucking gun away. I was supposed to destroy the communications modules, that's all. They didn't tell me they were going to sabotage the fuel. I didn't know we were going to flame out."

Brand felt a seething anger taking control of him. He looked into the sullen, bleeding face of the man who had nearly killed them. It would be easy to pull the trigger. Too easy. Brand forced himself to take a deep breath. In a level voice he said, "They? Who are 'they,' Sergeant?"

DeWitt coughed, squirting more blood out his nose. His

expression seemed to change. The look of abject fear was morphing into an expression of defiance. He shook his head. "Go ahead. Go ahead and kill me. You're not getting any more from me."

Brand kept his grip on the Sergeant's lapels. He wanted to keep beating him until he talked. But DeWitt was right. Brand could sense the moment slipping past when sheer terror would loosen DeWitt's loyalty to whoever he was supporting. More pistol-whipping wouldn't produce answers. All he could do now was turn DeWitt over to the Secret Service detail. He still didn't have the answer. Who? Who had tried to bring down Air Force One?

Brand glanced up at the front of the cockpit. Batchelder looked stunned. Morganti was no longer yelling about the mistreatment of the sergeant. His eyes were narrowed, as if he were trying to comprehend what he'd just witnessed.

Switzer was glowering at DeWitt. "You sonofabitch. If they don't shoot you, I'm going to do it myself."

<>

"That's it," said Major Gen. Jim Ripley in a flat voice. "Angel is down. Gone from the screens."

Ripley and the acting Chairman of the Joint Chiefs, General Vance McDivott, stared at the six-foot plasma display. The two officers were alone in the situation room, deep beneath the ground floor of the Pentagon. The half dozen communications technicians normally assigned to the array of plasma screens had been sent out.

For half a minute McDivott's eyes stayed riveted on the display. The pulsing yellow symbol of Shell 22—the KC-135 tanker that was previously joined with Angel—was still on the screen. Still flying westward toward its base at Dover, Delaware. The symbol for Angel—Air Force One—was no longer visible.

"Radio comms?" asked McDivott. He already knew the answer.

"None," answered Ripley. "No transmissions, no emissions, no data-link."

"What about SAR? Who's been alerted?" The search and rescue effort for Air Force One, McDivott already knew, would be on a scale never seen before.

"En route from both sides of the ocean. At least a dozen Coast Guard vessels and as many aircraft. More as soon as dawn comes. Eight ocean vessels are diverting to the spot. They'll converge on the last reported position."

Which would buy time, McDivott reflected. Air Force One's last reported position was more than five hundred miles from where it actually went down. A day or more could elapse before the actual debris field would be spotted. It depended on how much flotsam was on the surface. The handling of recovered wreckage would be carefully managed by Capella members already positioned on the recovery teams.

McDivott walked back to the command desk in the front of the situation room. He took a seat and picked up the red Pentanet handset, through which his voice would be broadcast into every room in the Pentagon. Intended as an emergency warning device, the Pentanet system had been installed a few days after the September 11, 2001 crash of American Airlines Flight 77 into the west wall of the Pentagon. Until today, the Pentanet had never been used.

McDivott had rehearsed this scenario in his mind a hundred times. He sat motionless for nearly a minute, cradling the handset between his hands. What he was about to say would have historical significance.

He put the handset to his ear and pressed the talk button. "Ladies and gentlemen of the Pentagon, this is Gen. Vance McDivott. It is my very sad duty to inform you that our commander-in-chief, the President of the United States, has died. We have a confirmed report that Air Force One, while en route across the Atlantic Ocean, has been hijacked and destroyed by agents of a foreign power. Although search and rescue efforts have been launched, it seems certain that the President and all the occupants of Air Force One have been lost."

McDivott paused, imagining the impact his announcement had on its audience. "This is a time for mourning," McDivott continued. "Let us bow our heads in prayer." He could hear his voice resonating through the rooms and halls of the Pentagon. It had a somber, ethereal quality. Befitting the occasion.

"Almighty God, we ask you to cast your blessing on our fallen leader and our fellow Americans who have perished in this tragedy. We pray that you give us the wisdom to understand the meaning of this evil act. We pray that you continue to shine your bounty on our beloved nation. And lastly, dear God, we beseech you to grant us the righteous strength to punish those who have brought harm to our great nation. Amen."

McDivott replaced the Pentanet handset in its cradle. *It's done,* he thought. *We have fulfilled our duty as patriots. God's will be done.*

He saw Ripley coming from across the room. He was carrying another wireless phone. Ripley covered the mouthpiece and said, "It's Speaker Atwater. Do you want to talk to him?"

McDivott considered, then shook his head. The Speaker of the House could wait. Atwater needed frequent reminding that he *wasn't* the one in charge. Nor would he ever be, even after taking office as President. Fred Atwater's rise to leadership in the House of Representatives had been carefully tended by his fellow Capella members.

McDivott knew why the Speaker was calling. As the next in succession to the Presidency, Atwater was anxious to be sworn in. *Too* anxious, thought McDivott. This was a historic moment in the United States, and it would be unseemly to act too quickly. The news of the death of the sitting President had to be disseminated to the world. The 25th Amendment to the Constitution, adopted in 1967, was fuzzy about the rules of succession. Atwater would have to tread lightly until his Presidency was legally established.

Then would come Fred Atwater's first official act as President.

He would submit the name of the man he had chosen to be the next Vice President. Though many members of congress and most of the liberal media would howl like banshees, the majority of Americans would applaud the selection. In such a moment of national crisis, the appointment of a warrior-statesman like Gen. Vance McDivott to the second-highest office in the land would be perceived as an act of brilliance. Only the inner circle of the new administration—all Capella members—would know the truth. Fred Atwater was President in name only. The real commander-in-chief was Vance McDivott.

<>

"Fuel remaining?" asked Brand.

"Maybe six thousand pounds," said Switzer. "Maybe less. No way to be sure."

Brand nodded. It was going to be close. He could see the coastline of Greenland. It was an uneven gray silhouette against the blackened sea. Narsarsuaq was less than sixty miles away, at the mouth of a twisting fjord.

He'd landed here before, but never under these conditions. Never without a flight plan, never without radio communication or a functioning instrument landing system. The Danish-owned facility was a refueling stop for smaller aircraft and an emergency landing field for two-engine airliners. According to Brand's briefing sheet, the facility wasn't manned at night.

Which he hoped was true. If they were lucky, no one would realize they'd arrived until they were on the ramp. With more luck, Mike Grossman's Secret Service team would deplane and secure the operations shack before anyone on the ground could transmit the fact of Air Force One's presence.

"What about runway lights?" asked Morganti. "Will they be on?" Morganti's demeanor hadn't become any warmer, but he was keeping the cockpit dialogue curt and businesslike.

"Depends on whether some airline has designated Narsarsuaq on their flight plan as a diversion airport."

"What do we do if the lights aren't on?"

Brand shrugged. They both knew the answer. "We land anyway. We look for the fjord, then try to pick out the runway when we get in close."

Morganti said nothing. Neither man needed reminding about the huge risk of landing on an unlighted runway in a landscape like Greenland. Narsarsuaq had been constructed in World War II as a refueling stop for U. S. warplanes headed to Europe. The single runway was only 6,000 feet. Too short for routine airline and heavy jet transport operations. If they didn't find the runway on the first pass, they'd have to thread the high, blackened terrain of a fjord as they climbed back out. In any case, Brand doubted that they had fuel for more than one attempt.

No one was talking about the subject that was foremost on their minds. Someone had just tried to kill them. Sergeant DeWitt was part of it. Who else might be involved? Since the encounter with DeWitt, Brand had sensed a change in Morganti. The copilot was no more respectful than before, but he had become less contentious.

Mike Grossman and two Secret Service agents had come for DeWitt. Blood still encrusted the sergeant's face and his shirt. One eye was nearly swollen shut. The sergeant had maintained a stone-faced silence, making no attempt to resist when they bound his wrists with tie-wraps and hauled him back to the cabin.

Brand was already thinking about what would happen after they were on the runway. Switzer had managed to restore some of the basic electrical systems. Would the engine thrust reversers work? Switzer thought so, but they wouldn't know for sure until they'd touched down and Brand pulled the reverser levers back. Same with the brake anti-skid system. Without anti-skid, stopping the big jet on the short runway would surely blow some of the tires. They'd be stuck at Narsarsuaq.

Morganti was leaning up over the instrument panel visor, peering out at the darkness ahead. "I see something," he said.

"Two o'clock low. A beacon."

<>

Don't land long. Put it down in the first thousand feet. Brand told himself that it was just another short field landing. Just like any of the hundreds he'd made on primitive runways in third world countries. Except those hadn't been with a half-million pound jumbo jet. Brand reminded himself that the wheels were nearly a hundred feet behind and below him. The cockpit was perched thirty feet above the nose wheel, like the bridge of a ship.

They were descending through 1,500 feet. Maybe. They had no accurate altimeter reading, since the last setting was over five hours old. The barometric altimeters could be off by several hundred feet.

The landing gear was extended. Brand could see the dark terrain of the offshore chain of islands sliding beneath them as they neared the mainland.

"Forty degrees flap," he called.

"Forty flap," Morganti responded and clunked the flap lever into the final detent.

Still no runway in sight. Morganti had spotted the rotating beacon atop an airport building, but nothing else. No approach lights, no runway lights. Brand slowed the Boeing, configuring for landing. He was still turning to the final heading—072°—when he saw them.

Runway lights. He felt like rejoicing. Two rows of runway edge lights. They looked impossibly short, but he knew that was a nighttime illusion. The rows of lights would appear foreshortened when viewed from this angle.

But the runway *was* short. Too damned short for a loaded 747. It didn't matter. Brand nudged the throttles back, slowing to final approach speed.

"Five hundred feet," said Morganti. It was a guess, both pilots knew.

Narsarsuaq had no approach lights—the illuminated ladder on

the ground that guided pilots to the end of the runway. The black void of the sea extended nearly to the end of the runway.

The green-lighted end of the runway swept beneath them. Brand nudged the nose of the jet up. He eased all four throttles back and felt a *whump* as the main gear trucks made contact with the concrete. He could see the far end of the runway rushing toward them at 130 knots. He wrapped his hand around all four reverse levers and pulled them up to a vertical position. And waited.

"Four in reverse," called out Switzer. "Reversers are working!"

They were, bellowing in full thrust. Brand applied brake pressure, carefully at first, not wanting to blow tires. In his peripheral vision he saw the blue lights marking either side of the narrow runway zipping beneath the wings.

A thousand feet of runway remained when Air Force One shuddered to a slow crawl. Brand carefully steered the jet onto the narrow taxiway that led to the operations complex and a broad apron. Time was precious now. The thunder of the massive reversers would have alerted any airport staff to the arrival of a large aircraft. He brought the jet to a halt on the ramp and shut down the engines, leaving only the auxiliary power unit in the tail running.

Brand peered down at the dimly lighted ramp. He saw figures running from beneath the left wing. It was Grossman's team heading for the main hangar. Making sure that the presence of their boss, the President of the United States, remained a secret to the outside world.

<>

"Certainly, we can fuel your aircraft," the man said. His name tag identified him as Johan Fischer, Airport Director. He was a slightly-built Dane with an unruly crop of reddish hair. "And tell me, please, who is going to pay?"

They were standing on the tarmac. One of Grossman's Secret Service agents stood on either side of the Dane.

Brand thought he was joking. "The President of the United States. As you may have noticed, this is her airplane."

"Will she be paying by cash or by credit card?"

The truth dawned on Brand. The guy was serious. "Uh, credit card, I suppose."

"Since you arrived without transmitting an advance fuel order, it will take some time. I'll have to clear your card with our verification service."

Brand stared at him. "Look, Mr. Fischer, we don't have time for that. And I have to tell you that there can't be any form of communication about our arrival here."

"This facility is not the property of the U. S. government, Colonel. If you wish to obtain any services from us, you will have to deal with the official representative of the Danish government."

"Let me guess. That would be you?"

Fischer drew himself to his full height. "You are correct."

Brand tried to suppress his exasperation. This idiot was ignoring the obvious. Air Force One's security team had already shut down the airfield's communications facilities. Brand could simply hold the Dane under temporary arrest while they completed fueling. But without the help of Fischer's fueling crew, it would be a tedious—maybe impossible—task purging the contaminated tanks and refilling them.

"Mr. Fischer," said Brand, "this is an emergency situation. We may have to dispense with some of the usual formalities."

Fischer's expression remained unchanged. "This is a commercial enterprise, Colonel. I must insist that your credit be verified and a proper request made for—"

The Dane jerked his head, suddenly aware of the woman in the blue jump suit who had walked up behind him. A look of alarm flashed over his face. "Ah, Madame . . . I mean . . . let me introduce myself . . ."

"I'm Libby Paulsen," the woman said, thrusting out her hand. "I'm honored to meet the official representative of the Kingdom of

Denmark."

The Dane stared as if he were seeing an alien from space. He took her hand. "It is . . . my pleasure . . . Madame President."

"Mr. Fischer, Denmark and the United States have a long history of mutual assistance. I will personally thank the Prime Minister for the invaluable help we have received from your facility. I can assure you that your actions will be highly praised."

The Dane continued staring at her. A look of pure ecstasy spread over his face. "Yes . . . I think . . . in this case, of course. . . we can certainly make an exception to the requirement for verification." Fischer drew himself up to his full height. "You have my assurance that our staff will fuel your aircraft and have it ready to depart as soon as possible. Is there anything else we can do for you, Madame President?"

Libby shot Brand a quick glance. "I'm sure Colonel Brand and his crew will be most appreciative of any help you can render. You have my sincere thanks, Mr. Fischer."

Fischer brought his heels together and gave Libby a courtly bow. Studiously ignoring Brand, he headed off across the darkened tarmac.

Brand watched the Dane march away. He shook his head. "Amazing."

"What's amazing?"

"The way you charmed that guy. It's incredible."

"It's not incredible. It's an act. It's what I do best, remember?"

She said it without smiling. Brand detected a note of toughness in her voice. That was good. Maybe she was regaining some of her composure after being nearly killed over the Atlantic.

Or maybe she was still acting.

CHAPTER NINE

"Five more minutes, Madame President," said Switzer.

"Thank you, Sergeant." Libby shivered in the pre-dawn darkness. She could see the refueling truck finishing its task on the right side of the aircraft. Standing with her on the tarmac were Jill Maitlin, a pair of Secret Service agents, and Johan Fischer, the airport director. The only sound on the ramp was the dull rumble of the auxiliary power unit in the 747's tail.

"Is there anything more we can do for you, Madame President?" asked Fischer.

"Just one thing," said Libby. At this she saw Jill Maitlin easing in closer so that she could hear. "We are in a . . . sensitive national security condition. I must ask you not to release any messages or calls that mention our presence here. Not for at least twelve hours."

She expected that the Dane would balk. Then he surprised her. "You have my assurance, Madame President. I will personally see to it that your request is honored."

Libby didn't know whether to believe him or not. It didn't matter. There was nothing more her team could do about it short of destroying every telephone and radio apparatus in Narsarsuaq. "You have my sincere thanks, Mr. Fischer." She realized she was using her actor's voice again. "I will convey my appreciation to your prime minister."

It was the right thing to say. Fischer's face again lit up at the mention of a commendation. Maybe the guy needed to score some points back in Copenhagen to atone for whatever he'd done that got him sent to this desolate place in the first place. Or maybe he was just a bureaucrat who liked being stroked.

Or maybe he was an actor too.

Libby gazed around her. The fueling truck was pulling away.

She could see stars twinkling through the thin veneer of clouds. In the darkness beyond the runway she could barely make out the jagged silhouette of the ridgeline. Narsarsuaq looked like the end of the earth. The kind of place where she could vanish.

It was a thought she'd been having since they'd landed here. She could drop out. Disappear. Let the crazies who wanted her dead take over. Being President had always terrified her. Libby had managed it with brains and, most of all, acting. But this—this was scarier than anything she'd ever dreamed.

The other passengers on Air Force One—the non-essential crew, including the members of Congress and the two Iranian diplomats—had been offered the chance to disembark here at Narsarsuaq. None wanted to stay behind. If the President was leaving, they were too. Libby wished she felt as secure as they did.

"Time to board," she heard Jill Maitlin say.

Libby didn't move. She stood at the foot of the boarding ladder, arms wrapped around her. A thought kept whirring through her mind. *You're the President. You don't have to do this.*

Brand and his crew were already in the cockpit, ready to start the engines. Why had she let him persuade her to continue this flight?

"Libby . . ." Jill was speaking in a low voice so that Fischer and the agents couldn't hear. "We have to get aboard. *Now.*"

Libby caught the emphasis on *now.* Jill had always been bossy, but lately she'd been more so. Jill Maitlin comported herself more like a mother superior than a White House advisor.

Libby gave it a few more seconds, mainly to show that she was still in charge. She took a deep breath and trudged up the boarding stairs. Jill and the Secret Service agents followed in close trail. At the top of the stairs Libby stopped. She turned and looked back. In normal times this would be a photo op. This was where the President would pause to wave farewell to the press and the assembled politicos and the curious public.

Here in Narsarsuaq there was no press. No curious public.

Only Johan Fischer, watching from the darkened ramp. Libby waved. Fischer waved back. *Goodbye*, she thought and stepped inside the cabin of Air Force One.

<>

Brand knew it was trouble as soon as the Secret Service team leader burst into the cockpit.

They had nearly reached the end of the runway. Grossman came to the front of the cockpit. "Sergeant DeWitt's missing."

Brand stopped the airplane. He turned to look at Grossman. "What the hell happened?"

Grossman wore a pained expression. "It's my fault. I assigned one guy to watch him. DeWitt seemed subdued, in a stupor. I wasn't worried about him. I needed all my team for the security sweep when we landed, so I had DeWitt locked up in the galley pantry. No one bothered to check on him until we were taxiing out. Sometime while we were parked the sonofabitch found a way out and slipped away."

"You're sure he's not on the airplane?"

"My guys are searching, but it's my guess that he's back there on the ground somewhere. Looks like he removed a floor panel in the pantry, then went out through the belly of the airplane. Shit, I'm sorry, Colonel. We can still go back and try to root him out."

Brand considered. They had only about three hours before sunrise. Chasing after DeWitt would use up what darkness they had left. Darkness was their friend.

"We can't go back," said Brand.

Grossman nodded. "Understood, Colonel. And, ah, like I said, it was my responsibility, guarding that sonofabitch, and . . ."

"If he's in Narsarsuaq, he's not going anywhere. You can deal with him later."

The Secret Service agent looked relieved. "Yes, sir. I'll make sure of it."

Brand resumed taxiing. When they reached the end of the runway, he swiveled the big transport around on the 150 foot wide swath of concrete. They'd be taking off in the opposite direction they'd landed, climbing seaward instead of toward the rising terrain of the fjord. Their charts showed that even with the five-mile-per-hour tailwind, the 747 would require slightly less than 5,000 feet to become airborne. Ahead stretched the twin rows of white runway edge lights. At the far end they could see the red flicker of the runway end lights. Beyond, only darkness.

Switzer was reading the takeoff check list. The PA system still wasn't working, so there would be no takeoff announcement. Brand had to assume the cabin occupants, including the President of the United States, had enough sense to fasten their seat belts.

Brand brought the aircraft to a stop in the center of the runway. He wrapped his hand around the four throttles. Air Force One would leave Narsarsuaq the same way it arrived—no communication, no announcements. Only the thunder of its four fanjet engines. No one on the ground would know they'd been there except for Fischer and a handful of aircraft handlers.

And Chief Master Sergeant Bruce DeWitt.

<>

Through the streaked glass window DeWitt watched the shape of the Boeing 747 rumble down the runway. It was unlike any departure of a VIP transport he had ever witnessed. No lights, no clearances, no escort vehicles with flashing beacons. Just the deep-throated roar of the Pratt & Whitney engines propelling it like a ghost ship into the night.

When the big jet vanished in the darkness, a flood of relief swept over DeWitt. In the space of a few hours he had seen his life spin out of control. He'd gone from second flight engineer on Air Force One to systems saboteur to near-victim of a mid-Atlantic crash to prisoner to . . . what?

Patriot, he reminded himself. Distasteful as the sabotaging of the aircraft had been, DeWitt knew that history would remember him as a red-blooded American who had helped remove a treasonous leader. That he had survived the near-downing of Air

Force One was a God-sent miracle. An even greater miracle was that he had managed to extricate himself from the aircraft. The Secret Service agent who locked him in the pantry hadn't bothered to remove the Leatherman tool on his belt.

It had taken only a few minutes after their arrival in Narsarsuaq for DeWitt to free himself of the plastic tie wraps. Then he used the screwdriver blade to unfasten the floor panel. With his intimate knowledge of Air Force One's layout, DeWitt found his way through the darkened passages of the airplane's belly compartments, into the forward cargo compartment. The dooor had been opened to remove equipment on the ground. DeWitt peered around to make sure the open door wasn't being watched, then he made his exit.

What he hadn't anticipated was the fall—twelve goddamn feet to the blackened pavement. He'd hit the concrete like a dropped log, and now he could barely straighten his left leg. His left ankle was sprained, maybe broken. He'd hobbled over to the edge of the ramp, then scurried along behind a row of parked tow vehicles to the complex of hangars and Quonset huts. He knew where he needed to go. He'd easily picked out the hangar from the others by the antennas mounted on the circular roof. He let himself in the unlocked door. He'd taken several minutes to make sure he was unobserved. He gritted his teeth against the pain in his ankle, he ascended the ladder to the loft.

As the rumble of Air Force One's engines slowly subsided in the west, DeWitt returned his attention to his surroundings. By now his eyes were adjusted to the darkness of the loft where he'd concealed himself behind pallets of insulation material. The shop space directly beneath him contained the station's high frequency radio. Watching from his hiding place, he'd been surprised when the three Secret Service agents burst into the building. To his relief they weren't searching for him but for the high frequency radio. DeWitt observed them fumbling with the console, discussing how best to disable it, finally settling on the simple expedient of severing a bundle of wires leading to the main panel.

It was then that DeWitt understood. They were disabling communications from Narsarsuaq because they didn't want anyone disclosing the fact that Paulsen was alive. They intended to takeoff again. Bound for the U. S. or back to Europe? DeWitt couldn't be sure, but his gut instinct told him that Air Force One would be returning to the U. S. One thing he was certain about: they'd be doing it without operative radios. He'd taken care of that. It would take a team of avionics technicians and a truckload of new equipment to restore Air Force One's communications modules.

Dewitt waited another five minutes. When he was sure no one else was approaching the building, he hobbled down from the loft, gritting his teeth against the pain from his left ankle, and let himself into the radio room. He almost laughed when he examined the severed wire bundle. His specialty as a technician in the Air Force was avionics. Even in the darkness, using only the Leatherman and a roll of electrical tape he found on a bench, he figured he could splice all the wires in less than fifteen minutes.

It took him ten. Before booting the radio back up, he sat on the floor massaging his ankle while he considered his next move. The radio was a Micom 2E, which meant that he could use the discrete frequency reserved for Capella to make a direct connection with an office in Washington. What he didn't know was whether the radio was monitored anywhere else on the airport. Had the airport authorities been ordered *not* to report the passage of Air Force One? How would they react when they eventually discovered the presence of a left-behind cockpit crew member?

It didn't matter. He'd come up with a story. The only thing that mattered was that Air Force One didn't make it to North America.

DeWitt slipped on the headset with the attached boom mike. He flipped the master switch and was rewarded with the glow of amber panel lights on the Micom console. As quickly as he could he punched in the discrete frequency, listening to the changing static patterns while the digital radio channeled to the correct wave length.

The static abruptly subsided. He heard the ringing of a telephone. "Tomahawk," said a voice over the headset. DeWitt nodded. "Tomahawk" was the code name for the Capella duty officer.

"This is Pacer Four," said DeWitt. "I'm calling from Narsarsuaq, Greenland with an update on Angel."

Several seconds passed. DeWitt felt a grim satisfaction as he imagined the flurry of excitement in the Capella duty room. *You bastards thought I was dead.*

"I need you to authenticate, Pacer Four."

"Unable to authenticate from this radio. Here's what you need to know. Angel landed in Narsarsuaq an hour ago, and is now airborne again."

For several seconds DeWitt heard only thin static over the radio. Then a different voice. "Pacer Four, confirm your last. Confirm that Angel is airborne."

"That is affirmative. Angel refueled in Greenland and departed fifteen minutes ago."

Several more seconds passed. "Pacer Four, say Angel's route and destination."

"No destination was disclosed." DeWitt waited a moment, then added, "It's very probable that Angel is westbound." DeWitt knew whoever was in the duty room was trying to decipher why Pacer Four, who they knew was a Capella member and the second flight engineer aboard Air Force One, was no longer aboard the jet. He also knew that without encrypted communications, the question wouldn't be asked over an open radio frequency.

"Are you speculating, Pacer Four, or do you have hard information?"

DeWitt felt a surge of anger. As in a recurring nightmare it came back to him that these were the assholes who'd almost dumped Air Force One in the Atlantic—with *him* aboard. They'd sent him on a suicide mission. Now they were treating him like he was some kind of street snitch.

"I just told you. It's an educated guess, and I don't give a shit what you do with it. I'm running out of time and I have to sign off." He'd done his duty—*more* than his duty—by disabling Angel's communications modules, then by escaping on the ground and reporting to them that their target was still not destroyed.

"Okay, okay, Pacer four. We need you to remain on this line so we can—"

DeWitt held down the channel-changing toggle, cutting off the transmission. Fuck them. When the digits had shifted half a dozen channels from the frequency he'd been using, he flipped the master switch off. Then he settled back against the wall and massaged his ankle. It was time to think about what he was going to tell his hosts in Greenland.

CHAPTER TEN

"**I** don't believe it," said General Vance McDivott.

Jim Ripley watched his boss ranting at the plasma display. Not one of the six plasma screens on the wall was showing the telltale yellow triangular symbol of Air Force One. When McDivott rotated the thumb wheel on the remote view selector, all he could pull up were the pulsing transpondor symbols of *other* military aircraft. Dozens of them. Most were en route to the point in the mid-Atlantic where they'd been told Air Force One had gone down.

But now this. If the latest report was to be believed, Air Force One *hadn't* gone down. The goddamn thing had landed in Greenland, refueled, and taken off again. And it was emitting *nothing*. No transpondor squawk, no datalink, no radio transmissions. Air Force One had become a stealth jet.

McDivott turned to Ripley. "This guy—what's his name?—is he considered reliable?"

Ripley looked at the two staffers with him in the room. They were bird colonels, Capella members, and both were shrugging. "DeWitt," said Ripley. "The second flight engineer on Angel. He was considered reliable, very motivated. He'd been recruited to Capella over two years ago. Somehow he got off Angel in Greenland. He transmitted the report that Angel had refueled and taken off. He didn't know the destination. Then he went off line."

"Off line? Was he compromised?"

"We don't know," said Ripley. "According to the duty officer, Sergeant DeWitt sounded agitated. He just hung up."

"Agitated? Why would that be?"

Ripley resisted the urge to laugh. Sometimes he couldn't believe McDivott. "Well, it could have something to do with discovering that he was supposed to die with the President."

It seemed not to register with McDivott. He glowered again at the screens. "Okay, assuming the report is reliable, where the hell is Angel headed?"

The colonels fidgeted, looking at Ripley. "Two possibilities," said the one nearest McDivott. "Maybe to Europe, but not likely. Most of the British Isles and the western continent are in instrument weather conditions and we don't think Angel has that capability. Most likely they're headed west."

"Sneaking back to home plate," said McDivott. "That's exactly what Brand would try to do. That means we have to bring NRO's satellites into the game."

Ripley nodded. That was going to be tricky. The National Reconnaissance Office, the agency that controlled the U.S.'s network of spy satellites, was directed by a civilian named Bernard Kruse. Kruse was not a Capella member. He reported directly to the Secretary of Defense, also non-Capella. Kruse was a problem.

One of NRO's satellites, a fifteen-ton Lacrosse-class radar-imaging craft, was already deployed in the search for Air Force One's wreckage. Like the other searchers, the satellite was scanning the wrong piece of the Atlantic. It was looking for wreckage where Air Force One had supposedly crashed.

Ripley knew what would happen next. McDivott would order him to request more satellite reconnaissance, this time to locate the aircraft headed for North America. Ripley wouldn't tell Director Kruse the rest of the scenario. When they had located Air Force One, they were going to kill it.

<><>

Through his cabin window Mahmoud Said peered into the darkness where Greenland had vanished from sight. Said felt a pang of regret.

He glanced over at his fellow Iranian, Kamil Al-Bashir. Al-Bashir's face was a reflection of Said's own thoughts. "We should have stayed," said Al-Bashir.

Said nodded glumly. Al-Bashir was right. The two Iranian diplomats had been offered the opportunity to deplane in

Greenland. Against his innermost instincts, Said had agreed to continue the journey.

Said was sure that something was badly wrong with the airplane. Over the darkened Atlantic their lights had failed. Then, for what seemed an eternity, the engines had gone silent. After they'd landed in Greenland, one of the pilots, the one named Batchelder, had come to the cabin to give them a sketchy explanation. Something about an electrical anomaly. An interruption of power to the ship's electronic nerve center, which had caused systems to fail. The pilot insisted that the problem had been repaired, that Air Force One was perfectly safe to resume flying.

Said didn't believe him, and he suspected that many of the other passengers didn't either. But if the President of the United States— the most-protected figure in the world—felt secure aboard Air Force One, then it must be safe enough for the rest of them.

Now Said regretted the decision. He turned to look again at the figure sitting on the opposite side of the cabin. He was a young man with a short haircut and a blank expression. He was one of the President's Secret Service detail, and he didn't bother concealing why he was there. The agent hadn't let the two Iranians out of his sight since departing Tehran.

Typical American paranoia, thought Said. While they were hosting the Iranians aboard Air Force One, they were also guarding them. As if they were potential terrorists. It was insulting.

Said made a show of looking at his watch. He said to the agent, "It is time for me to communicate with my office in Tehran. They are expecting my report." It was the fifth, perhaps the sixth time he'd made the request.

The agent gave him the same answer. "Sorry, not possible. The aircraft's long-range communications equipment is still not working."

Said knew it was a lie. The Americans had promised that he would be able to communicate with Tehran all the time they were airborne.   It was one of the conditions President Hosseini had demanded before dispatching Said and Al-Bashir to Washington.

Was it all part of some intricate plot? Was the story about the Vice President being assassinated a ploy to lure the Iranians aboard this flying sarcophagus?

It didn't make sense. Nothing made sense. Mahmoud Said wished he had never left Tehran.

"I must speak with the President," said Said. "That is why we came on this flight."

Again the agent shook his head. "Sorry. The President is still tied up. Her senior advisor says that they'll let you know as soon as you can have a meeting."

Said fumed silently. Such disrespect was inexcusable. He and Al-Bashir, the personal emissaries of the President of the Islamic Republic of Iran, were being treated like goat herders.

Mahmoud Said made a vow to himself.   If the peace negotiations between the two countries ever resumed, this woman President would be surprised. The concessions she demanded from Iran would not come as easily as she thought.

<>

"This is insane," said Morganti.

Brand glanced at the copilot. Morganti was being Morganti again. Disagreeable and acerbic. Brand said, "What's bothering you?"

"This flight. It's crazy. Flying a severely disabled aircraft, the President aboard, no clearance, no radios, no knowledge of what we're flying into. You're going to get us all killed."

"If you believe that, why didn't you get off in Narsarsuaq?"

Morganti gave him a withering look. "I'm a professional officer. Something you wouldn't understand.   I follow orders, not necessarily from you but from the commander-in-chief, even if I think they're stupid. But you can be sure that I'll be taking this to the general as soon as we get back to Andrews."

Brand didn't bother replying. It was as much as he could hope for that Morganti was still doing his job. Morganti had been quarrelsome since the trip began, even more so after the landing in Greenland. He had sat through the pre-departure procedure in a surly silence.

But Brand was worried about more than Morganti's attitude. The conspiracy that had tried to bring Air Force One down included at least one crew member, DeWitt. Could Morganti be part of it?

It defied logic. Why would a planted crewmember sacrifice himself to bring down the President's airplane? DeWitt had blurted that "they" hadn't told him about contaminating the fuel and causing the engines to flame out. His role had been to sabotage the communications modules, not to go down with the airplane.

If Morganti was a plant, was he willing to die?

Brand didn't think so. To be safe, he could relieve Morganti of his duties. Batchelder was fully capable of taking over the copiloting job. But Brand couldn't rule out the possibility that Batchelder or even Switzer wasn't part of the conspiracy.

You're getting paranoid, Brand. And for good reason. Never had he felt so alone in a cockpit.

Switzer had gone to the avionics bay to try to restore more radios. So far he'd gotten one of the three autopilots operating. One inertial navigation system was aligned. Though they had no map display, the inertial unit was giving them geographical coordinates. With those they could plot their course on a navigation chart. The good news was that the inertial unit emitted zero electronic signals. Nothing to betray their presence.

Switzer returned. His uniform shirt was sweat-splotched. He looked frustrated. "The communications modules are trashed beyond repair, Boss. I might be able to get a VHF radio back. Or maybe not. You want me to keep trying?"

"No." Brand wanted Switzer in the cockpit in case something else stopped working. They'd proceed in radio silence.

Brand had to shake his head at the irony. Air Force One had eighty-five telephone terminals, a third of them capable of scrambling, as well as multiple faxes, internet connections, and nineteen active television screens. None of it was working.

For the moment that was okay. With their first electronic emission, the fact of the President's survival and her precise location would be known. Even without transmitting, it was only a matter of time before they were picked up by long range radar. Or by a surveillance satellite. Fighters would intercept them long before they reached the U. S. shore. What would happen then? Brand didn't know.

He peered again at the night sky. At this latitude the *aurora borealis*—the northern lights—shimmered like a curtain in the northern sky. In normal times Brand liked gazing into the star-filled heavens. The feeling of being a tiny speck in the universe gave him perspective. But tonight he felt exposed. The glow of the aurora was making them visible.

Maybe Morganti was right. Maybe flying back to the U. S. *was* crazy. Maybe they should have stayed on the ground in Greenland and waited for whatever happened next. It would have been the logical thing to do.

Brand's inner voice was telling him otherwise. Getting back in the air was the right decision. He knew in his gut that it was their best chance.

His thoughts were interrupted by the opening of the cockpit door. The Secret Service agent posted outside entered the cockpit. With him was Sergeant Lowanda Manning, Air Force One's chief flight attendant. She was a tall, solidly built African-American woman in her early forties. Manning was wearing her blue jacket with the presidential airlift squadron patch over the left breast. Her dark-skinned face was nearly invisible in the dimly-lighted cockpit.

"Colonel Brand, this just came over the text messaging machine in the ship's galley." She handed Brand a printed sheet.

Brand held the sheet beneath the single standby light on the instrument glare shield and read it.

05190218Z
Att: Chief Flight Attendant, SAM 28000
From: Duty Officer, Catering office, 89 AW, Andrews AFB.

SAM 28000 order for reprovisioning and specific quantities of onboard stocks not yet received. Request updated inventory of onboard stocks and special requests prior arrival Andrews. Please reply ASAP.
/s/ Sam Fornier, Capt. USAF

The message looked legitimate.   SAM 28000 was the identification for this aircraft.   It was one of the two nearly-identical B-747s that alternated duty as Air Force One.

But it didn't make sense.

Brand turned to Switzer. "How can the text messaging machine in the galley be working when all the comm modules shut down?"

"It can't," said Switzer. "No way." The sergeant was peering at the overhead communications panel. Nothing was powered. "No way unless somehow in one of the retrofits, the galley texting machine circuitry got isolated from the communications modules. If so, maybe it just got powered up when I restored some of the galley power."

"Look at the time this message went out," said Brand.   "It was sent over three hours ago."

Switzer was nodding his head.   "That was before this catering officer would have known that we were missing.   It means the message has been sitting somewhere for three hours waiting for our machine to come back to life."

"What do you want me to do, Colonel?" said Sergeant Manning. "Reply to this guy?"

"Do you know him?"   Brand glanced at the message again.

"Capt. Sam Fornier?"

"No. Must be one of the new ones. They rotate real quick through that job at Andrews."

Brand gazed outside again, thinking. It could be a set up. They could be expecting the Air Force One crew to reveal their intentions by texting a reply. The text messaging machine could have been spared for a reason.

Were they that clever?

Yes. More clever than he would have imagined. But Brand's gut feeling was telling him something else. The message didn't have the feel of a set up. The note looked like a hundred other bureaucratic communications he'd seen from bored supply officers.

A plan was emerging in Brand's mind. A long shot. Maybe the only shot they had. It all depended on an Air Force captain named Sam Fornier.

Brand pulled the steno pad from his flight kit. When he was finished scribbling, he showed the note to Morganti, Switzer, then Batchelder. Brand tore the page out of the pad and handed it to Manning. "Show this to the President. If she approves, send it exactly this way. Let me know as soon as there's a reply."

Manning's large eyes grew larger as she scanned the note:

05190603Z
From: A/C commander, SAM 28000
To: Capt. Sam Fornier, Duty Officer, Catering office, 89th AW,
Andrews AFB.
Despite info you may have to the contrary, the President is
alive and en route to home plate. There are ongoing attempts
by unknown parties within the military to destroy SAM 28000
and eliminate the President. Due to the extreme sensitivity of
this message, I ask that you immediately contact Lt. Gen. J. H.
Cassidy at (703) 756 6505 and establish comm link via this
channel. Absolutely critical that you share this with NO ONE
except Cassidy.
  Acknowledge.
  /s/ Col. P. T. Brand, Commander, Presidential Airlift
Squadron

The sergeant headed for the door. "I'll let you know, Colonel."

CHAPTER ELEVEN

The uniformed attendant peered inside the unmarked black Lincoln. He took the time to study the ID cards of each occupant. Then he stepped back and gave the limo a swipe with his scanner. All clear. The attendant stood at attention and rendered a salute while the grated iron gate raised. The Lincoln rolled through the club entrance, rounded the horseshoe-shaped driveway in the courtyard, then entered the enclosed passage that contained the massive front door of the Briar Club.

Another attendant, also in uniform and armed with the same concealed automatic weapon, opened the passenger door. He stood at attention while Gen. Vance McDivott stepped out. Behind McDivott appeared Major Gen. Jim Ripley. Ripley followed McDivott up the long stairs and through the front door.

The Briar Club on Massachusetts Avenue was notable not so much for its gilded age opulence as for its air of mystery. The magnificent building had been bequeathed to Capella by a wealthy shipping magnate named Lewis Magnuson, one of Curtis LeMay's early disciples. Access to the club was restricted to members. No roster had ever been made available to curious reporters or investigators. The arrivals and departures of Briar Club members occurred behind the iron gate and within the enclosed entrance. Unlike the other exclusive clubs of the District's ruling class, the Briar Club held no Christmas ball, no charity events, no open house. Each Briar Club member was also a member of the secret society known as Capella.

With Ripley in trail, McDivott marched through the carpet-lined entrance hall. Brocaded chairs and settees lined the paneled walls. Persian carpets lay before each of the three matching fireplaces. A crystal chandelier hung from the gilded ceiling.

The furnishings of the club were an eclectic mix of 1920s glitz and twenty-first century technology. The lower level contained a ten thousand-volume library. There was a linear series of chambers including a dining room, a conference hall with neoclassical columns at each corner, a massive stone mantelpiece, and a fifteen-foot-diagonal plasma screen that slid from the ceiling.

McDivott nodded to the two uniformed staffers behind the desk as he continued straight to the elevator entrance. First McDivott, then Ripley paused at the console while a retina scanner identified them. The ID check took less than two seconds for each man. The elevator door slid open with a hiss.

Vance McDivott enjoyed the perks that attended being Vice Chairman of the Joint Chiefs—the limo, the Pentagon office with instant access to the latest intelligence, the deference accorded him by the highest military and civilian officials. The post had gained him and his wife, Roseanne, admission to glittery District social events and salons that were closed to ordinary government toilers. Most of all, what McDivott liked about his Pentagon job was the exercise of raw power. There was nothing like it. Almost.

The Pentagon was nothing compared to the Briar Club. The military was an inefficient bureaucracy of drones and ass-kissers that deferred to the even more inefficient Congress and executive branch. Capella deferred to no one. As the head of Capella, Vance McDivott wielded more raw power than anyone on the planet.

McDivott and Ripley exited the elevator on the third floor. McDivott's office in the Briar Club was not as spacious as in the Pentagon, but from his headquarters in the club he was linked to the Capella network around the world. The antenna array that festooned the exterior of the Briar Club lacked some of the Pentagon's assets, but it could access almost all of the Defense Department's satellite-provided surveillance imagery.

McDivott stopped at the desk console in his office just long enough to check the message screen. There was nothing of importance. Just another plaintive message from Atwater.

McDivott glanced at it, then deleted it.

Ripley was standing behind him. "Is the Speaker on his way?"

"I sent him to the White House," said McDivott. "He has to deal with the cabinet, at least as many as they can round up at this hour. The cabinet has to designate Atwater as Acting President. It's his job to get them to sign off."

McDivott paused for a moment to stare at the brass bust standing on a pedestal beside his console. The bronze image of Old Iron Pants glowered back at him. Now, more than ever, McDivott could feel the spirit of Curtis LeMay here in the sanctum of the Briar Club. This was the moment in history that LeMay had always warned would come. It was the reason he founded Capella.

What would Old Iron Pants say now? McDivott knew. He knew because he considered himself to be the living embodiment of Gen. Curtis LeMay. He and LeMay were cast from the same mold. *Do it,* LeMay would tell him. *Do your duty. Save your country.*

McDivott shed his uniform coat and draped it over a chair. With Ripley behind him he headed down the corridor to the conference room that served as Capella's command post. Half a dozen men, all in shirtsleeves and loosened neckties, were huddled around the conference table. A plasma screen on the wall showed a satellite image of the northeast coast of the U. S.

McDivott spotted a tall, muscular man standing at the fringe of the group. McDivott gave him a wave. Rolf Berg, head of the security contracting company called Galeforce, was a key member of the Capella high command. Berg was a tough ex-special ops officer. His security force was prepared to enforce Capella's seizure of power in Washington.

"There you are," said a ruddy-faced man with white muttonchops. "You had us worried."

"You can stop worrying, Casper," said McDivott. "The situation is under control."

Casper Reckson, chairman of the Sterling International Media

Group, was frowning. "We can't keep the lid on the story much longer. The President is either dead or she's not."

"Or she's in the hands of terrorists. In which case it doesn't matter whether she's dead or alive. To avert a tragedy like 9/11, we're forced to take them all out."

"Has that been accomplished yet?"

McDivott didn't like Reckson's pushy attitude, but he forced himself to be respectful. Like it or not, McDivott—and Capella—needed Reckson. The old titan had an iron-fisted control of the nation's largest broadcast and newspaper syndicate. Reckson's empire was crucial to Capella's success. "Something happened," said McDivott. "Air Force One somehow made it to Greenland. They've refueled and they're airborne again, without communications."

"How could that happen without your people stopping them?"

"We think they had help on the ground in Greenland. But we're tracking them now. They're apparently en route to the U. S."

"Apparently?" Reckson's face darkened. "This is preposterous. You're in charge of the Air Force, General. Can't you order fighters to shoot them down?"

"Of course," said McDivott, straining to keep his tone courteous. "But we need to be very specific about who receives the order. It has to go through one of our Capella officers. Whoever carries out the order must be convinced of its authenticity."

What McDivott wasn't telling this pompous civilian was that every Air Force fighter squadron on the east coast fell under the command of the First Air Force, which was run by a four-star named Brent Younkin, a loyal Capella member. The problem was that only a few of Younkin's wing and squadron commanders were Capella members. Any order to shoot down Air Force One had to be carefully routed through one of them.

"And that order, I presume, has already been given?"

Reckson's tone was becoming more than annoying. Before McDivott could snap an answer, Ripley stepped in as he usually did when he sensed that McDivott had reached a boiling point. "Yes, sir. As we speak, our assets are en route to engage Air Force One."

The hard lines in Reckson's face softened. "How much longer then?"

"Twenty minutes. By then, I assure you, this situation will be resolved."

< >

Capt. Sam Fornier ripped the paper off the machine. The officer stared at the incoming message. No way could this be happening. This was some misguided idiot's idea of a prank. Or another boneheaded Air Force readiness exercise to simulate a make believe shit-crisis somewhere in the world.

Except that this shit-crisis wasn't make believe. Since Fornier had transmitted the original reprovisioning request, the world had changed. According to the hotwire on the briefing board, Air Force One had gone missing. No other official information had come over the electronic briefing board, but every television channel was filled with speculation about what might have happened to the President's airplane. Very heavy shit.

Now this.

Fornier knew exactly what to do with this message. Take it to the air wing command duty officer in the main hangar. Let him deal with it. That's what colonels got paid for. Fornier rose from the desk.

And sat back down again.

The young officer read the message again. The same bothersome line kept jumping off the page.

...ongoing attempts by unknown parties within the military to destroy SAM 28000 and eliminate the President...

Fornier glanced around the catering office. No one else was on duty at this hour. Fornier was solely in charge of the texting equipment that connected the Andrews catering facility with every special air mission aircraft currently deployed. Only one aircraft—Air Force One—fit that category.

Sam Fornier had a low tolerance for military bullshit. Being a catering officer for pampered politicians hadn't been Fornier's first choice for an action-packed career in the U. S. Air Force. It was a dead end job. All Fornier wanted was to put in the obligated service time, stay in shape, run a few marathons, play with computers, get the hell back to civilian life.

Now this. The message—supposedly from SAM 28000, the aircraft assigned as Air Force One—had trouble written all over it. *Unknown parties within the military.* What was that supposed to mean? Some kind of coup attempt? Or a cover up for a terrorist action? Whatever, it was too hot to handle. Way above a captain's pay grade. Let one of the mush-wit lifers in air wing staff earn his keep.

Fornier rose from the desk, message in hand, and paced behind the row of desks in the windowless duty office. After a solid minute of pacing, the officer returned to the desk.

Fornier picked up the duty phone, began punching in a number, then abruptly returned the phone to its cradle.

Shit. Another half minute passed. The young officer retrieved the cell phone from the backpack on the desk. Fornier pecked at the keyboard, then stared again at the message printout while the phone rang.

On the fourth ring a gravelly voice came on the line. "Cassidy."

<>

Libby was in the jump seat behind Brand. She looked over Brand's shoulder while he read the newly received message that Sergeant Manning had just delivered.

051906301Z
From: Capt. Sam Fornier, Duty Officer, Catering office, 89th AW, Andrews AFB.
To: A/C commander, SAM 28000

Your message relayed. Cassidy requires that you answer following: Who was Bitch Mistress? Who is Queenie? Who was the idiot who punched out Maddox?
Immediate reply expected.
/s/ SF

"What's that all about?" said Libby. "Bitch mistress? Queenie?"

Brand was shaking his head. "Stuff that only Jack Cassidy would know to ask."

And then Libby remembered. "General Cassidy was your boss when you were in Africa. I met him. The cranky general."

"Same guy." Brand held up the printout. "And there's no doubt this comes from him."

Libby didn't know whether that was good or bad. Maybe they were exposing themselves to more danger by opening a communications link. Maybe the conspirators—she was still having trouble accepting the idea—would home in on the source of the message. Brand seemed to think it was worth the risk.

"How do you want to reply to this, Colonel?" asked Sergeant Manning.

Brand was already scribbling on his steno pad. He tore off the sheet. "Send this. After the President clears it."

Libby squinted at the handwritten message. She looked at Brand. "Bitch Mistress was an airplane?"

"The name my crew painted on the nose of our C-130 in the Sudan airlift. Cassidy hated it, but he pretended he never saw it."

Libby nodded, still looking at Brand's handwriting. "And Queenie? Okay, that's Cassidy's dog. What's this about an idiot punching out Maddox? Who's Maddox?"

Libby thought she saw Brand wince. "A brigadier general. He and I, ah, had an . . . altercation one night in Okinawa."

"Let me get this straight. You were the idiot who punched out a general?"

Brand nodded.

"I presume there was a reason for this."

"There was. He needed punching out."

"Colonel Brand, how is it that you're still in the U. S. Air Force?"

"Good question. Maybe you should ask Cassidy."

CHAPTER TWELVE

S am Fornier hated this shit. The young officer was pacing the narrow passage between the desks in the duty office, waiting for Cassidy to call. Sit tight, the general had said. Talk to no one. He'd get right back.

That was ten minutes ago. He hadn't gotten back. It was just a matter of time before the combined wrath of the United States military descended on this place. Fornier snatched the cell phone off the desk, keyed the "recents" tab, and was about to punch the entry with Cassidy's number.

And then stopped. Could they trace this cell phone? It was one of the phones issued by the air wing. It was designed to be trackable—but not with the hack that Fornier had recently applied. Now the damned thing was about to get Fornier into unbelievably deep shit. The best move was to trash the hacked phone. Get rid of it and run like hell.

The phone was buzzing.

"Captain Fornier," blurted Sam, thinking too late that this might not be a good time to use real names.

The same gravelly voice came on the line. Fornier guessed that the general either had laryngitis or was a heavy smoker. As Fornier held the phone with one hand, scribbling Cassidy's message with the other, a mounting wave of anxiety swept over the young officer. *Well, Fornier, you've done it. You've gotten yourself in it this time.*

When Cassidy had finished, the captain took a deep breath. "Yes, sir, I understand the urgency. I'm sending it right now."

<>

Libby was in the cockpit, still in the jump seat behind Brand, when Manning burst through the door. Wordlessly the sergeant handed the printout to Libby.

Libby felt a cold chill come over her as she read the message. She passed the sheet around the back of the seat to Brand.

05190632Z
From: Catering officer, 89th AW, Andrews AFB
To: A/C commander SAM 28000
Cassidy sends urgent warning. You have been tagged as a hijacked aircraft and considered hostile. An F-15C has been scrambled with orders to engage over international airspace between Greenland and coast of Canada. Cassidy urges you exercise all available options.
/s/ SF

"How do they know where to intercept us?" said Libby. "How do they even know we're alive?"

To her surprise, Morganti answered. Until now the copilot had been silent and sullen in the right seat. "Sergeant DeWitt," said Morganti. "The security detail let him escape back in Narsarsuaq. Now he's telling the whole world that we're alive and headed for the U. S."

Libby detected the hostility in his voice. Morganti still worried her. Where did all the hostility come from? "*Are* we headed for the U. S.?" Libby asked. "Or someplace else?"

Brand answered. "We're headed for North America. Depending on what we learn from Cassidy, we either land in Canada or continue offshore to some point in the U. S." Brand paused, then added, "With your concurrence, Madame President."

With your concurrence. Libby couldn't tell if Brand was saying that for the benefit of the others or not. It didn't matter. She had no idea what they should do. The whole situation seemed incomprehensible.

She looked at the message again. "What does he mean by 'all available options?'"

Brand exchanged a quick glance with Switzer. "We have the ATADS," said Brand. "Air-to-air defense system. The trouble is, it isn't working."

"Maybe," said Switzer. "The ATADS is tied to a different module from the comms. I can give it a try."

"Go for it. Lou will cover the engineer seat."

Libby watched the engineer leave the cockpit, canvas satchel in his hand. Batchelder settled himself into the seat facing the engineer panel. None of this was making any sense to Libby. Someone was going to intercept them. The engineer was going to fix something. "What does this ATADS do?" she asked.

She nodded, her eyes widening, as Brand told her.

<>

"No," said McDivott. "You shouldn't be sworn in. It's too early."

McDivott was taking a break from the claustrophobic command post at the Briar Club. He was standing in the corridor outside his office, listening to Fred Atwater's whiny voice over the scrambled phone.

"It will reassure the nation," Atwater was saying. "The American people need to know someone is in charge."

"Someone *is* in charge," snapped McDivott. He felt like reminding the dumb shit that the someone in charge definitely wasn't Fred Atwater. Nor would it ever be. But this wasn't the time. McDivott forced himself to wait a second, then he said in a conciliatory voice, "It's too soon, Fred. We have to be meticulous about the rules of succession. You have to get a majority of the cabinet to sign off on designating you the Acting President. That's as far as we want to go at this time."

Atwater still wasn't buying it. "I know the rules of succession, and I've read the 25th Amendment a hundred times. My lawyers tell me that it's clear enough. I can be sworn in now. The Supreme Court can make it official later."

"Tell your lawyers to take a hike. We need to have evidence that the President is dead. So far she's only missing. We need a body or clear proof of death."

"And when will that be?"

McDivott didn't answer immediately. There was no point in telling Atwater that not only was the President *not* dead, the traitor was in the air, headed westward. The removal of Libby Paulsen had still not been accomplished.

But it would very soon. Vance McDivott still commanded the most powerful air force in the world. No way was Air Force One going to reach the United States.

"Very soon," said McDivott. "It's being taken care of."

<>

Contact.

The blip appeared just outside the hundred mile ring on Slade's APG-70 radar. He swung the nose of the F-15C thirty degrees to the left to establish an intercept course.

Colonel Tom Slade—call sign "Blazer"—sucked a lungful of oxygen through his mask. On the Plexiglas of his canopy Slade could see the dancing reflections of the northern lights over the Labrador Sea. He shifted his position on the hard pad of the ejection seat. Slade's butt was already numb and it would be more numb by the time he'd executed the mission and returned to his base at Westfield, Massachusetts.

Slade had been surprised—and pleased—when he received the scramble order back at fighter wing headquarters. His mission was to intercept Angel—the name assigned to Air Force One—which had somehow *not* crashed in the Atlantic and had been reported airborne after a stop in Narsarsuaq.

Airborne to *where*? The U. S.? Which base? The Capella command post reported that Angel was headed westward across the Labrador Sea. Looking at the APG-70 display, Slade saw that they had reported correctly.

The F-15C was a big fighter. It was sixty-four feet long, weighing over 60,000 pounds fully loaded. It was armed with heat seeking missiles and two varieties of radar-guided missiles—the AIM-7 Sparrow and long range AIM-120. More than enough firepower for a mission like this one. The conformal tanks and three externally-mounted ferry tanks provided enough fuel to execute the mission and return to base without inflight refueling.

Slade knew that most fighter pilots would find this mission abhorrent. Killing a fat and unsuspecting target like Air Force One violated their code of honor. Tom Slade had sworn allegiance to a higher code. His loyalty was to God and country, not to a left-wing traitor like Paulsen. A traitor who wanted to destroy everything that Slade and patriots before him had fought for.

Early in his Air Force career, when Slade was still a captain and Vance McDivott was his squadron commander, Slade had been recruited into Capella. It was a natural fit. To a man like Slade, patriotism was a warrior's highest calling. Slade had often prayed that if Capella were someday forced to save the United States, the task would fall to him.

Tonight his prayers had been answered.

Slade would not get maudlin about the innocent passengers and crew aboard Air Force One. Some of them—White House staffers and bleeding heart liberal congressmen and the Middle East ragheads Paulsen collected—weren't so innocent. The others, well, God had placed them there for a reason. Slade would not question the will of the Almighty.

The UHF tactical channel was quiet. Unless Slade received an abort order from headquarters, there would be no radio communications. No target report, no kill verification. After he'd acquired and identified the target, he would execute the mission in radio silence. He'd fly a pursuit curve, swooping around to a close trail position, slowing to the target's speed. He'd descend to the transport's altitude, which the APG-70 was showing to be 29,000 feet.

At this closure speed, nearly 1,200 nautical miles per hour, he'd engage the target—Slade did a quick calculation—in five minutes.

He reached down to the multi-function display on his panel and toggled the screen to the weapons page. He selected the box labeled "AIM-7." A semi-active radar-guided Sparrow missile.

<>

Morganti saw it first. "There it is. We're lit up."

It was the first time the copilot had spoken since they'd gotten the warning from Cassidy. Brand snapped his attention to the overhead panel. Morganti was right. The amber warning light on the RWR—radar warning receiver—was blinking. An air-to-air radar was tracking them.

Whose radar? Where? It was what Brand had been expecting—and dreading. Hundreds of miles before they approached U. S. airspace they would be picked up on radar. And intercepted. Had to happen.

But not yet. Not out here over the Labrador Sea.

If everything had been working on Air Force One, the situation display on the instrument panel would show the position of any radar-emitting aircraft in the vicinity. The screen of the situation display was blank, like every other screen on the panel. All victims of DeWitt's sabotage.

Brand kept his eyes fixed on the RWR light. Maybe it was just sensing magnetic disturbances up here in the northern latitudes. He'd seen it before. Something to do with the aurora borealis. The light would flash intermittently, then it would go out.

The light kept flashing. The flashes were coming quicker.

"Eyes outside," said Brand. "See if we can spot this guy. Lou, go to the cabin and get people looking out both sides. Maybe we'll see who it is."

The amber light was flashing in a steady pattern. Amber meant they were being tracked by a search mode radar. It could be any kind of military aircraft. Patrol plane, tanker, another transport. Anything equipped with radar.

A flashing red light was something else. Red was a target acquisition warning and it meant one thing. A fighter had locked on to them. The radar warnings were among the few systems Switzer had been able to restore. They were part of the ATADS, which included the radar receivers, chaff dispensers, decoy heat-emitters, and the battery of tail-mounted AIM-9 Sidewinder heat seeking missiles. The ATADS emitted no electronic signals. Nor did the heat seeking missiles.

Okay, the RWR light worked, Brand thought. What about the rest of the air defense system? Would the decoys deploy? Would the missiles fire? He wouldn't know. Not until they were needed.

Brand peered into the milky darkness outside his cockpit window. It was like staring into an empty void. The sea and the sky melded together in a velvety blanket. He saw nothing except the twinkle of stars. He tried shifting his gaze back into the cockpit, refocusing his eyes, then outside again.

If it was a friendly fighter, Brand figured, he would show himself. He'd have his navigation lights on. That was the procedure. He'd fly alongside, flash his lights, then escort the radioless aircraft to a suitable airport.

What was that? Something, a gray-hued shape, swimming in and out of the gloom. To the left and slightly behind. Brand saw it, then he didn't. He tried refocusing his eyes inside, back outside. Nothing. The shape was gone. Which meant . . .

Batchelder came through the cockpit door. Directly behind him appeared Libby Paulsen. She was wearing her blue jump suit with the presidential patch. Her hair was tousled and she wore little make up. Her gray eyes looked more serious than Brand had ever seen them.

Libby said, "We spotted something out the left side."

"What did it look like?"

"We just got a glimpse. Definitely an airplane, all gray, maybe the size of a fighter jet."

"Could be an F-15," said Batchelder. "Hard to say. No lights. While we were trying to ID it, the thing disappeared."

"Disappeared in what direction?"

"Behind us."

Brand nodded. That was bad. If a fighter were that close to them, he'd have no problem identifying them. He'd be coming alongside, flashing his lights, exchanging signals. This guy didn't want to be spotted.

Something caught Brand's eye. He swung his attention back to the RWR panel. The amber light was extinguished. The red light was flashing.

<>

There was no mistaking that shape. Like a giant whale, thick-bodied, wings nearly invisible against the night sky. No navigation lights, and only an occasional dim flicker through the cabin windows. But the dancing glow of the aurora borealis offered enough illumination to make identification easy. Slade had no problem making out the American flag on the vertical stabilizer. Clearly visible was the blue and white paint scheme. Just as visible was the lettering emblazoned on the fuselage: *UNITED STATES OF AMERICA*.

It was as positive an ID as Slade needed. He didn't want to remain in view any longer than necessary. Even in the darkness, the glow of the aurora might make him visible to anyone who happened to be looking outside. Slade eased the throttles back and slid the F-15C into trail a quarter mile behind the 747.

He could see all four engines suspended beneath the nearly-invisible wings. In the center of each tailpipe glowed a yellow plume of flame. Unlike the heat seeking AIM-9 Sidewinders, the radar-guided AIM-7 Sparrow would home in on the dense mass of the 747's fuselage.

Slade took his time. He toggled the Master Armament switch to "On." On the multi-function display he superimposed the target acquisition box over the radar symbol of the 747. Slade eased the fighter slightly higher and into an offset trail position. Enough to keep him clear of the debris field. He'd ripple fire two missiles, then observe the results. If by any chance the aircraft was still flying, he'd shoot again.

Whatever it took.

<>

It was happening too fast for Libby.

The red light on the overhead panel was flashing like a fire alarm. "The sonofabitch is targeting us!" she heard Morganti say.

Brand turned to Switzer. "Arm the ATADS."

"Already done." Switzer was wearing a grim expression as he pointed to the console. The latched door that covered the console was open and Switzer had the switches armed. "Ready to shoot," said the sergeant.

Libby felt as if she were watching a bad movie. A sci-fi drama with fake technology. She remembered a briefing on Air Force One's air defense system. She recalled hearing about the ATADS, that it was some kind of last-ditch ploy against an unanticipated air threat. They told her that it had only been used in test platforms, never to fire real weapons. She knew that Air Force One had some kind of anti-missile system as well as protection against the electromagnetic pulse of a nuclear blast. Somewhere in the tail section of Air Force One was a battery of missiles. Each missile had its own self-contained guidance system. All the missiles needed was a positive heat signature from a target somewhere behind the aircraft.

And a command from the cockpit.

Switzer had his hand on the firing button. His eyes were fixed on Brand, waiting for the order. Brand turned to lock gazes with Libby.

Libby looked back at him. She hated this. She hated the decisions that went with this job. Brand was still looking at her, giving her a nod.

"Yes," she said.

CHAPTER THIRTEEN

Slade wished he could transmit a "Fox-one." It was the brevity-code call that a semi-active radar-guided missile was being fired. He could imagine the effect back in the Capella command post. He would love to follow up with an eye-witness report of the descending fireball. He would be the sole witness to the death of the traitor queen.

But Slade knew the rules, and he understood the reason for them. Nothing, not even the record of a scrambled radio call, would be available for investigators. In total anonymity Col. Tom Slade was going to change the course of history.

Slade eased his finger over the trigger on the control stick. He gave the multi-function display a final glance. The target acquisition box hovered neatly over the symbol for the 747. The scenario was playing out exactly as he had rehearsed a hundred times in his mind.

He returned his scan to the outside. He wanted to see the missiles hit their target. He'd fire from a slight offset, get the Sparrows in the air, stay away from the cloud of flaming debris that would—

What the hell? A flash. Something in the tail of the 747, like a tiny explosion.

Then he saw it. It looked like a firefly in the darkness, making tiny course corrections as it homed unerringly for its target. Slade had witnessed the flight of over a hundred air-to-air missiles. He'd never seen one from this angle.

The sonofabitch was coming at *him*. More by instinct than conscious thought, Slade slammed the stick to the left and racked the F-15C into an eight-G turn. He knew it was futile. The only effect of the maneuver was to block his view of the missile homing in on the intake of his right engine.

When the impact came, Tom Slade's only sensation was a

blinding light. Then darkness.

<>

"My god," whispered Libby. "Did we do that?"

The flash emanated from behind and to the left, momentarily lighting up the sky. Through Brand's side window Libby could see the pulsing yellow glow, descending behind them. The glow lasted several seconds, then faded.

"Our missile," said Brand in a toneless voice. "It took out the bandit."

Libby felt a wave of revulsion come over her. In her year and a half as President she had given her approval to operations that resulted in someone's death. Sometimes the deceased was an enemy of the United States. Sometimes the deceased was an American she'd sent into action. In each instance she was removed by several thousand miles and multiple layers of responsibility from the actual carnage.

This was different. She had given the order to fire. She hated it.

Libby continued staring out the window. The yellow glow was gone. The sky was dark. "It was one of ours, wasn't it? An American?"

Brand said nothing.

She knew. She could tell by the way Brand was looking at her. Whoever was flying the fighter was on the same team that had tried to kill them over the Atlantic. Her fellow Americans. She was their commander-in-chief.

A silence fell over the cockpit. In the semi-darkened cockpit Libby could see Brand's profile. He was gazing out the windscreen, out where the aurora was shimmering in the northern sky. His expression was reflective, as if he were deep in thought.

She remembered that expression. She'd seen it before. In another lifetime.

<>

They are anchored on the eastern shore of Maryland. Libby is looking around the boat. She peeks into the aft cabin, then the forward cabin. Each is neat, as if a housekeeper has just tidied up. Brand actually lives on this vessel. He also has an apartment in Alexandria, but she knows it is mainly for his books, an office, and a more spacious place to spread out his painting equipment.

In Libby's experience, few men are neat. It stands to reason that in order to live on a boat you have to have a certain sense of order. The interior of Brand's boat is orderly, yet somehow homey. Not at all like sailboats she's seen before. Brand's boat looks like a floating studio. The home of an artist who also happens to be a technocrat. The nearly invisible hi-fi produces acoustics, to Libby's ear, like those in a symphony hall.

Arranged on the bulkheads of the cabin are half a dozen unframed canvases. Brand's foldable easel stands in a corner.

She squints at one of the paintings. Libby doesn't qualify as an art critic, but she knows what pleases her and what doesn't. Brand's watercolors are mostly aquatic scenes. Harbors filled with the masts of moored vessels, a yacht much like Andromeda *heeled over under full sail, a pelican gazing from his perch on a boat's rail.*

"They're. . . different," she says.

"Astute observation," says Brand. "Different from what?"

"Each is different from the others. Some have a broad field of view, with an object in the foreground, like this one"— she points to a scene of a seashore view from over the prow of a boat — "and some, like this pelican here, are up close, with the background sort of . . . unfocused."

Brand nods. "Like a photograph?"

She stands back, appraising the painting. "Yes, it has that quality."

"I shot each of the scenes with a camera. Several times, actually, different perspectives and fields of view. When I saw what I was looking for, I painted it."

Libby tilts her head, looking at each painting in turn. She nods her approval. "This stuff could grow on you."

"Which do you like best?"

She squints at the paintings again. "This one. The pelican."

"Do you want it?"

"I don't think I can afford it."

"You can." He takes the canvas down from the bulkhead and hands it to her.

She gazes at it for several seconds. "It's beautiful. But I don't see the artist's signature."

"It's better that way."

She thinks about it for another moment. She knows what he means. Gifts of art invite scrutiny. And questions. Who is the painter? Someone we've heard of? Brand is right. Let the artist remain anonymous. It occurs to her that Brand is better at protecting their secrecy than she is.

"For now," she says. "Someday I'll ask you for the artist's signature on the painting."

He gives her that bemused half smile again. "Someday."

Libby just nods. There's that word again. Someday. She and Brand use it a lot. It's the closest they can come to talking about the future.

<>

Snick. Snick. Snick.

The Nikon clicks off the shots in rapid succession. Beldner pulls his head back to glance at the stored images, then returns his eye to the viewer and notches the shutter speed up one click.

Snick. Snick.

They are staying a good seventy, maybe eighty yards away, but that's close enough. The big 600 mm. lens—Beldner calls it the Howitzer—is bringing the targets up close and personal.

"Get any with her top off?" asks Manson from the nearby rail.

"Lots. Nice mole on her left boob," reports Beldner. "Looks like she and the guy are about to get it on right there in the wheelhouse."

"They paying any attention to us?"

"He gave us a look over, but didn't bother with binocs. Guess they're not worried about being surveilled."

Beldner isn't concerned about being spotted. The Howitzer is well concealed in a pile of orange life preservers and coiled lines. Only the 6-and-a-half-inch diameter end of the telescopic lens is peeking through an opening. The non-reflective filter eliminates any telltale glint of sunlight. The trawler is creeping along at something less than three knots. The three men with fishing rods are going through the motions of casting and retrieving their lines. Manson has even caught some kind of fish. The thing is still flopping around in the well on the aft deck.

This is the second time the targets had come out here to the east Chesapeake in the sailboat. Beldner can see why. They can anchor in one of these little coves in the archipelago across the bay from the mouth of the Potomac. No traffic, shoreline nearly deserted, no intruders. Just the odd slow-moving trawler, like this one, with the three guys fishing.

And the 600 mm. Howitzer.

Beldner doesn't know the guy's name. Wouldn't be hard to find out if he were curious. He's already figured out that the broad is a Congresswoman by the name of Paulsen. By the way they're nuzzling each other you know that the guy isn't her spouse, which is undoubtedly the reason for the shoot. Beldner has been in this business long enough to know that you don't ask questions about the job. Or the client. You get the shots, get out of sight, collect your money. You don't care what the client does with the photos. Could be blackmail, could be a tabloid spread, maybe even espionage. Beldner has seen it all. It doesn't matter. All that matters is that he gets paid.

Snick. Snick. Snick.

"It's getting better," says Beldner. "They're playing grabass again. Hands all over each other."

Snick. Snick. Yeah, they are definitely getting worked up, the guy's hand between her thighs, she stroking him like a cat. Are *they going to do it out there in the open? Beldner hopes so. The broad seems ready, but the guy is saying something, looking up and glancing around. He peers over at the trawler with the disinterested fishermen still working their lines, then nods to the woman. Holding her hand, he leads her down the open companionway to the forward cabin.*

Beldner gets off another half-dozen frames, some good skin shots, before the couple vanishes into the darkness of the cabin. "Ease us around," he calls up to Edmunds on the helm. "Keep a good distance and get me a better angle through that cabin door." If they don't close the door he might get a few shadowy shots of the real thing. Some good old-fashioned bonking. Even if they are only silhouettes, he can make the images clear enough with the computer.

Beldner keeps shooting as the trawler moves in a slow arc around the cove. They have a straight-on view of the stern of sailboat. The cabin door is still open, the interior of the cabin mostly dark. Beldner won't know if he is getting anything good until he's done the enhancements back in the office.

Doesn't matter. What he's gotten today is hot. Real hot. Images sharp and unmistakable, targets clearly frozen in activities that leave nothing to the imagination. Just what the client ordered.

<>

"Nice painting," says Ken Paulsen.

Libby looks up from the Washington Post. *She's sitting at the breakfast table. Early spring sunshine is slanting through the kitchen window. She has fifteen minutes before she has to be out the door. The opener on her agenda is the meeting of the House Committee on Agriculture, of which she is the junior member.*

"Painting?" says Libby. Her husband is standing in the kitchen doorway. He is in golf attire—jet blue slacks, web belt, polo shirt over a long-sleeved jersey. Paulsen is a two-handicap player, and the natty wardrobe matches his game. As far as

Libby can tell, most of Paulsen's business as a Washington lobbyist is conducted on the fairways of the District's country clubs.

Then she sees it. Paulsen is holding up an unframed canvas. A watercolor of a pelican perched on a boat rail.

"Not bad," says Paulsen, "if you like birds crapping on boats. Where'd it come from?"

Libby doesn't hate Ken Paulsen. Not any longer. In the twelve years of their marriage her emotions have run from love to contempt to what she feels now—a studied indifference. That she has remained in a loveless marriage is, she often reflects, more a commentary on her own ambition than on her feelings about wedlock. The truth is, being married to the handsome and likable Ken Paulsen has been good for her career. Divorcing him would crush her approval rating in the heavily Catholic district she represents.

Falling out of love with Ken had taken her less than a year. It began the first time she was confronted with his philandering. The girl was a vapid blonde named Susie, one in a long succession of interns, reporters, lobbyists, secretaries, and one married female naval officer. The first occasion was followed by an ugly spat, denials and recriminations.   Next morning came the apologies and a tear-filled promise that it wouldn't happen again.

It did. Again and again as she learned that Ken Paulsen was a man hardwired for adultery. There were more pitched battles, accusations and denials, more promises of fidelity. At some point Libby stopped caring. The only requirement she now asks of her husband is that he not jeopardize her career by flaunting his affairs in public. He has complied, more or less. She has come to regard Ken Paulsen not as a husband but an associate with whom she has to maintain a civil if not an intimate relationship.

"That painting?" she says again. Her voice has a tinny sound, and she hates it. Damn. She neglected to put the painting away. Ken must have found it in her office. He's holding it up like a *specimen.*

She says, "Oh, some little gallery in Annapolis. I bought it on a whim."

Paulsen is giving her a curious look. "Why were you in Annapolis?"

"Business," she says. She doesn't like his tone. What the hell does he care where she picked up a watercolor of a pelican? "Lunch with someone."

He looks at her for another moment, then nods. "Didn't know you were into cheap art. Who's the artist?"

"Who knows? I liked it, so I bought it." She picks up the paper again and resumes reading, her signal that the conversation has ended. She feels a flash of anger, not so much at her husband— she knows better than to let Ken Paulsen push her buttons—but at herself. This feeling of guilt. It is ironic that she should be lying to him, the crown prince of liars. About a damned painting. And the painter.

CHAPTER FOURTEEN

Sam Fornier stared at the blank screen. Something was going on. Fornier was trying to log on to Gourmand, the dedicated server that relayed text messages to the galleys of the squadron aircraft. Fornier's laptop, which was Wi-Fi linked to the master server, was displaying a message: ERROR CODE 351: GOURMAND IS UNAVAILABLE. PASSWORD RESET REQUIRED.

Bullshit, thought Fornier. The Gourmand server, which was physically located somewhere in Virginia, had never been unavailable. And never had it been necessary to reset the password. And if it ever was required, it would be the air wing information technology officer who issued or changed passwords.

And that officer happened to be Capt. Sam Fornier.

Ooookay. The game was heating up. Someone was screwing around with Gourmand. And given the total craziness of what had happened with Air Force One, Fornier had an idea who. The same someone who had picked up on the texting link between Air Force One and the catering officer at Andrews.

Oh, shit. As the realization sank in, it took all Fornier's will power not to grab the laptop, yank the running shoes out of the backpack, put them on and run like a baboon with its ass on fire.

Instead, the young officer went back to the laptop. Typing as fast as possible, Fornier pecked in a new password for the Gourmand server.

And then logged off.

Just as quickly Fornier opened up a new connection, this one to Chowhound, the secondary server which Fornier had set up out of boredom one night when there was nothing else to do in the catering office. Chowhound used a discrete address and had only one admissible user: Sam Fornier.

Or so Fornier hoped. Sam was loading the password for the secondary server when the sounds came from the hallway outside.

Footsteps. Lots of them. With trembling fingers Fornier pecked at the laptop, closing down the Chowhound connection.

The door to the office burst open.

<>

Is McDivott a psycho?

It wasn't the first time the thought had occurred to Major Gen. Jim Ripley. Back when Ripley was a new brigadier and McDivott was looking for his first star, Ripley had watched McDivott maneuvering his way up the military pyramid. To his followers, Vance McDivott was a warrior in the mold of Alexander or Napoleon. A mix of religiosity and brazen courage. To his detractors, McDivott was something else. He was a dangerous firebrand with the power to mesmerize an entire nation.

Ripley knew the truth. McDivott was both.

"So what happened to Blazer?" McDivott asked.

No one answered. Each of the officers in the room gazed back at McDivott. They knew it was a rhetorical question. Blazer—the call sign for Tom Slade, pilot of the F15C dispatched to intercept Angel—had vanished from the screen. Like Angel, Blazer was emitting no electronic signals.

"It seems pretty clear," offered Ripley. "Blazer has been morted."

McDivott looked at him. "By what means?"

Ripley knew this was coming. Another rhetorical question. That was McDivott's style, asking questions to which he already knew the answers, just to see if he'd missed something. "How else?" said Ripley. "We know that Angel has air-to-air defense weaponry."

"Were we not assured that their avionics capability had been neutralized? No radar, no data link. How could Angel have gotten a lock on Blazer?"

"They're getting help," said an Air Force major. His name was

Blackwell, and he commanded the special communications section of Capella. "We've homed in on a data link that seems to be emanating from Andrews. We think that an officer in the VIP catering office, maybe with the help of someone in the Pentagon, alerted Angel to the threat over an open comm channel."

"Open channel?" said McDivott. "How did that happen? And why hasn't this catering officer been nailed?"

"It's happening as we speak. We've already shut down the server they've been using, which should put Angel out of communications permanently."

"What about this source in the Pentagon? Who the hell could that be?"

Blackwell shook his head. "We don't know yet, but we're getting close. We're monitoring every registered device. If they try to open up another comm line, we'll be on them."

McDivott clasped his hands behind him and seemed to lapse into deep thought. After several seconds he peered around the room again, pausing to fix his gaze on each of the officers present. McDivott rose from his chair and stood stroking his chin. "It's all very clear, gentlemen. By firing a missile at Tom Slade's aircraft, the terrorists have displayed hostile intent."

"Terrorists?" said Ripley.

"The ones who have taken control of Air Force One. By this overt act of war, they have revealed their intentions. We have all the justification we need for shooting them down."

"Ah, General, won't that be stretching the rationale a bit, considering that the F-15 was on its way to—"

"This is the U. S. Air Force, not the Cub Scouts, General Ripley. The F-15 was fired upon and destroyed. When we're fired upon, we fire back."

Ripley knew when to shut up. McDivott's eyes had taken on a messianic glow. Ripley had it seen before and he knew what was coming.

"Let us pray," McDivott said. His eyes swept the room,

commanding each of the half dozen officers to join him. He bowed his head. "Heavenly father, we ask that you bestow your blessing on the soul of our departed hero, Tom Slade, and welcome him to the kingdom of glory." McDivott paused for effect. Then he continued in a more strident voice, "And we beseech thee, Father, to give us courage. Give us the courage to complete the crusade on which you have sent us. We ask your guidance and divine help to strike from the sky the oppressors who would destroy our nation." He paused again before saying, "Amen."

"Amen," echoed the officers in the room.

Jim Ripley was a religious man, but not as religious as McDivott. Did McDivott really believe that God was directing him? Was the general a religious fanatic who had gone over the edge? If so, he was taking an entire country with him.

Ripley uttered his own silent prayer. He prayed that God would forgive them for what they were about to do.

<>

"What about the Iranians?" said Jill.

Libby looked up from her desk. "Iranians? What about them?"

"The reason we made this trip, remember? The two diplomats who are supposed to be your negotiating partners. You need to talk to them."

Libby rubbed her eyes for a moment. So much had happened in the past eight hours she'd forgotten about the pair of Iranians who boarded Air Force One in Tehran. "How do you talk about a peace accord when someone is trying to kill you?"

"Fake it," said Jill. "We've been their Great Satan for thirty years. These guys don't trust us anyway, and now they're scared to death."

"For good reason. So am I."

"If you want to pull off this peace accord, you have to reassure them."

Libby sighed. *If you want to pull off this peace accord.* They both knew the truth. The Iranian peace accord had been Lyle

Bethune's idea, but it would have had no chance of succeeding without the involvement of the President. That involvement had just earned for her the everlasting hatred of the right wing. And maybe a death sentence.

"Okay, send them in."

Jill stepped back into the passageway. Seconds later she returned with the two diplomats in trail. The Iranian Foreign Minister, Mahmoud Said, looked like a befuddled professor in his rumpled black suit and thick spectacles. The other man, Kamil Al-Bashir, was a younger and scruffier version of Said. Each wore a graying stubble of beard and the same glowering expression.

Said didn't offer to shake hands. He positioned himself in front of Libby's desk. "We are outraged about our treatment aboard your aircraft."

"Your treatment?" Libby caught Jill's furtive nod. "Oh, you must mean—"

"We are being watched like criminals. No one has kept us informed. We have not been permitted to communicate with our superiors as we were promised."

Libby remembered. Gritti and Grossman were worried because the Iranians hadn't undergone a security check. It was Grossman's idea to keep them under constant watch.

"I apologize, Minister Said. My security people sometimes become overly protective of me. They are especially worried because of the . . .unfortunate death of our Vice President."

"Have we become suspects in this matter?"

"Certainly not. I will order our security chief to discontinue watching you and Mr. Al-Bashir." Libby ignored the scowl from Jill Maitlin.

Said nodded. His voice became less strident. "Does that mean we will be allowed to speak with our ministry in Tehran as we were promised?"

"Yes, of course. As soon as we have restored our long range communications network." She paused and gave him a wan smile.

"I understand your frustration. Believe me, I am just as frustrated. It must seem unbelievable that such an airplane—" she made a sweeping gesture with her hand —"would have this sort of failure. Our Presidential Pilot tells me he's never experienced such a thing."

She thought she saw a softening in the Iranian's hard expression. "Madame President, is there some other danger we haven't been told about?"

Libby tried to read the Iranian's face. Like all the occupants of Air Force One, he knew about the electrical failure and the descent over the North Atlantic. Like the other passengers, he had chosen to stay aboard in Greenland. What else did he suspect? Did he have any idea that they had nearly been shot down by a friendly fighter?

"No danger," said Libby. "Our crew assures me that our aircraft's problems are minor. We will be arriving in Washington right on schedule."

"Then we can resume our negotiations?"

"Certainly. The accord between our countries will be my highest priority. You have my sincere promise."

It seemed to be working. Libby could sense the change in the Iranian's demeanor. She saw Said exchange glances with the younger man, who nodded his agreement. Said turned to her. "Thank you for your openness, Madame President. Mr. Al-Bashir and I are prepared to cooperate with you in completing this difficult process."

Libby came from around her desk and took the Iranian's hand between hers. She gave each a smile. "Gentlemen, I am honored to be your negotiating partner. We will reach an accord that will serve both our countries. Together we will make history."

Each man was nodding his head affirmatively as Jill ushered them from the suite. When the door was again closed, Jill said, "That was masterful. Just what it took. You reassured them."

Libby said nothing. She slumped back into the chair behind her desk. She didn't feel masterful. She felt like an actor. *You reassured them.* Maybe, but Libby knew the truth. She was the one who needed reassuring.

<>

The girl with the pony tail looked up from the desk. "Can I help you?"

There were four of them, all carrying semi-automatic pistols. Were those Glocks? The girl didn't know. Guns were guns. These guys looked like goons and they were after something. Or someone. They had the look of rent-a-cops. Blue nylon jackets, thick necks, short haircuts.

Two of them didn't wait. The pair charged past her desk, pistols at the ready, yanking open cabinets and peering beneath desks, .

"Hey!" she said. "What do you think you're doing in here?"

The guy in front of her desk, a barrel-chested man who appeared to be in charge, demanded, "We're looking for Captain Sam Fornier. Where is he?"

The girl crossed her arms over her chest. "Who are you?" She tried to appear unintimidated, even though they were intimidating the crap out of her. "Stop waving those guns around or I'm calling security." It came out squeaky. It was the best she could do.

"I don't give a shit who you call, lady. This is a matter of national security. I'm asking you as nice as I can, where is Captain Fornier?"

She met his gaze for several seconds before she answered. "He left about five minutes ago. He said he was going over to the east hangar to check on something."

"The east hangar?" The man yanked out his cell phone and stared at the screen. A map of the base, the girl guessed.

The man looked back at her. "Where in the east hangar?"

"He didn't say. Maybe the materiel office. Would you tell me what this is about?"

"No." The man was waving to his colleagues to rejoin him.

"Should I tell Capt. Fornier to get in touch in with you?"

He leaned across the desk and glowered at her. "Don't tell anyone anything. Stay here, don't move, and we'll be right back. Understand?"

She felt like telling this cretin to shove it up his rectum sideways. She thought better of it. "I understand," she said. "I'm not going anywhere."

She waited until the sound of their footsteps on the epoxied floor of the passageway had faded. Then she unfolded her arms from the front of her utility uniform. She glanced at the lettering embroidered on the nametape over the right breast pocket: FORNIER.

Okay, now what? Samantha Fornier didn't know. She only knew with a growing certainty what she *wasn't* going to do. She wasn't going to hang around this goddamn office until the goons wised up and came back to arrest her. She had to get to the parking lot before it was too late. *Haul ass, girl.*

Sam flipped the lid down on the laptop. She yanked the power supply from the wall socket and stuffed it along with the laptop into her backpack. She removed her boots and yanked off the trousers and blouse of her utility uniform. From the locker next to her desk she pulled out a warm-up suit and running shoes. *Haul ass, girl.*

Three minutes later Capt. Sam Fornier was hauling ass.

<>

It was eerie, thought Cassidy. The Pentagon at three in the morning felt like a ghost town. The building's sprawling complex of parking lots, normally filled with over 18,000 cars, was nearly deserted. A squad of security guards checked his ID at the main entrance. To Cassidy's surprise, they weren't the same guards as usual. These were civilians in blue uniforms with a black emblem that read "Galeforce." Cassidy could see more security teams with the same uniforms prowling the other lots and the grounds of the Pentagon.

When Cassidy reached the wedge-shaped section that housed

the Air Force's Manpower and Personnel Branch, he encountered yet another blue-uniformed group. The portico of the building was flooded with light. One of the guards mumbled something into his shoulder-mounted radio mike while another waved Cassidy on through the entrance.

The cavernous corridors of the building were nearly empty. Except for the duty officers and skeleton crews manning the desks of their departments, no one was there. Cassidy knew that would change in a few hours when over twenty thousand military and civilian personnel poured into the Pentagon. By then they'd all be talking about what happened to the commander-in-chief.

Cassidy could hear the echo of his footsteps on the hard tiled floor of the hallway. A lone blue-uniformed security guard at the top of the escalator to the upper floor gave him a cursory nod. Cassidy continued down the hallway to the third door on the right.

The Air Force Manpower and Personnel Branch was Jack Cassidy's first and—he had already vowed to himself—his last non-flying post. He'd taken the job with that stipulation. No more desk jobs. His next assignment would be one of the major air commands—Pacific or Europe. That or retirement.

Or so he had thought. Given the events of the past few hours, it seemed likely that neither would happen.

The duty officer at the front desk, a major named Loomis, looked up in surprise. "Oh, it's you, General. Guess you've come out because of Air Force One?"

If you only knew, thought Cassidy. He had no intention of getting into a discussion with Bill Loomis, a non-stop motor mouth. Cassidy kept walking. "I'll be in my office, Bill. Make sure that no one gets past this desk. Not before you give me a heads up, okay?"

Loomis looked perplexed. "Yes, sir, no problem. Is this something I can help with?"

"Keep my lines to the major commands open and secure. Everything outgoing encrypted."

Another quizzical look. "You've got it, General."

Inside his windowless office, Cassidy locked the glass door behind him, rolled down the slatted blinds, and settled into the big Aeron office chair. His condo in Arlington was ten minutes away. Even though he had phone access from his home office to the major Air Force commands, it wasn't secure. What he had to do now required the encrypted connections of his Pentagon office.

During the drive to the Pentagon, he'd had time to think about who was behind this mess. By the time he'd reached his office, he was sure. For years he'd known about Capella. The right wing clique was comprised mostly of military officers, but also some high-ups in the government and the media. From time to time Cassidy had received hints that his career might be better served if he belonged. Cassidy had ignored the hints. In his opinion, the loonies on the right were as dangerous as the loonies on the left.

Now time was running out. He guessed he had an hour, maybe less. Who to call? It had to be commanders he personally knew. Guys he could trust. And therein was the problem. He had no idea how deep this conspiracy went.

After he thought about it, he picked up the phone that would connect him to the headquarters of the 1st Air Force. The connection was supposed to be encrypted. What he didn't know was who else besides the recipient could unscramble the conversation. Were the connections monitored? Yeah, bet your ass they were. But by whom?

Cassidy distrusted computers and longed for the days when people exchanged post cards and called each other on land lines. Now they had all this high tech crap and nobody knew how to make it work except the IT geeks. Geeks like this kid, Fornier.

With that thought, he checked his cell phone again. Where the hell was the geek?

<>

The street in front of Sam Fornier's apartment was deserted. It was still too early for the joggers and bikers and the pre-dawn worker bees headed for the city. Sam's headlights played on the rows of parked cars along the curb. Both sides of the street were filled. She'd have to park in the back, in the narrow slot behind the dumpster where the Mini Cooper would barely fit.

Just to be on the safe side, she would make one pass down the street before going into the apartment. She didn't think the goons had yet figured out who she was and where she lived. She'd taken a chance going out the gate at Andrews. The military facility was already in lock down mode. All *inbound* traffic was being blocked at the entrance while military police searched vehicles, but they were still letting personnel exit with only a cursory ID check. That would change as soon as the goons figured out that Capt. Sam Fornier had gone missing.

Easing down the street, Sam gave each parked car a good look. The brick-facade apartment buildings were uniformly dark, no sign of life. As she approached number 32 on the right side, she slowed almost to a stop. Her apartment was on the second floor. The blinds on the living room window were open. Had she done that? Sometimes she forgot. When had she left? This morning, a little past seven. It had been daytime, so maybe she hadn't noticed.

She was almost past the apartment when she saw it. *A light in the window.* It was momentary, just a flicker. A flashlight? She glimpsed it again, this time a sweeping beam. Definitely a flashlight. Probing the darkness inside her apartment.

Oh holy flaming shit. Sam stepped on the accelerator, and in the same instant she noticed movement on her left. One of the parked cars, a black SUV with smoked glass windows, maybe a Toyota. It was moving. Pulling into the street, making a U-turn to go her direction. No headlights.

Sam jammed the pedal to the floor. At the corner she wheeled to the right. The Mini's tires screeched on the pavement. In the mirror she could see the dim shape of the SUV. It's headlights were still off.

The street was sparsely illuminated by widely spaced

streetlamps. Sam flicked off her own headlights. In the sudden darkness she could barely make out the dark rows of parked vehicles blurring past on either side. At the next corner she threw the Mini into a skidding turn to the left. Just in time she swerved to miss the back end of a parked panel truck. In the mirror she saw the dark silhouette of the SUV veer around the corner.

The goons were getting closer.

Sam fought against the panic that was swelling inside her. *Faster. Don't let those assholes catch you.* She jammed harder on the accelerator, then realized it was already floored. At this speed she saw only the blurred shadows of the parked cars. Another corner was coming up fast.

Sam yanked the wheel hard to the right. Too late she felt the Mini's rear wheels slide out. The boxy little car was trying to swap ends. Sam fought to keep control, steering into the skid, trying to straighten the Mini's careening path.

It didn't work. The rear end swung around like a pendulum. The car hurtled into the intersection. Disoriented, Sam sensed the world spinning around her. The Mini had nearly made a complete revolution when the dark shape of a parked sedan swelled in the windshield. Sam felt the glancing impact as the right front corner slammed into the side of the sedan. The metallic *whang* deafened her. Sam had only a dim awareness of the car flipping over. She felt herself flung sideways across the seat, into the ceiling, the sudden gray presence of the deployed airbag jamming against her.

The flipping ended. Sam sensed the Mini skidding across the pavement on its roof. With a final *whump* the car slammed into a parked vehicle on the opposite side of the street. Sam lay in the overhead panel of the car. She tried to orient herself. The car's motor was racing. A hissing noise was coming from somewhere in the engine compartment.

Her brain was in slow motion. *What the hell happened?* Nothing was making any sense. Why was she here? She had gone to her apartment to—

Oh, shit. In a flash of understanding it came to her. The goons. They were here.

CHAPTER FIFTEEN

"**W**e have just a few minutes," said Libby. "Colonel Brand can't be away from the cockpit for long. After he's briefed us, we'll discuss our course of action."

It was Jill's idea to use the conference room. It was the largest compartment in the aircraft. "They'll be writing about this in their memoirs someday," Jill had said. "Let's make sure they write that they were included."

Libby wasn't so sure. She avoided large staff and cabinet meetings. Her Presidential style was to go one-on-one with her advisors. That way she could announce decisions post facto, which spared her the unruly cabinet debates and the long-winded spiels from self-important secretaries and policy specialists.

Libby sat at the head of the long conference table. To her left she saw the solemn faces of Gen. Gus Gritti and Mike Grossman. At the far end was Karl Ozinsky, senior senator from Ohio. Ozinsky was a member of the Committee on Foreign Relations and, in Libby's opinion, a pompous demagogue. Two election cycles ago Ozinsky had taken a shot at his party's Presidential nomination before losing the New Hampshire primary. With his white-maned, patrician good looks and imperious manner, Ozinsky had become a fixture on the political talk shows.

Libby didn't like Ozinsky, but she had to give him credit. He wasn't afraid to take flak for crossing party lines on issues that were important to him. It was, in fact, why the senator had been included on the Tehran junket. "It signals our transparent approach to foreign policy," Jill said. "Get Ozinsky on board and we're halfway to getting the treaty ratified." Libby didn't believe it. She expected the opposite, but at least the cranky senator's presence gave her Iran mission the appearance of being a bipartisan effort.

Next to Ozinsky sat Lester Vosges, White House senior director for Middle East Affairs. A witty and erudite Columbia professor, Vosges brought an air of civility to heated policy debates. On Vosges's right was Josh Fortenoy, the thirty-year-old deputy White House chief of staff. Fortenoy was a brash young man whose job as gate keeper and scheduler had been mostly expropriated by the President's senior adviser, Jill Maitlin.

Jill sat in her customary place at Libby's right. The seat on Libby's other side was filled by the Presidential Pilot. Brand was wearing a blue windbreaker with the Air Force One emblem over his khaki uniform shirt, no tie.

Libby nodded to Brand. Brand glanced around the room. "As you know by now," he said, "Air Force One has become a target. An entity still unknown to us is trying to remove the President. Our communications capability has been sabotaged, which means we're not able to transmit our position or our intentions. We have opened up one very tenuous line of communication and our situation has been reported to a senior officer in the Pentagon."

"Who would that be, Colonel?" asked Senator Ozinsky.

Brand hesitated. "I don't think that it's—"

"A general named Cassidy," offered Jill Maitlin. "He's supposedly a friend of Colonel Brand's."

Brand said nothing. His eyes bored into Jill Maitlin.

"Let Colonel Brand finish," said Libby.

Brand unfolded an aerial chart. "Here's my plan. From our present position"—he pointed to a spot off the coast of Canada—"we parallel the coast of North America, remaining a couple hundred miles offshore. Then we turn to enter U. S. airspace over the northeast coastline. We'll make an immediate landing at a suitable base on the coast."

"What's to keep them from shooting us down?" asked General Gritti.

"Nothing," said Brand. "Nothing except our single communications link—and our own defense capability."

Ozinsky was peering over the rims of his reading glasses. "Defense capability? Would you explain that, please?"

"No, sir."

The senator leaned forward, glowering at Brand. "Colonel, I asked you a question. I expect an answer."

"Considering our circumstances, Senator, I prefer not to discuss it."

Ozinsky's eyes blazed. "Now you listen to me, I want to—"

"Excuse us, Senator," said Jill Maitlin, "but that's not why we're here." She turned her attention to Brand. "The real subject of this discussion is *where* we are going to arrive. And for your information, Colonel Brand, you've got it all wrong. Air Force One should return to the nation's capitol. We shouldn't be landing anywhere except back at Andrews."

Libby glanced from Jill to Brand. She saw Brand's expression harden. Jill's expression was just as obdurate.

"With all due respect," said Brand, "that would be the stupidest thing we could do."

Jill's face reddened. Before she could reply, Mike Grossman spoke up. "Ms. Maitlin has a point, Colonel. The President has the best security coverage in the world in Washington. What can happen to her there?"

"That's the point," said Brand. "We don't know. We don't know the extent of this conspiracy. Even if we didn't get shot down before we approached Washington, we don't know who's waiting for us on the ground."

"That's why we have the Secret Service," said Jill Maitlin. "To protect the President."

"From whom?" said Brand. He looked around the table. "Who is the enemy? We know they've planted at least one agent inside the Presidential Airlift Group, one of our flight engineers. We know they've deployed at least one interceptor against us and, probably, the air refueling ship. It would be a mistake to assume they don't have agents inside the Secret Service."

"Now wait a damn minute," said Grossman. "If you're suggesting that one of our agents—"

"It doesn't matter what the colonel is suggesting," said Jill. She gestured with her hand around the table. "Let me remind you once again, Colonel Brand, the people at this table are the President's advisors. It's our job to counsel her, not yours."

Brand said nothing. His face remained expressionless. A silence fell over the table. Libby could feel the eyes on her. Another impasse. They were waiting for her to decide, as if she were a damned referee. What should they do? Go to Washington, or land somewhere else? Jill or Brand?

The obvious answer was Jill. Throughout Libby's political career—House to Senate to White House—she had depended on Jill Maitlin. Jill was the wise one. The tough one. The behind-the-scenes decider. She trusted Jill.

Brand was another matter. There was a reason she'd made Pete Brand the Presidential Pilot. It had less to do with qualifications than it did with instinct. As if she had known a day like this would come. A day when her life might depend on Brand.

Jill Maitlin was drumming her fingers on the yellow legal pad in front of her. She made a show of glancing at her watch. Jill's standard method of prompting Libby into action.

"Colonel Brand is right," Libby announced. "We shouldn't land in Washington."

Jill Maitlin's eyes flashed. "That's crazy. We have to talk about this."

"We've talked about it." Libby tried to sound more decisive than she felt. "Colonel Brand has a plan, and I think we should go with it." Libby rose from her chair. "I'd like for the rest of you to start working on a ground strategy after our arrival in the U. S."

The assembled group rose in unison. All except Jill Maitlin. She remained in her seat with her arms crossed, her face a frozen mask. Libby glanced at Brand. He gave her a nod, then walked out of the conference room.

Watching him leave, Libby felt a familiar queasiness rise in her. Why was she trusting Brand? He was one in a succession of male figures in her life whom she had trusted. Each had abandoned her.

With the queasiness came a memory. She could close her eyes and see them, the images from nearly four years ago. Rain, darkness, boat masts, a blackened harbor. A night that changed her life. The night Brand betrayed her.

<>

Libby parks where she always does, two blocks up from the marina. It has become a ritual, this weekend trip to the boat. She follows the sidewalk downhill, past the row of shops and restaurants, through the gate where she punches in the four-number code, then across the long dock out to the slip where Andromeda *is tied.*

The weather has turned nasty. The raw wind is driving sheets of early autumn rain across the sky. A ceiling of grey-black clouds scuds low overhead. She left the umbrella in the office. No matter. When she reaches the boat she'll slip out of her damp work clothes into the warm ups she keeps aboard.

With the dreary weather has come an early darkness. Libby walks across the wet planking, wiping the moisture from her eyes. She peers through the gloom toward the end of the dock. All she sees are the dim shapes of boats tied next to each other. She tries to pick out the familiar silhouette of Andromeda. *She can't spot it.*

She continues down the dock, along the row of boat slips. Still no Andromeda. *The Severna Marina is huge, hosting over five hundred vessels. Maybe in the rain she has meandered down the wrong pier.*

No. She stops and looks around. She knows where she is. There is Brand's slip. It's empty. Leaning away from the slanting rain, she pulls out her cell phone and punches in the coded number she uses for Brand. Wisps of wet hair dangle in her eyes. She shelters the phone with her other hand while it rings.

No answer. After five rings it stops. No voice mail

announcement. That's a change.

Libby is getting a bad feeling.

She is still standing on the dock, staring at the empty slip where she knows the boat is supposed to be, when she becomes aware of padded footsteps behind her. She turns to see a young man in a yellow rain slicker coming down the dock.

"Ms. Paulsen?"

She doesn't answer for a moment. It makes her nervous when strangers know her by name. "Can I help you?" she says.

"I'm supposed to give you this." The young man hands her a clear plastic zip bag. Without waiting, he turns and heads back up the dock.

Libby hesitates. Her feeling of unease is worsening. Now she is sure. Something isn't right.

Inside the bag is an unmarked, sealed envelope. Trying her best to shelter the envelope with her body, Libby tears it open and pulls out the folded paper. At a glance she recognizes the precise handwriting.

Dearest Libby,

This may seem a clumsy way to deliver this message, but I think you will agree that the subject is too painful for us to discuss face to face.

After much consideration, I've concluded that our relationship must end. Please know that you have done nothing wrong, nor have I. From the beginning we both knew that what we had together couldn't last. Our worlds have always been too far apart, too incompatible.

Before we make an irrevocable mistake, it's best that we break off this relationship now. We should not see each other again, nor should we communicate.

You have a brilliant career ahead of you. I wish you the greatest success and happiness.

With all my love,

Pete

Libby stares at the note. The ink is beginning to run as rain drops spatter the soft paper. She looks up the dock where the silhouette of the young man is vanishing. She wants to call him back. This is a mistake. This can't be for her. Pete Brand—the real Pete Brand—would never do this. He loves her too much. He wouldn't hurt her like this.

She wads the paper in her fist. Rivulets of rain mix with the tears streaming down her cheeks. After several minutes she steps to the edge of the dock and drops the crumpled paper into the water.

A wave of desolation sweeps over her. A little girl's voice from years ago speaks to her. You should have known. She has again committed the mistake of entrusting her happiness to a man she loves. A man who, she thought, loved her in return.

The rain has turned cold. Libby doesn't notice. Hands at her sides, she trudges back up the marina dock. She walks through the gate, up the lamplit sidewalk past a micro-brewery filled with boisterous young people. She keeps walking, past the parking lot where she's left her car, on up the hill and through another tree-lined neighborhood of boutiques and cafés. For twenty minutes she walks, oblivious to the rain.

She will force a meeting with him. Make him to talk to her. There has to be more than "our worlds are too incompatible." What is he thinking?

No. It won't work. Not with a man like Pete Brand. He doesn't reach a decision like this and then change his mind.

Nor would she. The role of spurned lover isn't Libby Paulsen's style. The relationship with Brand has been an illusion. Another bitter chapter in her life closed. Over and done with. She should have known.

She continues walking to the end of the shopping district. Then she walks back down the opposite side of the street. By the time she reaches the parking lot where she'd left the car, she knows what she has to do.

<>

"Are you sure?" The voice of Ben Marx, chairman of the national committee, sounds croaky.

"If I weren't sure, would I be calling you at this hour?" Libby knows that her voice is strident, almost combative. She doesn't care. It's a perfect reflection of her mood at the moment. "I told you I wanted some time to think about running for the Senate. Well, I've thought about it. You have my answer."

Marx is silent for a moment. It is nearly midnight on the East Coast, and Libby is sure that she has awakened him. She doesn't particularly like Ben Marx. He's a notorious bully, a one-time Pennsylvania governor and a leftover from the days when a cadre of machine bosses picked the party's candidates for national office.

"Well, I guess I should say congratulations," says Marx. "May I ask what it took to persuade you to go for the nomination?"

No, you may not, she thinks. After several seconds pause she gives him the answer she has spent the past hour composing. "I want to serve. As trite as it sounds, I happen to think I can serve my state—and our party—better than anyone else out there. With the support of you and the national committee, I'll do that."

"If you really mean it, then I can speak for the committee. You'll get the support. Now let me go back to sleep. Tomorrow we'll figure out how we're going to announce this."

"Thank you, Ben. Good night."

In her darkened study Libby refills her glass with brandy. She gazes through the blinds at the deserted street outside. Ken hasn't come home, which is fine with her. Whatever he thinks about the upcoming Senate race—or anything else—no longer matters. It's done. In the space of one handwritten note and a phone call, a might-have-been life is finished. A new one has begun. The campaign will be brutal, consuming all her time and energy.

Exactly what she needs.

And what if you win?

She takes another sip of brandy. She can feel it, that old queasiness in her stomach. And what if you win? *She knows the answer and it terrifies her.* You'll be in over your head.

CHAPTER SIXTEEN

Run, Sam, run.

The soles of Sam Fornier's running shoes skimmed over the damp asphalt. From behind she could hear the chuffing of the two men running after her. She wondered how good these guys were. She'd gotten only a glimpse as they were piling out of the SUV to come after her. They looked muscular and mean, wearing the same polo shirts and khakis as the four who came looking for her at Andrews.

It had been close. She was still kicking open the passenger side door of the Mini when the black SUV rolled up. Sam yanked the backpack out of the upside-down Mini, slipping it over her shoulders while she bolted down the street.

She rounded a corner and notched up the speed. Sam's breath was coming in rapid gasps. She knew she couldn't keep up this pace. She was a triathlete, not a goddamn sprinter. She ran for the joy of running, not the race. Until now.

To her left was a darkened park. She knew the park. It had trails and large patches of trees and shrubs. If she could gain some distance on these goons, she might be able to hide. Or she could keep running. She could head for the strip mall a few blocks ahead where there would be lights and people.

Or she could just call 911.

Bad idea, she immediately decided. However this played out, it would be over before any cops showed up. And Sam was growing more certain by the minute that whoever these guys were, they had connections in high places. The law wouldn't be on her side. Screw 911. She'd take her chances as a fugitive.

She wondered why they hadn't just shot her. They could have dropped her right there in the street while she was still exiting the Mini. Because they wanted information? The joke would be on them when they found out the truth. She was a nobody computer geek who had been minding her own business when she was sucked into a communications loop between a crotchety general and the pilot of Air Force One.

A hundred yards to the next corner. By the sound of the chuffing behind her, she knew she was opening up some distance. Cut left into the woods, or keep running straight? A couple blocks ahead and to the right was a strip mall with an all night convenience store. Maybe she could—

Ploom. It was a muffled sound, like a hammer blow inside a bucket. At almost the same instant Sam felt the bullet zing past her left ear. *Ploom.* The next round ricocheted from the pavement a few inches from her left foot.

Now she knew. The goons couldn't catch her, so they were going to shoot her. The thought sent a fresh surge of adrenaline through Sam Fornier's veins. She veered to the left. The park was straight ahead. Ten more yards.

Ploom. Ploom. She felt the spatter of concrete dust against her heels. Sam darted right, then zagged back left. Two seconds later she was sprinting into the darkness of the park.

<>

"Sam Fornier?" asked Ripley, squinting at the display screen. "Who the hell is he?"

Keppler glanced up from his console. "A pissant catering clerk out at Andrews. Take a look at this." Keppler clacked a series of keystrokes and a fresh image appeared on the screen. It was an ID photo of a short-haired young woman, blonde, no make up. She looked like somebody's college-age daughter except for the blue uniform with captain's bars on the shoulders.

Ripley peered at the image. "A woman? That's the Sam Fornier who's been texting Air Force One? Why haven't they shut her down?"

Keppler snorted. "Because the Galeforce dipshits at Andrews let her slip off the base, that's why. Then they missed her again when they tried to grab her at her residence."

"You mean she's still at large?"

"Still at large, still communicating. Even though we shut down her server. She's apparently cobbled together some kind of workaround. And it looks like she's hacked the tracking mode on the issue phone she swiped at Andrews. Our scanners are having a bitch of a time getting a lock on it."

"If this is some insignificant catering clerk, how is she able to stay ahead of your SigInt guys?"

Keppler gazed for a moment at the face in the screen. "Because she's good. I've seen kids like this before. Hackers who crack the system just to prove they can. Dangerous as hell if they figure out how to breech your security net. It's like this one had it already figured out, just waiting for a chance to use it."

Ripley thought he detected a note of admiration in Keppler's voice. Ripley had observed this phenomenon among the techies who ran the cyber warfare panels. They tended to regard their adversaries not as enemies but as opponents on a game board.

Keppler's official title was Director, Information Systems at the Defense Intelligence Agency. A recent recruit to Capella, his job was to coordinate the signals intelligence feed to the Briar Club headquarters. Keppler was like most of the SigInt spooks Ripley had ever known. Twenty-some pounds overweight, thinning slicked-back hair, black-rimmed glasses, acerbic disposition. The opposite of military officers like Ripley and McDivott.

Ripley asked, "Where's Fornier getting the information she's feeding to Air Force One?"

"From somebody with access to major command encrypted sources. Probably in the Pentagon."

"Probably? You can't locate him either?"

Keppler let out another derisive snort. "Look, General, let me explain in a way you can understand. What we've got here is a moving target with an untrackable phone. She's calling one of about twenty-thousand possible numbers, which may or may not be cellular and may or may not be trackable. This may take a little while."

"What am I supposed to tell Big Mac?" asked Ripley. Big Mac was Capella's in-house name for McDivott. "That Paulsen is still the President because you guys can't stop some skinny girl from relaying classified information?"

Keppler shrugged and turned back to his console. "Tell him we're getting close. We're getting a fix on the leak at the Pentagon. When we get that leak plugged, trust me, the game's over."

<>

Thank God for the darkness. The night was Sam Fornier's only advantage.

She knew the park, even in the pre-dawn darkness. She ran these same paths nearly every day. She could hear the goons crashing through the brush behind her. Rounding a corner on the narrow path, Sam glimpsed what she was looking for. She took a running leap and grabbed the hanging limb of a sprawling Ash tree. Sam hauled herself onto the limb, then shinnied up the trunk of the tree until she was twenty feet above the ground. She was still trying to enclose herself in the leafy folds of the top branches when the pair came trotting down the path.

They stopped almost directly beneath her.

"Where the fuck did she go?"

"She's close. I could hear her running, and now I don't."

Sam's heart was pounding like a jackhammer. The beam of their high-intensity flashlight was probing the bushes. The light swept up, down, through the trees. Sam wrapped herself tighter around the tree trunk. She tried to shield her white face with her shoulder. The beam flashed through the tree, paused, then slowly moved lower again.

"Like chasing a cockroach. She could be anywhere in here."

"Or headed for the other end of the park."

They started on down the path, probing the bushes on either side with the light. Sam didn't move. Dawn was coming in another hour. She couldn't stay in this damned tree. She had to get back on the line with General Cassidy, and she didn't dare do it from here. She had to get the hell out of this place.

Sam waited until she no longer heard them moving through the bush. Carefully, making no sound, she slid down the trunk of the ash tree. At the low branch she paused, listened again, then dropped to the soft ground.

She trotted quietly back the way she had come into the park. She stopped long enough to peer up and down the darkened street. No cars. No sign of the goons.

Sam darted across the street and into the shadows of the buildings on the far side. At a slow trot, stopping every half minute to gaze around, she worked her way toward her target. She slipped down an alley, coming out on the far side, then turned left again down a residential street with rows of adjoining townhouses.

At the end of the next block she saw it, and—*thank God*—the place appeared to be open. The store was lighted inside. The sign glittered over the entrance: *Starbucks*. Sam darted inside and took a table at the back.

<>

This mission sucks, thought Lt. Col. Stu Apte. His F-15C was climbing through 20,000 feet, outbound over the Atlantic. The rim of the eastern horizon was turning pink.

It wasn't the first time the thought had occurred to Lt. Col. Stu Apte. In the briefing at their base in Westfield, Massachusetts, Apte had experienced a sinking feeling when the wing commander, Col. Darrell Waugh, told him what they were going to do. This was bullshit. A hot potato scramble like this was supposed to be led by the squadron commander, Lt. Col. Fred Walstrum. Then Waugh shows up, bumps Walstrum off the mission, and orders everyone out of the room except Apte.

"Intercept *what?*" Apte had said when they were alone.

"You heard me. Air Force One has been hijacked, and the terrorists are going to crash it into Washington. It's our job to intercept them."

Apte was stunned. "May I ask who's ordering this mission?"

"No, you may not. It comes down from the Joint Chiefs and forwarded by the Commander, 1st Air Force. That's as much as you need to know."

"How do we confirm that they've been hijacked?"

"It's been confirmed. Now we follow the rules of engagement. ID, determine compliance or non-compliance."

Apte wasn't liking it. Not a goddamned bit of it. "Compliance with what?"

"With orders to land at Dover. If they don't, we take them down."

"What weapons?"

"AIM-9 Sidewinders. I'm the shooter, you're the back up."

Apte nodded. The Sidewinder was a heat seeker. It could be fired from any angle, but best was from behind where the missile could get a lock on any of the four jet tailpipes. The Sidewinder was a passively-guided weapon, emitting no radar signal.

Apte had never liked Waugh. He'd known him for nearly twenty years in the Air National Guard but never warmed up to the guy. Waugh never mixed with the other Guard pilots. He seemed to be on a track of his own, making squadron commander way out of seniority, then advancing to wing command. Waugh had already been named as the next state Air National Guard commander, with the rank of brigadier general. It was obvious that Darrell Waugh had a patron somewhere high up in the chain of command.

Now Apte was keeping his F-15C in a loose combat spread off Waugh's left wing. They already had the bogey on their radars— seventy five miles on the nose, level at about 28,000 feet. It was a fat target. The size of a 747.

At twenty miles Apte had a visual. He knew the rules. The two fighters would swoop beneath the target, pull up in a high reversal, drop back to a parallel track with the bogey. The rules of engagement required the lead fighter—Waugh—to fly up the left side of the 747. He was supposed to exchange hand signals with whoever was in the cockpit. *Determine compliance.*

Apte couldn't shake the feeling that Waugh had his own interpretation of compliance. As if the decision had already been made to take out the bogey. Apte was just along to provide cover.

"Bulldog One tallies the bogey, twelve o'clock low." Waugh, call sign "Bulldog One," was reporting that he had his own visual on the target. Apte stayed with Waugh's fighter as the F-15Cs pulled up and offset their heading twenty degrees to the left. Topping out nearly abeam of the 747, the two fighters made a hard turn back to the right. Apte had a good view of the 747. He could see the graceful swept wings, the four engine pods, the distinctive bulbous nose. Even from this distance he could make out the blue-and-white paint scheme. They had the right target.

Apte's bad feeling worsened. This *really* sucks.

CHAPTER SEVENTEEN

*D*o it, Fornier. *Do it, then disappear. Disappear before they kill you.*

Sam's heart rate had slowed almost to normal. She was seated at a table near the rear of the shop where she couldn't be seen except from the counter where a lone attendant was restocking the pastry display. She sipped at a Venti Café Mocha while she pulled the laptop out of the backpack. She kept her eyes on the counter while she awakened the computer. *WhooHoo*—this was what she loved about Starbucks. There was the little symbol for a solid Wi-Fi signal.

Now for the real test. Sam tried logging onto the Chowhound server. Another *WhooHoo*. There it was, still working. The numbnut techs at Comm Security Ops hadn't yet figured out how to shut the makeshift server down. She opened up the message template, then began typing.

To: *A/C commander SAM 28000*

Colonel Brand:
This is my final message. For your information, a force of civilian security agents in blue uniforms are swarming over Andrews. Since our last comm I have been pursued by these guys, shot at, and have now gone into hiding. My career is ruined and I fear for my life. If I'm not dead in the next few hours I plan to move to another country. Maybe another planet.
Very respectfully,
Capt. Sam Fornier

PS: I hope you make it.

Sam gave the message one more read. She shouldn't send it. It had no purpose other than to let this guy Brand know how she really felt. And, in case he cared, to let him know that she was still alive and running. She should delete it. Whenever they got around to an official investigation of what happened to Air Force One, her messages would become part of the historical record.

Tough shit. What difference would it make if she was dead? Without further hesitation, she hit SEND.

Sam finished the Café Mocha. One more time she checked her phone. The screen was blank. To hell with it. She logged off the server and shut down the laptop. She stuffed the computer back in the backpack and took it with her to the ladies' room. When she emerged a few minutes later, she gazed around. The shop was still empty. After half a minute's hesitation, she returned to the table in the back and booted up the laptop again.

There was a fresh message on the screen.

To: Capt. Sam Fornier
From: SAM 28000

Sorry about the rough treatment you've been getting, but it is critical that you remain in the loop with Cassidy.   The President needs you. Your country needs you.
Hang in there, son.
Col. Pete Brand

Sam almost laughed. *Hang in there, son.* All her life she'd played games with her first name. She loved the effect when the truth sank in that the tough-talking, butt-kicking Sam Fornier was a girl. But this was the best ever.

Why should she hang in there? Out of loyalty to some failed politician like Paulsen? Forget it. There was only one reason she would hang in there one minute longer. Because she wanted to see Brand's face when they finally met. If, of course, they managed to live through this.

It was then she became aware of the buzzing of the cell phone in her backpack.

<>

It was the same croaky voice. "Cassidy."

"I know," said Sam.

"Is your phone secure?"

"I think so."

At least she *hoped* so. Sam and her sometime boyfriend Jake, who was an IT officer in the wing and a certifiable ubergeek, had made a game of seeing if they could break the trackability mode on the phone. The one time they had tested it, the thing appeared to be secure. And untrackable.

The trouble was, there was no way of knowing whether the bad guys—whoever the hell they were—had locked on to Cassidy's phone. Sam could only hope that they hadn't yet figured out that he was in the loop with Air Force One.

Sam told the general about the goons invading her office and her near miss in the woods.

"That's bad," said Cassidy. "It means they've infiltrated the security apparatus at Andrews. It also means they're probably here in the Pentagon and Christ knows where else."

"Who are these people, General? Why are they doing this?"

"You'll find out, Captain. I'm not going to tell you over the phone. Where are you now?"

She gave it a beat. This was too good to resist. "You'll find out, General. I'm not going to tell you over the phone."

She thought she heard a chuckle. "Good answer," said Cassidy. "Are you able to text-message our client from where you are?"

Shit, thought Sam. All she wanted was to get the hell out of here. Away from this mess. Hide until it was over. She should tell him no. "I think so," she said.

From her table in the back of the Starbucks shop Sam could watch the front door. Her laptop was in front of her. She was logged in to Chowhound, the connection she had set up to replicate the official server called Gourmand.

"Okay," said Cassidy. "Here comes a message for the client. Ready to copy?"

"Go ahead," Sam said, then added, "Sir." She still hadn't gotten over the bizarreness of the whole scenario. A snot-nosed captain having this conversation with a three-star.

Cradling the phone to her ear, Sam listened to Cassidy's message. *Unbelievable,* she thought as she pecked the words on the keyboard. *This is getting crazier by the minute.*

<>

Brand gave the message a quick read, then handed it to Morganti.

To: *A/C commander SAM 28000*

Alert from Cassidy: Flight of two F-15s en route with orders to intercept and escort you to Dover Air Force Base. Imperative that you comply with intercept orders and take no actions that may be interpreted as hostile. Working on a suitable reception at Dover.
Updates as available. Stay tuned.
/s/ SF

"He'd better be right," said Morganti. He pointed to the RWR—radar warning receiver—light on the overhead panel. It was flashing amber. "We're already lit up. Somebody's got us on their radar."

Brand saw it too. He wasn't surprised. There had been no chance they could approach the east coast of the U.S. *without* being intercepted. It was just a matter of when. And by whom.

"Arm the ATADS, boss?" asked Switzer. His hand was reaching

for the console.

Brand considered. They'd already destroyed one F-15, whose intentions were definitely hostile. What about these new arrivals? Defending Air Force One against the Air Force's Eastern Air Defense Sector assets was impossible. The big lumbering 747 was an easy target.

"No. Our only chance is to do as Cassidy says. We won't give them any excuse to take a shot."

Switzer looked skeptical as he withdrew his hand from the ATADS console. Morganti wore a scowl, keeping his silence.

Brand didn't like it either. What happened next would be out of their control. He peered outside, scanning the pink sky for the specks of incoming fighters. He saw nothing except a puffy layer of rose-tinted cumulus. Where were the fighters?

<>

They were high and behind the 747.

Peering down at the transport, Buzz Apte remembered what they'd been told about Air Force One's air defense assets. Who would have believed that a fat people-hauler like this converted airliner would have the firepower to shoot down fighters? Apte didn't know it until an hour ago in the briefing. The rules of engagement were clear. If they received any indication that they were about to be fired on, they would blow the 747 out of the sky.

Apte didn't like it. There were people on board that jet. If the intelligence report was correct, some were terrorists. The others were his fellow Americans. One was the commander-in-chief, either dead or alive.

This mission sucks.

So far Waugh, the flight leader, was complying with the rules of engagement. The two fighters were easing down alongside the 747's left side. There was no longer any doubt about the identity of the airplane. The sun was glinting off the familiar blue-and-white paint scheme. Apte watched Waugh's fighter approaching the left side of the airliner.

And then dropping back.

"Bulldog One," called Apte, "did you get a signal exchange with the bogey?"

"Stay off the air," Waugh replied. His fighter was sliding back behind the 747.

Apte fumed in his cockpit. *Asshole.* The rules of engagement required Waugh to exchange hand signals with the cockpit of the Boeing. Why the hell was he ordering Apte to stay off the air?

Only one reason. Because Waugh didn't want any of what was about to happen to be recorded. Apte eased his throttles back to stay abreast of Waugh's fighter. He saw Waugh dropping back to a trail position behind the Boeing 747.

Into missile firing position.

Apte was still steeling himself for the inevitable when he heard a high-pitched *deedle deedle* over the earphones in his helmet. The aural alert for an incoming datalink message. Apte shifted his gaze to the multi-function screen in front of his right knee.

The text flashed across the monochrome screen of the display:

GEN CASSIDY TO BULLDOG ELEMENT: WEAPONS STATUS RED AND TIGHT. DO NOT FIRE ON AIR FORCE ONE. HIJACKING REPORT IS BOGUS. PRESIDENT IS ALIVE AND ABOARD. PROVIDE ARMED ESCORT TO DOVER AIR FORCE BASE.

Thank God. Apte keyed his microphone. "Bulldog One, check your datalink. Weapons tight. Don't fire."

"Get off the air," Waugh snapped over the radio. His F-15C was a quarter mile behind the 747, slightly high and offset to the left. Optimum Sidewinder range.

A flood of questions surged through Buzz Apte's brain. Who the hell was General Cassidy? Why was Air Force One not able to communicate? Who wanted it shot down? Why was Waugh so willing to pull the trigger on the President's plane?

Would he really do it?

Apte was still processing this last question when the answer appeared before him.

CHAPTER EIGHTEEN

Apte saw the Sidewinder leap from its station beneath Waugh's left wing. Trailing a plume of fire, the missile zigzagged like a bat, then settled on a steady course, racing toward the big swept-wing jet a quarter mile ahead. The thin gray smoke trail told Apte everything he needed to know.

The flight of the Sidewinder took two-and-a-half seconds. The missile made a final zigzag then bored in a straight line for the tailpipe of the outboard engine beneath the 747's left wing. Even in the pale light of dawn, the orange flash was bright enough that it forced Apte to close his eyes for an instant.

When Apte opened his eyes, he expected to see a massive fireball. Instead, he saw a cloud of smoke and debris spewing from the left wing. Pieces were streaming like confetti from a shattered piñata. The 747 was descending, rolling to the left. Through the trail of smoke Apte could see that the outboard engine was gone. So was the outer panel of the left wing. Fuel was gushing in a solid stream from the damaged wing.

Apte glanced again at Waugh's fighter. The F-15C was maneuvering back into position behind the stricken 747. In an instant of clarity, Apte understood what was happening. *He's going to take another shot.*

Waugh's first Sidewinder had homed in on an outboard engine. If the missile had exploded inside either of the two inboard engines, the 747 would be in a death spiral to the ocean.

Waugh was going to finish the kill.

A storm of emotions whirled through Buzz Apte's brain. He was an honor bound military man. A faithful soldier who followed orders. But his instincts as a man and a loyal American were raging at him. He knew what he had to do.

Apte yanked the nose of his F-15C to the right. Peering through the HUD—Head Up Display—in the windscreen, he slewed the targeting box to the aircraft just to the right of his nose. Almost instantly he received the aural acquisition tone in his earphones.

Apte hesitated—but only a millisecond—and then squeezed the trigger on the control stick. He felt the faint rumble of the Sidewinder leaving its station beneath his right wing. He forced himself to watch the bat-like flight of the self-directed missile streaking toward its target.

The tail of Darrell Waugh's F-15C erupted in a bright flash. As if in slow motion the big twin-engine fighter broke in half. The flaming tail section tumbled back, downward and out of Apte's sight. The forward half of the F-15C tilted back and settled toward the ocean. Apte rolled into a bank so that he could keep it in sight.

It took three more seconds. *There.* Apte saw what he hoped to see. The canopy separated from the cockpit section followed by the pilot's ejection seat. Apte watched the drogue chute stream out, trailing the tiny speck of the pilot downward. He knew that at 15,000 feet the main chute would deploy, and Darrell Waugh would spend the next part of this spring morning bobbing on a life raft in the Atlantic.

For a moment Buzz Apte let himself think about what just occurred. *Kiss your ass goodbye, Apte.* He could not yet imagine the ramifications of this episode. He only knew that he, Lt. Col. Buzz Apte, formerly a respected officer and fighter pilot, was in very deep shit. Shooting down your wing commander, even in the Air National Guard, was never a good career move.

<>

Brand was fighting to keep the wings level. Something was causing the 747's left wing to drop. He had the yoke rotated full right and the right rudder pedal shoved in to keep the 747 from rolling into a dive to the left.

"What the hell happened?" said Switzer.

The question didn't require an answer. They all knew. From the time the F-15s dropped out of view behind them, Brand's inner warning system had been clanging in full alert. Cassidy's message said that the fighters were there to escort them. When the impact rattled through the airframe, Brand knew the truth. They'd taken a missile. The F-15s weren't there to escort them. They had come to kill them.

"Number one's shut down," announced Switzer. He pointed to the panel. "No RPM, no temperatures, no indications at all."

Brand turned to peer out his window. From the captain's seat of the B-747 the pilot had a view of the two engines on the left wing. Brand could see the number two engine, the inboard power plant, protruding ahead of the wing. There was nothing protruding where number one should be.

"It's gone," Brand said.

"What do you mean?" said Morganti. "Is it burning, or what?"

"It's gone. Missing. And it looks like the outboard wing is gone too. There's no fire that I can see. Lou, go back to the cabin and take a better look."

Batchelder nodded and exited the cockpit.

It was taking all Brand's attention to keep the 747's wings level. Flying on only three engines, they were forced to descend. Brand had reduced power on number four—the right outboard—to compensate for the lost thrust of number one. He had the wings level again, but it still required nearly full throw of the yoke.

"I knew it," said Morganti. "The F-15s took a shot and hit number one engine. We should have taken them out when we picked up their targeting radar. Now they're going to blow us away."

Brand didn't bother answering. Morganti could be right. Maybe the text message from Cassidy—TWO F-15s WILL ESCORT YOU TO DOVER—was a set up. Now what? Use the ATADS? Take a shot at the fighters? It would be futile. Before he could get a missile off, they'd be blown out of the sky. The F-15s were in charge now.

Batchelder was back in the cockpit. "You're right. Number one engine is gone. All of it, off the airplane. And so is most of the outer wing panel. An F-15 is perched back there, like the guy's inspecting the damage he did."

Switzer's hands were already moving on the fuel control panel, adjusting valves. "Fuel's no problem. Not yet anyway. The outboard tanks were almost empty."

Brand looked out again. Then he saw it. Off the left side, moving into position alongside them, coming abeam the 747's cockpit. A single F-15C.

For several seconds Brand and the fighter pilot gazed at each other. Brand could see the sleek shape of the Mach 2 fighter. He saw the external rails with missiles waiting to be fired. One of the rails was empty. A missile had been expended.

Brand felt a flash of anger. This was the sonofabitch who fired a missile into the airplane carrying the President of the United States. Where was the other one? Still back there, waiting to finish the kill?

The F-15C was rocking its wings.

Brand was momentarily puzzled. The wing rock was a signal used when air defense fighters intercepted straying general aviation aircraft. It meant *You have been intercepted. Follow me.* And it required acknowledgement.

Very carefully, Brand rolled the 747 slightly to the left. Then back right. *I understand.* It took almost full throw of the yoke to bring the wings level.

The fighter pilot gave him a nod. Brand saw the landing gear of the F-15C appear beneath the jet's belly, then retract again. Another signal. A command. They were going to land.

Again Brand acknowledged with a gentle wing rock.

"He wants us to land?" said Morganti. "Where?"

"His call," said Brand. "Dover maybe. It's straight ahead about two hundred miles."

"It had better be soon," said Switzer. "We've lost two hydraulic systems, and all the fuel in the left outboard tank is gone. This bird won't keep flying much longer."

Brand didn't need reminding. Without hydraulic pressure, the 747's flight controls wouldn't move. They would become an inert flying object.

Still descending. The F-15C was leading them at a slow airspeed, which was good. Brand couldn't shove the throttles up on the damaged 747 any more than he already had and still maintain directional control. Again he wondered what the F-15C pilot was thinking. Why would he put a missile into them and then lead them to a landing field? It didn't make sense. Nothing was making sense.

<>

Fifteen minutes passed. The F-15 was still there, still leading them toward the East Coast.

Sergeant Manning came back to the cockpit. "Another text message, Colonel."

Brand was busy. He was flying a loose formation on the F-15C. "Read it to us, Sergeant."

Maintaining her standard blank expression, Manning read from the print-out in her hand.

Cassidy sends: Comply with landing instructions. On arrival at Dover Air Force Base you will be met by security team. Base Cmdr is Col. Stockton, who can be trusted.

"Is this guy nuts?" said Morganti. "Isn't he the one who told us to trust the F-15 pilots?"

"I know Stockton," said Brand. "If he's in charge at Dover, we'll be okay."

"What do you want me to tell our passengers?" said Sergeant Manning. "Everyone saw the explosion on the wing and they're scared shitless— uh, you know what I mean. Those folks are plenty upset."

The passengers. In the minutes after the missile strike, Brand had nearly forgotten about them. Now he was too busy to go talk to them. "Sergeant, you'll have to brief the passengers. You can tell them that we expect to be landing in half an hour."

Manning nodded and headed for the door of the cockpit.

Brand said over his shoulder, "One more thing, Sergeant."

"Sir?"

"Tell the President that I'm coming back to confer with her for a couple of minutes. It will have to be quick because we're going to get busy up here."

The sergeant gave him another wide-eyed stare. "Yes, sir. I'll tell her."

<>

"Cassidy?" said Vance McDivott. "Are they certain?"

"Certain enough," said Ripley. He slipped the phone back into its sheath on his belt. "That was Keppler, the guy who runs the signals intelligence section. He says they traced the intercept countermand order from 1st Air Force back to the Pentagon. Then they zeroed in on the Manpower and Personnel branch. The trail led straight to Cassidy's office. Keppler just ran a file check, and it seems that Cassidy and Brand go way back. If you remember, we thought it was Cassidy who backdoored the appointment of Brand as Presidential Pilot."

McDivott nodded. He remembered. Cassidy. That sonofabitch. He'd been looking for an opportunity to get rid of Cassidy. Cassidy had never been a team player. Always an outsider in the Pentagon clique. Cassidy was a loose cannon who would never have been a good fit for Capella.

"What happened with the intercept? Do they know what went wrong?"

Ripley shook his head. "Only that the fighters got a datalink, apparently from 1st Air Force, not to fire. Probably initiated by Cassidy. Then one of the F-15s went down. We don't know if he was morted by Angel's ATADS or by the other fighter."

"What's the other F-15 jockey reporting?"

"Nothing. He went dark, no transmissions, not even datalink. Either he's gone rogue or something's happened to his jet."

Goddamnit. McDivott interlocked his fingers and flexed his knuckles, his standard gesture when he was trying to suppress his anger. Just getting the order to the fighters to make the intercept had required some delicate weaving through the order of command. Three general officers in the air defense chain had to be bypassed in order to get Waugh, the F-15 wing commander, in the lead fighter. It should have been a clean kill. Over and done with. Now this.

McDivott and Ripley were huddled in the far corner of the command post in the Briar Club. McDivott could see Casper Reckson and Senator Kent Stroud watching them. McDivott hadn't yet told them that Air Force One was damaged but still flying and would be on the ground in the U. S. within the hour. It would only invite more of Reckson's interminable questions. He'd wait until Air Force One was on the ground and the job was finished.

Ripley's phone was vibrating again. He put the phone to his ear and said, "Go." For half a minute he listened, nodding. Then he said, "Yes, absolutely. As many over there as you can get in the helos. Lock the place down. I'll inform General McDivott."

McDivott was watching him. "Well?"

Ripley returned the cell phone to its sheath. "SigInt desk again. Angel is definitely headed for Dover."

McDivott nodded. Then he signaled to the tall man in blue creased utilities watching him from a dozen feet away.

<>

Libby was behind her desk when Brand came in. Jill Maitlin occupied the chair at the end of Libby's desk. Mike Grossman and Dennis Morton, Libby's Deputy National Security Advisor, were in the chairs facing her.

Brand remained standing. He had shed the blue jacket. His collar was open. He looked tired, Libby thought. They all did.

"It's almost over," Brand said. "We'll be landing in Dover in about thirty minutes."

"Dover?" said Grossman. He frowned. "Who's going to be waiting for us?"

"Friends, if Colonel Stockton is in command. But the situation is changing constantly. We won't know for sure until we've stopped on the ramp."

"My orders are to defend this aircraft—and the President—to the last man," said Grossman. "After what we've been through, my people would be more than pleased to shoot some of the—" he glanced at Libby— "the sonsofbitches who've been trying to bring us down."

Libby nodded. She knew that she was the fourth President the big-shouldered, buzz-cut Secret Service agent had protected. She had no doubt that Grossman would willingly take a bullet for her. She was also sure that his loyalty was not to Libby Paulsen. It was to the Presidency itself.

Jill Maitlin said, "Shooting should be our last choice of actions. We have to assess the situation closely when we arrive."

"Assess?" Brand said. "Go over to the window on the left side and assess that situation. Either that F-15 or his wingman blew off our outboard wing and number one engine."

No one moved. They had all seen the fighter. Everyone had felt the explosion when the missile took out the engine.

Jill said, "If they really wanted to shoot us down, why haven't they done it already?"

"I don't know. We should consider the possibility that they plan to finish the job after we've landed."

"Leave that to us, Colonel Brand. I'll remind you that your mission is to fly the airplane."

Libby watched the exchange, saying nothing. The bad blood between Jill and Brand was getting worse. She wondered again where it came from. Jill Maitlin's contempt for Brand went deeper than just disapproving his assignment as Presidential Pilot.

Dennis Morton spoke up. "My feeling is that we shouldn't trust anyone on the ground when we land. No one should be allowed near the President until we've assessed the situation and established communications."

Good for Morton, thought Libby. Dry and pedantic, like the prosecuting attorney he had been in his previous life. Morton's great skill was to parse facts from speculation.

"I'll take care of that," said Grossman. "Between my team and Sergeant Ruiz's Air Force security team, we have enough men and firepower to turn Air Force One into a fortress."

Brand just nodded. He was already headed for the door. "Time for me to go back to the cockpit."

Libby rose from her chair. She felt Jill's hard-eyed gaze as she followed Brand into the passageway outside the office.

Libby closed the door behind her. She and Brand were alone in the narrow space outside the office.

"Are you ready for this?" Brand said.

She shook her head. "No. I'm afraid. I feel like I'm going to break down and cry."

"Don't."

"Why?"

"Because you're a leader. Your people depend on you, Libby. Don't let them see you cry."

Libby closed her eyes for a moment. *Don't let them see you cry.* How many times had she heard that? It was something her father used to say. It was bullshit. She felt like a terrified kid who wanted nothing more than to run away and cry.

And then she realized something. He had called her Libby. When was the last time they had used first names? Another lifetime.

"Remember Africa?" she said.

He nodded.

"The time you saved my life?"

He nodded again.

"Were you afraid then?"

"No," he said.

"Are you afraid now?"

"No."

"Why not?"

"There's no time for it. Fear is the enemy. If we let it take over, it drives our decisions. We have to jam it into a compartment, get it out of our conscious thinking."

"If it was that easy, everyone would be brave."

"I didn't say it was easy. It's hard. It's something you learn. You can do it."

She thought for a moment. "Remember that truck you stole in Africa?"

He shrugged. "Sometimes you do what you have to do."

"This is one of those times, Pete. Do what you have to do."

CHAPTER NINETEEN

"**I**'ll be there," said Berg. He was already moving, yanking out his own phone as he strode toward the exit.

McDivott watched the tall, muscular frame of Rolf Berg disappear. Yes, Berg would definitely be there. Rolf Berg always managed to be where the action was. As the director of Galeforce International, Berg had a reputation for taking hands-on control of the most sensitive operations. And what was about to happen at Dover was the most sensitive operation in modern history.

McDivott had been wary of Berg at first. The big, tough-talking spec-ops veteran was an anomaly among the service academy general officers and the ivy league-educated directors on the secret roster of Capella. Berg came from a different place. He had put in his time as an enlisted SEAL, rising to commissioned status, leaving the Navy with the rank of commander. He founded the company called Galeforce International, which quickly gathered CIA and State Department contracts, executing them with impressive precision. As Rolf Berg's reputation swelled, it was inevitable that he would draw the attention of high ranking military officers, including Vance McDivott. It was even more inevitable that Berg would be inducted into the secret society of patriots called Capella.

Under the patronage of highly-placed Capella members, Galeforce became the government's single largest security contractor. Galeforce units served in Iraq, Afghanistan, Somalia, Yemen, Libya, and a dozen other near and far east outposts. The largest single unit, comprising nearly five thousand contractors, was positioned close to Washington, D. C. And within striking distance of Dover Air Force Base.

<>

"He's starting down," said Morganti.

Brand saw it. The F-15C's nose was slanting downward, beginning the descent. On the horizon Brand could make out the dark line of the Delaware shore. A hundred miles ahead lay Dover Air Force Base.

Brand eased the throttles back to keep from overrunning the fighter. He still couldn't get over the feeling that they were a wounded trophy the hunter was dragging home so he could finish the kill. There was nothing he could do now to change the outcome. Once they were on the ground it would be up to Grossman and his shooters.

He could still see Libby's face. The gray eyes filled with uncertainty. The expectation that he would protect her. That he would do the right thing, whatever that was. Could he pull off a miracle? He doubted it. His intuition was kicking in again. He had the sure sense that this drama wasn't over. Something was happening that was going to change the country. And the Presidency of Libby Paulsen.

Another thought kept inserting itself in his mind. Something he had not allowed himself to think about for three years. Libby Paulsen. He loved her. Had loved her since their first night in Africa. She was the reason he took this assignment. The only reason.

Knock it off, Brand. It was exactly the wrong thing to be thinking about. They were the kind of thoughts that could get them all killed. What he had to do now required cold, intuitive thinking. Focus. *Do what you gotta do.*

"There it is," called out Morganti. "On the nose, about forty miles."

Brand glanced away from the F-15C long enough to scan the horizon ahead. He blinked once, then saw it. Dover Air Force Base, its buildings and bristling towers reflecting the morning sun. Coming up beneath the nose was the jutting peninsula of New Jersey. Across the bay, on the shore of Delaware, lay the sprawling airfield. Brand had landed there hundreds of times, hauling everything from cargo to VIPs to caskets of servicemen and women killed in Middle East wars.

In the distance, sixty miles beyond Dover, was Washington, D. C. and Air Force One's home base at Andrews. Close, thought Brand. So close that it was tempting to continue. There was no way. He was sure that if he ignored the F-15's landing order, they'd be blown out of the sky either by the fighter or by the surface-to-air missiles that ringed Washington.

The F-15C was slowing back to approach speed. Brand saw the fighter's gear emerge from beneath the belly. Time to configure for landing.

With the failed hydraulic systems, the checklist dictated that they add twenty knots to the landing airspeed. But there was no checklist for landing with part of the wing missing. They were in unknown territory.

"Better add another fifteen knots," said Morganti. "It will help controllability."

"Too fast. We're going to have trouble stopping."

Morganti had the airport diagram for Dover laid out on the console. "Runway three-two's got nearly 13,000 feet. That ought to be plenty, even with the high landing speed. Our brakes should be normal as long as we still have number four system. We've got reverse on three engines."

Brand nodded. As much as he disliked Morganti, he respected his knowledge. Morganti had over two thousand hours experience in Air Force One. "Okay," said Brand. "Your call. Let's set the reference speed to V-thresh plus thirty-five."

The trouble was, the reference speed was calculated according the aircraft's weight, which they could only estimate. Switzer came up with a number. Their reference speed—the airspeed at which they would fly the airplane to a landing—would be 169 knots.

It was fast. Too damned fast. The excess airspeed would make the airplane more controllable, but it would make it difficult to stop.

Following the checklist, Switzer began extending the landing flaps by the alternate system. It was a slow process, requiring nearly five minutes. Brand held the yoke carefully, alert for a control malfunction if the flaps failed on the damaged wing.

The flaps extended. No severe control problems. None yet.

<>

"This is some kind of silly-ass drill, right?" said Col. Ed Stockton.

"No drill, Ed."

The sun was up, though Cassidy had no way of seeing it from the cave-like interior of his office. He had just told the commander of the Dover Air Force Base that Air Force One, badly damaged and without communications, was about to land at his base. As Cassidy expected, Stockton didn't believe him.

Then Cassidy told him a military cabal was trying to bring down the President.

"If I didn't know you better," said Stockton, "I'd swear you've been up all night drinking."

"I've never been more serious. Trust me, this is the real thing."

"The last bulletin from the Joint Chiefs chairman says the President is dead. Air Force One is in the drink."

"It's a lie. There's been a coup attempt, and the joint chiefs are involved."

Cassidy could hear Stockton exhale hard into the phone. "Shit," said Stockton. "Even if what you told me is true, what am I supposed to do?"

"Uphold your oath as an officer in the United States Air Force."

"Meaning what?"

"Meaning do what you have to do to protect the commander-in-chief."

"Protect her how?"

"Use all your security resources. Defend her and her staff from whoever might show up to take her out. Get her to a safe place."

Stockton said nothing for a moment. "Who's the aircraft

commander? Morganti or the new guy?"

"The new guy. Brand. You know him from SpecOps. He was our guy in the Sudan operation."

"How could I forget? I can think of a dozen field grade officers who'd like to take out Brand."

"Brand needs all the help he can get, Ed. So does the President."

Stockton let several seconds elapse. He sighed into the phone. "I've got a real bad feeling about this. I think that after what happens here, you and I are going to be falling on our swords."

"We've had a good run, Ed. Maybe this is the right time to exit."

"Maybe. I'd better start getting our shit together here on the ground. I'll get back to you when we're in position."

Stockton hung up. Cassidy sat motionless for a minute, thinking about what had to happen next. Stockton had to get the President out of Dover before the cabal zeroed in on her location. Get her in a secure place. Surround her with loyal troops.

And he'd do it, if he could. Stockton was a good man. He and Cassidy had covered each other's butts on more than one occasion. With Stockton running the show on the ground at Dover, it meant —

The yellow light on Cassidy's communications console was blinking. The secure line from Dover again.

Cassidy yanked up the handset. Gritting his teeth, he waited the obligatory four seconds, listening to the squiggling sound of the encrypting program inserting itself.

Stockton's voice came on the line. "Jack, you're not going to believe what's happening here. I just got a call from Ripley over at JCS. He gave me a direct order to turn over base security to this Galeforce outfit. He says they're going to meet an inbound hijacked aircraft."

"It's Air Force One, like I told you. And it's not hijacked. It's a bogus story."

"Yeah, yeah, I believe you. I told him that I was still the base commander and we'd take care of it ourselves."

"Did he back off?"

"He told me I was summarily relieved. Fired. I'm supposed to get the hell off the base. My replacement would be in one of the helos."

"Did you tell him to get stuffed?"

"Sure, I did. I told him I had to hear it from McDivott or I wasn't—uh, oh, Jack. This is bad. They're already here. I'm looking out at the ramp from my office. Six, eight, maybe more, landing on the ramp. No markings on the helos. No inbound calls, no clearance. I can see them deploying across the apron now. These guys aren't military, Jack. Must be the Galeforce bunch. Some kind of blue uniforms."

Cassidy's mind raced, searching for options. "Listen up, Ed. You've got to buy us some time. Don't let them—"

The carrier tone in the handset went silent. The blinking yellow light was extinguished.

Cassidy stared at the useless phone. He slammed it down and snatched up his cell phone. *How much time do we have?*

Not enough. He heard a commotion in the hallway outside his office. Cassidy fumbled with the phone, squinting at the keyboard. He had to make another call, and he had to do it very damned quickly. He heard angry shouts from outside. Loomis's voice?

Then a thump.

Where the hell is the number? Cassidy had to put on his reading glasses. He found the number, embedded on the calls page, still encoded. He punched up the call sequence. Then he waited. He heard someone jiggling the handle on his office door. Through the latticed blind he could see the silhouette of someone behind the glass. The thought flashed through Cassidy's mind that just a few years ago he would have his service pistol in a desk drawer. No more. Not in the security-obsessed, post-9/11 Pentagon.

He heard the phone ringing on the other end. Twice. A third

time. *Come on, answer the goddam thing . . .*

The office door shattered inward. Shards of glass crashed onto the tiled floor, tinkling across Cassidy's desk. He saw an arm reach inside, going for the inside handle.

The phone was still ringing. Cassidy saw the intruder's arm groping through the gaping hole in the glass. Reaching for the handle, fumbling, finding it.

On the fourth ring there was a click. A voice came on the other end. "Yes?"

< >

Sam wasn't sure she heard correctly. "I'm sorry, say that again."

It was the same croaky voice, except that it sounded urgent and agitated. "Tell them not to land. It's a trap."

The voice belonged to Cassidy, but it wasn't making sense. "I'm not following you," said Sam. "If they're not supposed to land at Dover, where should I tell them to go?"

"It doesn't matter, for Christ's sake. Just tell them not to—"

Sam heard a clattering noise, as if the phone had been dropped. There were sounds of a scuffle, objects hitting the floor. Then a *pop.* Sam felt a chill sweep over her. There was no mistaking the sound she had just heard.

Still holding the phone to her ear, Sam gazed around. The Washington workaday routine was just beginning. Half a dozen early morning customers were in line at the Starbucks counter. They were a mix of men and women, most of them young, en route to the metro and downtown office jobs. Over the phone Sam listened to what sounded like footsteps crunching on broken glass.

Then a voice on the phone. It had a resonant, authoritative ring. Like God. "Captain Fornier?"

Sam froze. She pressed the phone to her ear, unable to move or speak. She heard the sound of breathing on the other end.

"I know you're there, Sam."

The voice cut through her like a skewer. *Sam.* They knew who she was. They knew everything. She wanted to hurl the phone to the floor and run. Run like a striped-ass ape. Find a place to hide.

"Who are you?" she made herself say.

"It doesn't matter. The game is over. General Cassidy is dead."

"What do you want?"

"Turn yourself in, Sam. You have one chance. Do it now and nothing will happen to you."

Sam Fornier felt the spirit drain from her. The guy who sounded like God was right. She had one chance. It was time to quit. This wasn't her fight. She was a catering officer, not a commando. She'd gotten sucked into this by that colonel on Air Force One. What was his name? She had to think. *Brand.*

In a flash Brand's words came back to her. *The President needs you. So does your country.*

Tears sprang to Sam Fornier's eyes. *Hang in there, son.* Brand was a blockhead. How was she ever going to show him who—and what—she really was? *Damn.*

Sam cleared her throat. This wasn't the time to sound like a wimpy kid. "Hey," she said with as much bravado as she could muster. "You still there?"

"Still here."

"I have a proposition."

"Go ahead."

"The gun you just shot General Cassidy with?"

"What about it?"

"I propose that you take that gun and shove it up your ass."

She didn't wait for the God-like voice to reply. She punched END and swung her attention to the laptop keyboard. As quickly as her trembling fingers could hit the keys, Sam logged back on to the server. She began pecking out the message to Air Force One.

She was still typing, shifting her gaze from the keyboard to the front of the shop, when she saw them. Two of them, thick-necked, short-haired, each wearing a blue nylon jacket. Though she hadn't gotten a good look in the darkness, she would swear they were the same ones who had chased her in the woods. The goons.

She rotated sideways in the seat, shielding her face with her shoulder while she finished typing. Sam keyed the SEND icon, then gathered up the computer and backpack. As she slipped from behind the table and headed for the ladies' room, she caught a blur of movement in her peripheral vision.

Blue nylon jackets. Coming after her.

CHAPTER TWENTY

"The text machine, Lowanda. Another incoming."

Chief Master Sergeant Lowanda Manning looked across the galley at Morrow, the flight attendant she had stationed at the text machine. She saw the paper emerging from the output slot in the machine. Amazing, she thought. The little stone age text machine was still working while all the gee-whiz technology on Air Force One—phones, TVs, SatComms, data links—were as dead as a bag of rocks.

Manning could feel the deck angle of the aircraft tilting downward. They were going to land soon, and that suited Lowanda Manning. This flight was supposed to be her last trip as Chief Flight Attendant aboard Air Force One. Thirty years active duty, stacks of commendation letters, four rows of service awards and decorations, and she'd never seen real combat. Never been shot at, which was fine with her. Now this. Not in Lowanda Manning's worst dreams did she expect that some crazy assholes might try to blow her—and the President of the United States—out of the sky on their way home.

Manning yanked the print sheet from the machine. Whatever the message, it was too late. The crew would be too busy to deal with it until they got this ship on the ground. As she started toward the cockpit, she pulled the readers from her jacket pocket and gave the message a quick scan.

And stopped. She had reached the end of the passageway, about to turn toward the stairway to the command deck. She gave the message one more quick read.

Oh, sweet Jesus. Sergeant Manning whirled to head up the stairs, then she abruptly stopped. She had just been joined by a familiar figure in a blue jumpsuit.

<>

Twenty miles. They were descending over Delaware Bay. The shoreline was coming up beneath the nose. Three miles beyond the beach lay the approach end of runway three-two.

"Here comes another landing without clearance," said Brand.

"Another violation," said Morganti. "Keep this up and we could get in real trouble."

Brand glanced to see if he was joking. He was. It was hard to believe. Morganti wasn't exactly smiling, but his face had shed most of its hostility. Maybe Morganti was coming around.

Or it could be a ruse, thought Brand. Setting them up for a trap on the ground. Maybe, but he doubted it. Still, he wasn't ready to trust Morganti. He would keep his guard up. Keep it up until they were on the ground and safe.

Brand was shifting his sight from the F-15C to the steadily approaching airport ahead. He had to hand it to the F-15C pilot. The fighter jock was maintaining a slow enough speed for the damaged 747. He was leading them down a good glide path for Dover's runway three-two. Someday, Brand told himself, he'd buy the guy a drink. Unless he turned out to be the sonofabitch who fired a missile at them. In which case Brand would flatten his nose.

According to Morganti's chart, the Dover runway was long enough, but the 150-foot width would be a problem. Keeping the wide-body jumbo jet in the center of the runway would be difficult without hydraulic power to the steering.

Brand ordered the landing gear down. Because of the hydraulic failure, the gear extension would take two minutes instead of the usual few seconds.

The wheels clunked into the down position. "Landing checklist complete," reported Switzer. Then he added, "Let's get this thing on the ground."

Brand nodded. They were descending through a thousand feet. He glanced out the side window. The F-15C was still there. Brand guessed that he'd be there until Air Force One touched down. Just to make sure.

They were over land. A patchwork of green fields and clumps of woods swept beneath them. The end of runway three-two was swelling in the windscreen. Brand was making tiny adjustments with the yoke, keeping the jet on the approach path, working the three throttles to maintain 169 knots.

"Two hundred feet," called Morganti, "more or less." They still had only the barometric altimeters with no current altimeter setting.

They were committed. From this point, with the failed hydraulics and missing engine, Air Force One couldn't abort the landing and power back into the sky. They would land at Dover.

Brand was tilting the nose of the Boeing upward when he heard the cockpit door open. "Message from Cassidy!" yelled Sergeant Manning.

"Not now," Switzer said to her. "We're landing."

"No," said Manning. "Don't land!"

"Twenty feet . . ." called out Morganti, ". . .ten."

Clunk. Brand felt the dull vibration of the main trucks rolling onto the concrete. He pulled the three throttles back and snatched the reverse levers into the detent. The big jet was decelerating on the runway.

"*We can't land!*" yelled Manning from the back of the cockpit. "Cassidy says it's a trap."

"Too late," said Morganti. "We're down."

Brand was already applying pressure on the toe brakes. His brain processed this new information. *Cassidy says it's a trap.* The runway was racing beneath them. Two thousand feet of precious concrete had already been used.

He snapped the reverse levers back into the forward detent. "We're out of here," he said and pushed the throttles forward. "Max thrust," he ordered.

"No!" said Morganti. He reached for the throttles. "We won't make it."

Brand slapped Morganti's hand away from the throttles. "Set the flaps for takeoff," he said. He shot a glance at Morganti. "Do it!"

Morganti blinked, staring at Brand as if seeing him for the first time. He hesitated, then reached for the flap handle. "Flaps coming up." He clunked the handle into the takeoff detent, then actuated the electrical switch for the alternate flaps.

The sides of the runway were blurring past them. In his peripheral vision Brand saw the F-15 flash overhead. Now what? Would the fighter blow them out of the sky after they took off?

If they took off. They'd already used up more than half the available length. Brand could see the far end of the runway rushing toward them. Beyond the runway lay an open meadow, then a stand of trees.

"A hundred knots," called out Morganti.

Brand nodded. Without hydraulic power, the flaps were retracting slowly. Too slowly. The extended flaps produced aerodynamic drag, slowing them down. With part of a wing missing, the Boeing needed speed. Lots of it.

"A hundred-twenty knots."

Not enough. The Boeing was accelerating too slowly. Brand wondered what he would do if they ran off the end. He pushed the thought away. The jet would fly. It *had* to fly. Somehow.

"A hundred-forty." Morganti's voice had a flat, fatalistic ring to it. "We're almost out of runway."

Brand didn't need reminding. He could see the runway end lights swelling like a signboard in front of them. It was a nightmare scenario he had rehearsed in simulators, never for real. The decision to takeoff again after landing was irrevocable. No looking back, no changing your mind. You lived or died with the outcome.

The runway end lights were rushing up beneath the nose. Brand tried to remember the Dover airport layout. Did the runway have approach lights protruding from the ground? If so, the light stanchions would rip through the belly of the airplane like a can opener.

"A hundred-fifty," croaked Morganti. "Rotate, for Christ's sake."

"I will." Brand waited. The end of the runway was nearly beneath the nose. He pulled back on the yoke, lifting the nose of the jet from the runway. The edge of the runway disappeared beneath them. Brand could see the grass-covered meadow and the trees beyond.

They were still on the ground. In the next instant the big main gear trucks rolled off the concrete onto the dirt. The airframe rumbled and vibrated as all sixteen wheels plowed through the earth.

"That's it," murmured Switzer. "We've bought it."

Instinctively Brand tried to push throttles further forward. They wouldn't move because they were already against the stops. The nose was in a high, climbing attitude, but the airplane was still on the ground. Brand nursed the yoke further back, willing the damaged airplane to fly, imploring it, using every ounce of skill he had accumulated in a lifetime of flying. *Come on, do it. Lift off. Fly.*

The rumbling continued. Brand felt a new vibration. A shuddering feeling, and he knew what it was. With the nose pointed so far upward, the tail of the airplane was scraping the earth.

The trees at the end of the meadow swelled in size. The tortured airframe of the Boeing rattled and groaned as it careened across the meadow. Brand lowered the nose a few degrees, held it another second, then gently tugged back on the yoke again. He felt connected to the airplane, willing it to lift from the earth.

The shuddering and groaning abruptly ceased. The wheels of the Boeing were off the ground, but barely. The massive aircraft was skimming the earth, clinging to the cushion of air beneath its wings.

"The trees . . ." Morganti was saying. " . . . watch out for the trees . . ."

"I see the trees," said Brand. And there was nothing he could do about them. Every movement of the yoke produced a clattering stick shaker, warning that a stall was imminent. The Boeing was on the thin edge of flight, suspended a few feet above the earth.

Brand forced himself to relax the back pressure on the yoke. Just enough to flatten the aircraft attitude a few degrees. Enough to let the jet accelerate a few knots. *Please climb. Just a little.*

The trees filled the windscreen. Again Brand nudged back on the yoke. Again the stick shaker clattered. The Boeing was about to stall. It didn't matter now.

The Boeing's nose tilted slightly upward, clawing for altitude.

It wasn't enough. A sound like thunder resonated through the metal airframe. Green foliage splattered across the windscreen. In a nose high attitude, the 747 was plowing through the tops of the trees.

"Oh, shit!" Switzer blurted. Brand was fighting to keep the wings level, to keep the aircraft from settling into the trees.

A bell jangled. Brand glimpsed a red light illuminate on the overhead panel. "Fire, number four," said Switzer.

"Leave it running," Brand ordered. Number four engine must have swallowed part of a tree. Now it was burning. Shutting another engine down would doom them. They needed the thrust of all three engines, even if one was burning.

It was a desperate balancing act. Brand was flying on the edge of a stall, willing the airplane not to plunge into the ground, praying that number four engine would keep running.

The thunder abruptly stopped. They were past the trees. Ahead Brand could see another field, a highway, and to the left a cluster of suburban houses. A glance at the altimeter showed two hundred feet. The Boeing was climbing. Barely.

There was no way to raise the landing gear. The flaps had finally reached takeoff setting.

"There goes number four engine," announced Switzer. "It's spinning down."

Brand felt the loss of thrust. The burning engine had lasted long enough to get them through the trees. "Shut it down, fire the extinguisher bottle."

As Switzer and Morganti were executing the engine fire procedure, the engineer said, "More trouble, Boss. Fuel's going down fast in the right outboard. We must have ruptured a tank going through the trees."

"How long do we have?"

Switzer peered at the gauges. "At this rate, two engines at max power, I'm guessing fifteen minutes. Maybe less."

The Boeing was struggling to maintain a thousand feet altitude. Below them swept the suburbs of Dover , then a patchwork of Delaware farmland. With just two engines running, the landing gear permanently extended, Air Force One had only minutes left to fly.

Brand remembered something else. *The F-15.* The fighter pilot had ordered them to land at Dover. The guy undoubtedly had orders to shoot them down if they didn't comply. Was another missile headed for them?

Brand stopped thinking about it. There were some things he couldn't control.

"Now what, Pete?"

Brand was startled by the voice behind him. He shot a quick glance over his shoulder. "How long have you been there?"

"Since we almost landed at Dover," said Libby. She was perched in the jump seat. Her eyes were glittering. "I came in with Sergeant Manning. I thought we were going to die."

Brand nodded. There was no point in telling her that they almost did. Or that they still might.

"We have to put this thing down," said Morganti. "Where do you want to do it?"

Brand glanced at the copilot. Morganti was being almost civil.

Almost a team player. Amazing what a near-death experience could do for teamwork.

"What do you see for airports close by?" Brand asked.

Morganti unfolded the sectional chart. He studied it for several seconds, then peered out the windscreen. A piece of foliage was still stuck in the windscreen wiper, whipping against the glass. "Straight ahead, almost on the nose. A place called Summit. It has—" he went back to the chart "—never mind. Forty-four hundred feet of runway. It won't work."

Brand thought for a moment. Forty-four hundred feet wasn't nearly enough. Not for a severely damaged jumbo jet with a too-fast approach speed. Losing number four engine had cost them another hydraulic system, which meant they were down to the reserve brake system.

"Number four's still burning, Boss," said Switzer. "We've fired the bottles and the light's still on. We gotta put it down."

"No choice," said Brand. "We have to land at Summit and make the best of it."

He could see the little airport coming into view just beyond the nose. Morganti was right. It *was* too short. The closer they came, the shorter the runway looked. And narrow as a pinstripe. Summit was a general aviation field, not a terminal for jumbo jets.

It didn't matter. The Boeing was a wreck. With one engine shot away, another shut down and burning, the airplane having been run through a Delaware meadow and then flown through a stand of timber, it was time for a replacement.

He needed to turn about twenty degrees to line up with the north-south runway. He ordered the landing flaps extended again. The controls felt stiff, which Brand knew was because of the limited hydraulic pressure. He felt a continuous vibration in the yoke from the damaged wing surfaces. *Hang together*, Brand silently urged. *Sixty seconds more.*

He remembered Libby. "This may get rough," he said over his shoulder. "You'd better go back to the cabin and strap in."

"I'm still the President, remember? This is my airplane and I get to sit wherever I want."

A stillness fell over the cockpit. Morganti swiveled in his seat and stared at her. So did Switzer.

Brand nodded. "Yes, ma'am. You're the boss."

CHAPTER TWENTY-ONE

The end of the runway swept beneath them. Brand chopped the two throttles back to idle. The main trucks of the landing gear thunked onto the tiny strip of concrete. Already he could see the far end of the runway coming at them fast. He snatched the reverse levers up, and the two remaining engines answered with a satisfying bellow. Brand applied pressure to the toe brakes.

"Careful," said Switzer. "We don't have anti-skid. You might blow the tires."

It was a needless warning. Keeping the main gear on the skimpy runway was impossible. The tires were already blowing as they rolled over the light fixtures on the edges of the runway.

Half the runway was behind them. Brand stopped worrying about the tires. He had the brake pedals fully depressed. The main gear was shedding its massive rubber tires. With the engines screaming in reverse and the wheels disintegrating, the 747 seemed to be shaking itself to pieces.

The thin ribbon of runway slipped beneath them like a fast-running stream. Brand could see the runway end—another runway end in the space of ten minutes—and the open field beyond. He knew what was coming.

It took five more seconds. "Hang on," Brand said. The big jet lurched off the concrete and lumbered into the open field. Brand guessed they were still going forty knots when the nose gear broke. The forward fuselage clunked to the ground. The added drag of the nose digging through the earth brought the jet to a grinding halt.

A cloud of dirt and smoke erupted around the big jet. Tilted forward in their seats, Brand and Morganti were busy shutting down the two remaining engines and discharging all the fire bottles.

The rumbling and vibrating stopped. An eerie silence fell over the cockpit. There was no sound except the patter of debris still falling on the aluminum skin of the cockpit. Brand saw that the fire warning lights were all extinguished. Air Force One was an inert hunk of twisted metal.

He turned to look behind him. Libby was wearing a dazed expression. She looked like a child who had just awakened from a nap. She was still clutching the back of Brand's seat.

It was Morganti who broke the silence. He turned in his seat. "With all due respect, Madame President, this would be a good time for you to get the hell out of here."

<>

The contractor, the taller and senior of the two, glanced both ways in the narrow hallway of the Starbucks shop. As he expected, the door marked *Women* was locked. The doors to both lavatories were in the hall, out of view from the counter and the tables in the front of the shop. No one was watching. The contractor slipped the Sig Sauer from its holster inside the nylon jacket and nodded to his partner. The partner stepped back, then lunged at the door with this right foot. The lock bolt snapped easily. The door slammed open and the contractors stormed inside.

There was barely enough room for the two of them. On one wall was a sink, a hand soap dispenser, and a motion-sensing towel machine. The window on the far wall was closed. Half the lavatory was taken by the enclosed toilet stall. Visible in the space between the floor and green panels was a pair of ankles, rolled down pants, sneakers with some kind of swoop emblazoned on the side.

The contractor studied the scene for a moment. This was good. He was sure the girl wasn't armed. Not unless she'd managed to acquire a piece somewhere between here and the woods where they'd lost her. Not likely. The trick now was to haul her ass out of here without causing a ruckus in the shop. Someone might call the cops.

Then he reassessed the matter. What was he worried about? To hell with the ruckus. The cops weren't a problem. One phone call and they'd be pussycats. If the smartass bitch fought back, he'd pop her right here. He should have done it back when they spotted her climbing out of the wrecked car. Who would have guessed she could run like a rabbit with its ass on fire?

The door to the stall was latched. She had to know they were there. The sneakers and the ankles with the pants rolled down hadn't moved. No place for her to go. This was working out better than he had hoped. The prospect of snatching a fugitive with her pants down sent a tingle of pleasure through him.

Aiming directly at the latch, the contractor gave the door a kick. The flimsy door flew open, banging against the wall of the stall. Exactly one and a half seconds elapsed while the contractor's brain processed what he saw.

A woman on the john. Pants down. Thighs like tree trunks, one of which bore a purple tattoo. Large, round face, wearing an enraged expression, all crowned by a mountain of reddish hair. But what grabbed the contractor's attention was the object in her hand. An instant too late, he realized what it was.

Pepper spray. The blast caught him in the upper chest and the lower part of his face.

"Get out of here, you fucking pervert!" the woman in the stall shrieked. "Touch me and I'll gouge your goddamn eyes out!"

The contractor staggered backwards. His throat and chin were on fire. He was still reeling from the spray when the stall door slammed shut again.

"Wrong bitch, was it?" said his partner, just a hint of mockery in his voice.

"She comes out of that stall, shoot her," said the contractor. He yanked off his nylon jacket and turned the tap on the sink. He could barely see through the flood of tears even though he'd managed to close his eyes just before the spray hit him. As he doused his face, waiting for the burning to subside, the contractor forced himself to think.

Where did the girl go? They'd checked the back door, the one at the end of the hall, before kicking in the door to the women's john. That left one other possibility. He should have thought of it.

His eyes were still burning as he barged back into the hall, his partner in trail. The adjoining door, the one marked *Men* was locked. Another kick from his partner sent the door flying on its hinges. Pistols at the ready, they stormed inside.

It was just like the women's lavatory except for the porcelain urinal against the wall. Same sink, soap dispenser, green-paneled toilet stall. The stall was empty. The window at the far end was the same except for one distinct feature.

It was open.

The contractor leaned out and peered each way. His eyes were still burning from the goddamn pepper spray. The alley outside was dimly illuminated by the gray light of dawn. To the left was the main street, where he could see traffic coming and going. The other direction appeared to be residential. Back yards and fences.

The contractor did a quick calculation. No more than two minutes had elapsed since she vanished from their sight in the hallway. It had taken her maybe half a minute to lock the door from inside, open the window and crawl out. She'd been on the ground no more than a minute. She was two hundred yards away, give or take a few, even at her speed.

"The bitch is close. Real close. This time we've got her."

<>

"Run for it," Morganti said to Brand. "Get the President out of here before the bandits show up. If they were waiting for us at Dover, they'll be swarming over this place in just a few minutes."

Brand knew Morganti was right. The problem was, he didn't trust Morganti. Morganti had tried to undermine Brand's authority since he came aboard. It could be a trap.

"It's my job to stay with the airplane and the passengers," said Brand.

"Your job is to serve the President," said Morganti. "I'll stay here and deal with the bandits. I'll buy as much time as I can while you and Ms. Paulsen run for it."

"Look, I'm in command here and—"

"Excuse me," said Libby, "I know you two don't get along. This time Colonel Morganti happens to be right."

"Lib—ah, Madame President, you may not have the whole picture here."

"I've always been a better judge of character than you, Pete. We have to trust Colonel Morganti. Let's do as he suggests and get the hell out of here."

Brand caught the personal tone in her voice. Never before had she called him by his first name in public. The others caught it too. Morganti and Switzer were wearing the same curious expression. In the back of the cockpit, Batchelder and Sergeant Manning were giving them quizzical looks.

Brand gave it a few more seconds. Libby was right. So was Morganti. Time to get out of Dodge. Brand nodded. "Okay, let's move."

As he rose from his seat, he saw that Sergeant Manning was still in the cockpit. There was one more thing he had to do. He sat down again and scribbled on his steno pad. He ripped off the page and handed it to Manning. "See if you can send this."

<>

Lowanda Manning had no idea whether the texting machine still worked. The thing had a mind of its own, as if it were disconnected from the rest of Air Force One. Clutching the steno pad sheet with Brand's scribbled message, she trotted down the passageway toward the galley. It was an uphill run. She'd never seen the deck tilted like this, at least when they were on the ground.

The little green light on the machine's console was still illuminated. How could that be? Did the machine have its own power supply? Maybe. Maybe the message would go.

Manning sat at the console, the steno pad sheet before her, and began typing.

> *To: Capt. Sam Fornier*
> *From: SAM 28000*
>
> *This is the last transmission from Angel. Inform Cassidy that we are down and evading. Please know that your gallant service will be recognized.*
>
> *Col. Pete Brand*

Manning felt a mounting sense of urgency as she pecked out the last line of the message. Any minute now she would hear the sound she'd been dreading—the *whop whop* of helicopter rotor blades.

The sergeant keyed the transmit button and jumped up from the console. As she raced back toward the President's office, she realized that she still had Brand's steno sheet in her hand. Coming up with no other quick solution, she ripped the sheet into tiny pieces. Now what? One wad at a time, Manning stuffed the paper into her mouth and forced herself to swallow.

Gagging, she thought again about this guy, Fornier. Where was he? Was he on the run too?

<>

Left or right?

Sam made the decision an instant after her feet hit the alley outside the window. Left led to the store front and the busy street. Cars, parking lot, traffic. Not good. That's where they'd be looking.

Had to go right.

Sam whirled and started down the alley. The narrow lane was still in deep shadow. The morning sun was hovering behind the tree line to her left. She leaned into it, cranking on the speed. *Run, Sam, run.* Nothing else mattered. Get the hell away. Put distance behind her, then find a place to hole up.

As she ran a thought nagged at her. How did they find her? Could have been luck, random searching of the area where they'd last seen her. She doubted it. The phone? Had they managed to figure out her trackability hack, somehow got a lock on her phone? Maybe, but as she thought about it, the answer came clear. The Wi-Fi connection in the coffee shop. Nothing secure about that network. She'd gambled that the spooks wouldn't be monitoring the net traffic this soon. She was wrong.

She'd covered almost fifty yards when she spotted them. In the shadows she couldn't see the color of their jackets, but she knew. Had to be blue. There were two of them, still a hundred yards away. Coming toward her.

Sam wheeled and reversed course. Sprinting back down the alley, she passed the back of the coffee shop with the open window. This was bad. Unless she made it to the street, got past the parking lot and into the residential area on the other side, the goons would be waiting for her.

They already were. A car was pulling into the alley. A dark SUV, no lights. She couldn't tell from this distance, but her gut told her it was the same one that had chased her last night when she wrecked the Mini. *Bastards.* Sam slowed to a trot, keeping her eyes on the vehicle. The SUV stopped, blocking the entrance to the alley. The doors on either side opened. Two men stepped out. More nylon jackets.

Sam shot a glance over her shoulder. The two behind her were maybe a hundred yards away. The pair in front no more than seventy-five. They were walking toward her. They weren't in a hurry. Sam did a quick appraisal. To her left were the rear walls of the low buildings adjoining the coffee shop. On her right were fences, each a different height, guarding the back yards of the one-story, mid-1900s homes of the neighborhood.

Sam wheeled and sprinted back toward the first pair of goons. She couldn't see their faces, but she could tell they weren't surprised. They were taking their time. They knew she was trapped.

She picked one of the fences, a wooden one, not so high that she couldn't make it over, but high enough, about eight or nine feet. High enough to slow down her pursuers. When she was nearly abeam her chosen spot she abruptly angled in toward the fence. Keeping up the speed, she launched off her left foot.

It was a good vault. Her old gymnastics coach would have applauded. She caught the top of the fence with her hands. Using her momentum, Sam swung herself up so that her chin was level with the tops of the vertical wooden planks. She hiked her right leg up and snaked her foot over the fence. Her leg was almost over the fence, arms still hauling her body up, when she felt it. An impact, like someone had jabbed her between the shoulder blades with a pool cue.

At almost the same instant she heard it—a muffled *ploom*. She recognized the sound because she'd heard it before. It was the same sound she'd heard when the goons were trying to shoot her. That time they had missed.

Sam Fornier felt no sharp pain, just a dull ache. Her ankle was still hooked over the top of the fence. It was as far as she could go. Already the strength was leaving her. She felt her grip loosening on the fence, gravity taking over, pulling her back to the alley. She stopped fighting and let herself fall. She'd almost made it. Almost. Like running a marathon, then bonking in the last mile.

So this was what it felt like to die. It wasn't as bad as she expected.

CHAPTER TWENTY-TWO

The first CH-53 touched down in a swirl of blowing grass and dirt fifty feet from the nose of Air Force One. Seconds later, four more of the big helicopters, one after the other, alighted in a circle around the wrecked airplane. Each troopship bore the same dark blue-gray paint scheme. No numbers, no distinguishing insignia. From each chopper spewed a column of men in blue camo fatigues. All carried automatic weapons.

A company-sized contingent took up positions around the perimeter. At the head of the first column strode a slender man in the same blue camos, combat boots, fatigue cap. He carried a Sig P-229 semiautomatic pistol at the ready in his right hand.

Seldom did Rolf Berg take hands-on control of an operation. He had tiers of competent unit commanders beneath him to direct routine operations. But Berg had no intention of turning over command of anything this critical. He hadn't come this far, put his ass on the line so many times, to let someone bungle the operation. Or take the credit.

Christ knew, there'd been enough bungles. Air Force One was supposed to be at the bottom of the Atlantic, not here in a Delaware country airport. Still, Berg couldn't help taking a secret satisfaction that the military brass and agency honchos had botched the job. Now it had come down to him. Rolf Berg and Galeforce.

A few paces behind Berg was J. D. Schlater, Deputy Director of the United States Secret Service. Schlater ranked only a few rungs below Berg in the Capella hierarchy. Schlater's task was to take control of the Secret Service contingent aboard Air Force One.

Approaching the open door of the lower passenger entrance, Berg didn't like what he saw. The belly of the aircraft was resting on the grassy earth. The lower passenger door was nearly at ground level. After a crash landing the passengers should have evacuated the aircraft. They should be standing out here in the field.

No one was standing outside Air Force One. No one except a handful of men at the lower passenger door. Each wore a white shirt and necktie. Each had the unmistakable look of a Secret Service agent. None was smiling.

The passenger door was open and the mechanical stairs were partly extended. At the foot of the stairs stood a white-shirted man holding a short-stock submachine gun, a Heckler & Koch MP5. Behind him stood two more men, also with MP5s, in the same white button down shirts and loosened ties.

"Stop right there," said the man in the doorway. Berg recognized him. His name was Grossman, and he was the chief of the Secret Service detail aboard Air Force One. "No one is coming aboard."

"Step aside, Mike," said J. D. Schlater, striding up behind Berg. "Your job is finished here. I'm in charge now."

Grossman stared at Schlater for a moment. His face took a hard set. "I'm not leaving my post, Mr. Schlater. You know the rules."

"I know the rules, Mike. I'm your boss. I'm ordering you and your detail to step over here and lay down your weapons."

Berg didn't like the way this was going. Grossman wasn't moving. These guys were holding up the show and time was critical. Schlater had a reputation for toughness, but he might be letting loyalty to his old team influence his thinking. There was only one way for this to end.

Berg glanced at Ricketts, the squad leader on his right, and nodded. Ricketts acknowledged with a nod. From six FN P90 submachine guns erupted a muted chattering sound like chirps from crickets. The nearly silent bursts lasted less than two seconds.

The two agents behind Grossman went down. Their weapons

made a clunking noise in the entranceway. Mike Grossman remained standing, a look of disbelief on his face. The agent's white shirt was laced with a pattern of reddish holes. As in slow motion, Grossman let the MP5 slip from his grasp, then toppled face forward onto the grassy earth beside Air Force One.

Berg nodded again to Ricketts. The first squad of six contractors rushed through the door. Trotting behind them, J. D. Schlater paused to gaze down at the body of his subordinate, Mike Grossman. Schlater's expression was impassive, as if he were inspecting fresh road kill. "It was your call, Mike. I gave you a chance."

Berg followed Schlater aboard. The remaining seven Secret Service agents had been rounded up and ordered by Schlater to turn over their weapons. Unlike Grossman, they grudgingly followed Schlater's orders. Ricketts and his squad came tramping down the stairway from the upper deck. "The cockpit's empty, Director. No sign of the crew."

"What about the passengers and the flight service crew?"

"All of 'em we could find we've herded into the main cabin. All except—" he glanced back down the passageway "—these two."

Berg saw two frightened-looking, middle-aged men, both bespectacled with disheveled black hair, being shoved toward him by a pair of Galeforce contractors. "The Iranians you were looking for," said Ricketts.

The older of the two stopped and glowered at Berg. "What's the meaning of this? What are you doing with us? We are diplomats on an official mission."

Berg ignored him. So these were the guys. Said and Al-Bashir. The Iranians Paulsen was selling her country out to. Too bad that they didn't much look like terrorists, but that could be fixed. These two were on a one-way trip to meet Allah.

"Keep them with us," Berg said. "We've got plans for these guys."

"Yes, sir. Some of the passengers are getting pretty vocal. That senator—you know, the white-haired guy named Ozinsky—he got confrontational with us. We had to cuff him and isolate him. It might be a problem later."

"Let Schlater take care of it. He knows how to handle it. Have you located Paulsen?"

"She has to be in the Presidential suite," said Ricketts. "The airplane's locked down, and we've covered every other compartment. We're sure some of the staff and maybe the cockpit crew's in the suite too. We've got it sealed off and waiting for your order."

Berg nodded. That was the plan. Isolate Paulsen from the other occupants of the airplane before taking final action. Do it with as few witnesses as possible. Eliminate the witnesses. Set up the Iranian terrorists as the perpetrators. Then hose the Iranians. Not elegant, but they could tidy up the details later.

When Capella had reached the decision to remove Paulsen, Rolf Berg had been one of the first to give his commitment. Now it was crunch time. Berg had the sure sense that what he did in the next minutes would change history.

Berg headed down the passageway. He kept the P-229 suspended at his right hip. He had never been in this section of Air Force One, but he knew the floor plan by heart. The Presidential suite occupied almost the entire nose section on the main deck. As he strode down the corridor, Berg could feel the deck tilted downward because of the collapsed nose gear.

He had almost reached the far end of the darkened passageway when the door to the Presidential suite opened. A man emerged, and he immediately clunked the door behind him. In the dim light Berg could make out the blue jacket, the Air Force insignia. The man didn't appear to be armed.

"Colonel Brand?" said Berg.

"Colonel Morganti. I'm the Deputy Presidential Pilot."

Berg gave him a quick appraisal. He knew Morganti from the briefing sheets. And he knew the type. That pompous manner was something chickenshit colonels seemed to acquire along with their orders to Washington. Morganti had been sent out here for no other purpose than to impede Berg's mission.

"Where's Brand?" said Berg.

"With the President."

Berg gestured toward the door. "Open it."

Morganti shook his head. "Not until I get the order from inside."

"When did it become the Deputy Presidential Pilot's responsibility to guard doors?"

"That's not something you need to know."

Berg sighed. Where did they get these assholes? "Have it your way," he said and fired a round into Morganti's forehead just above the right eyebrow.

The Air Force officer's eyes bulged, then rolled back in their sockets. Morganti tilted sideways against the passageway wall and dropped like a bundle of laundry. Berg motioned to Ricketts and his squad. He pointed at the door to the suite. They had to move fast. Berg's P-229 was fitted with a silencer, but the muffled shot was still loud enough to have been heard inside the suite. If anyone in there was armed, they'd be alerted.

This part they'd rehearsed. The door to the Presidential suite was heavy duty, not the kind that could be kicked in. Berg stepped back while Ricketts attached the plastic charge to the door handle. A few seconds later the mini-charge detonated with a muffled *whump*. A ragged hole appeared where the handle had been, and the door flopped open.

Led by Ricketts, the contractors poured through the doorway. Holding the P-229 at the ready, Berg followed them inside the Presidential suite. Berg had run this scenario a hundred times in his mind. No discussion, no hesitation, no explanations. The decision had already been made. Fast and neat. Identify the target, isolate her, get it done. It was God's will.

The President's office looked smaller and less grand than he expected. The L-shaped desk faced outward. The seat behind it was empty. The room was semi-dark, illuminated only by the morning sunshine slanting through the window on the right. Peering at Berg from the settee facing the desk was a youngish-looking man, maybe thirty, looking thoroughly terrified. Okay, that would be Fortenoy, the deputy White House chief of staff. Next to him sat a man with large metal-rimmed glasses and a serious frown. Berg recognized him from the brief sheet. It had to be Lester Vosges, another of Paulsen's stable of numbnut advisors. Standing in the corner was a heavy-set black woman wearing Air Force blues and chief master sergeant's stripes. Probably Manning, the chief flight attendant.

None of the three spoke. They stared at Berg as if he had just landed from Saturn.

Vosges, the one who looked like an owl, had a cell phone in his hand. If he was trying to make a call, he would have discovered that his cell phone was useless, like every other cell phone on Air Force One. At least they were supposed to be, but it seemed that everything Berg hadn't personally controlled today had gotten fucked up. Without a word Berg snatched the cell phone from Vosge's hand. Berg's contractors already had orders to confiscate every cell phone along with every weapon aboard the aircraft.

Ricketts appeared from the doorway to the left, the President's private suite. He looked at Berg and shook his head. The private suite was empty. That left only the medical office, which adjoined the President's office from aft. Berg dispatched two contractors to search the office. Half a minute later they were back, again shaking their heads.

Berg felt a mounting sense of frustration. This was turning into a cluster fuck. Not in any of the scenarios they had rehearsed was this a contingency. Missing were the Presidential Pilot and the other copilot, Batchelder. And Paulsen's chief of staff, the skinny bitch—what was her name? Maitlin, that was it. All missing.

And Paulsen. *Where the hell is Paulsen?*

As if reading his thoughts, the round-faced female sergeant broke the silence. "She's not here."

<>

"I told you, we're not taking calls." Jeb Kincaid didn't bother concealing the annoyance in his voice. The White House Press Secretary had been fielding calls all night from the news-hungry media hounds. The silky-toned manner that reporters loved about Kincaid was gone. No, he wasn't releasing any information at this time. No, he wouldn't affirm or deny that Air Force One had suffered a calamity. No, for the last time, he wasn't making any comments. Please show a little respect for the President and stay the hell off the phone. Wait for the press conference that was coming later in the morning.

"It's not the press," said Rosalind Diggs, the matronly secretary who ran the front desk in Kincaid's office. Diggs's eyes were red from the emotional stress of the past several hours. "It's General Gritti."

It took a second to register. Kincaid stared at her. Gritti was the burr-headed marine who served as the President's National Security Advisor. He was an insider, one of the President's favorites. *Gritti had been aboard Air Force One with the President.*

Kincaid snatched up the phone, then hesitated. He gave Diggs a two-fingered swiping gesture across his throat. It was their private signal. It meant, *Switch off recording.*

Kincaid waited until Diggs had left and closed the door. "General Gritti, thank God you're okay. What's the President's status?"

"Is this a secure line?"

"Yes, sir. Just you and me."

"The President's okay," said Gritti. "At least for the moment. She needs your help."

"I'm listening," said Kincaid. He lowered himself into his desk chair and squeezed the phone between his neck and shoulder so that he could jot notes.

"Every one of the cell phones on Air Force One has been locked out. We don't know how the bastards did that. I'm calling you from the desk phone in the airport terminal in a place called Summit. That's where Air Force One has landed. I don't know how long I'll be able to talk before someone shuts this one down."

"Okay, keep talking."

"The President is airborne again. In a Gulfstream exec jet. They commandeered it here at Summit."

"They?"

"She and the Presidential Pilot and some staff."

"Airborne to where? I don't understand. I thought that—"

"I'll tell you in a minute. It's critical that you be discreet with this. The President wants you to contact people you trust in the media, have them on the ramp to meet her when the Gulfstream lands. Tell them to bring local law enforcement with them. Got that? Local police, not the feds. The President will be safe as soon as she's in the media spotlight and protected by real cops."

Kincaid knew Gritti from the previous administration, back when Kincaid was a Defense Department spokesman and Gritti was on the Joint Chiefs staff. He and the general had never been close. Gritti was like a lot of the senior officers Kincaid had met at DOD. Dismissive with lower-ranking civilians, especially thirty-something appointees like Kincaid who had no military credentials of their own.

"General, shouldn't we get the Secret Service in the loop? And Homeland Security?"

"Absolutely not. This is a conspiracy we're dealing with. A big, complex, well-organized coup attempt, and the military is deeply involved. Beyond that we don't know who's in it or who we can trust. The President's only move is to get outside the federal net, at least for now, and go public. Are you clear on this?"

It was Gritti being Gritti again. Talking down to civilians. "I'm clear," said Kincaid. "Where and when will she be landing?"

Gritti told him. Then he repeated his warning to exercise the most extreme discretion. The President was counting on him. Get it done.

After the line went dead, Kincaid finished jotting down what the general had told him. For another minute Kincaid remained in his office seat, thinking about what Gritti had said. This was explosive stuff. In normal times White House Press Secretaries were spokespersons, not conduits of power. But this was different. What Jeb Kincaid was being asked to do would be pivotal in the future history of the country.

He picked up the phone again and punched in a number he knew by heart. On the second ring, a familiar voice came on the line.

"Ripley."

<>

"I see it," said Ingram. He lowered his binoculars and pointed to the speck of the incoming aircraft. "Lined up on runway zero-four."

As the jet neared the runway threshold at the Easton airport, the Gulfstream's graceful features were becoming visible. Long pointy nose, tall slanting tail, thin swept back wings. Ingram couldn't help reflecting on the strangeness of the situation. No flight plan, no landing clearance, no official party to meet it here on the ground.

None except Ingram's group of thirty-some reporters and cameramen and the two dozen uniformed police officers. They'd gotten here only minutes before the tower controllers reported the Gulfstream on final approach. Behind them was the row of vans with the markings of networks and local affiliates. According to the controllers, the Gulfstream had flown a slow, meandering flight path down the Delaware peninsula, giving the team time to make it across the bay to the Maryland east shore. In the distance, high and beyond the shoreline, Ingram could make out the shapes of the four fighters trailing the Gulfstream.

The Gulfstream's tires squawked down on the 5,500-foot-long runway. The two turbofan engines rumbled in reverse thrust, slowing the jet enough that it easily made the turn off two-thirds of the way down the runway. Ingram could feel the tension heightening in the group around him. This was an arrival and reception unlike anything a President had ever received.

Ingram's cameraman eased up beside him. "Where do you want me?"

"Right behind me. We'll go in together."

Ingram had been designated the lead media representative. For the past quarter hour he had been rehearsing in his mind the role he was assigned to play. He and the cameraman would be the first to board the aircraft. First to meet its occupants. First to greet the President of the United States on her arrival back in the United States.

The Gulfstream exited the narrow taxiway and turned on to the sprawling ramp. The pilot spotted the media group assembled in front of the one-story airport terminal building and turned in their direction. The high-pitched whine of the engines swelled in volume as the jet approached. No one in the group spoke as the jet wheeled across the ramp. Instinctively, Ingram put his fingers in his ears to block the noise.

The Gulfstream slowed, did a neat ninety-degree turn, and came to a stop with its sleek nose pointed toward the terminal and the waiting group of reporters. Ingram could see the faces of the pilots through the slanted glass windscreen. He had to hand it to these guys. Flying a 747 all night across an ocean, crash landing in a pea patch airport, then taking off in a commandeered executive jet.

First one, then the second engine whined down. Ingram removed the fingers from his ears. For a minute nothing happened. The jet sat motionless and silent. The pilots' faces were no longer visible in the windscreen.

Ingram motioned to the cameramen, then walked to the left side of the aircraft. The other reporters followed, forming an arc from the front to the rear of the Gulfstream.

Ingram rapped on the aluminum skin of the main door. As if in response, he heard a metallic click, then the door unlatched. The door swung fully open. A boarding ladder dropped out from the base of the door and tilted outwards until it reached the pavement.

Ingram didn't wait. He clambered up the ladder, two steps at a time. He felt the ladder give slightly as the weight of the cameraman hit the bottom step behind him. By the time Ingram had taken his first step into the cabin he had the Glock out of its holster. It had already occurred to him that he'd be the first to take a bullet if there were agents aboard. The Capella briefer had said they believed that the President hadn't brought Secret Service agents along on the Gulfstream.

The briefer was right. There were no agents. There were no White House staffers. There was no President. The only visible occupants of the cabin were two men in Air Force uniforms. The cockpit was empty, which meant that these two must have flown the Gulfstream into Easton. One wore the leaves of a lieutenant colonel. The other had sergeant's stripes on his sleeve.

"Check the lavatory," Ingram told the cameraman, who was no longer carrying a camera. The reporter-cameraman facade had ended. He had his own Glock out of its holster and at the ready.

A few seconds later the cameraman was back, shaking his head. "Nothing."

By now two more reporters, also carrying semi-automatics, were in the forward cabin. The narrow space between the cockpit and the main cabin was filled with hunched-over, weapon-carrying Galeforce contractors.

Ingram turned his attention to the two Air Force men. So far neither had spoken. They were seated in the second row on each side of the aisle. They were eyeing Ingram like spaniels watching a Doberman.

Ingram felt the anger well up inside him. He had come to perform the patriotic service of removing a treasonous President.

Instead he was standing here looking at an empty cabin. Empty except for these two smug blue-suited assholes.

Ingram pointed the muzzle of the Glock at the forehead of the officer. His nametag read *Batchelder*. "Where is she?" Ingram demanded.

The officer didn't blink. He kept giving Ingram the spaniel look. "Where is who?"

CHAPTER TWENTY-THREE

"Tell me again," said Libby. "What is this thing called?"

"A Piper Apache," said Brand from the left seat. "Currently known as Air Force One."

Libby nodded. She knew the protocol. Any fixed-wing airplane carrying the President received the call sign "Air Force One." Never before had the label been applied to a clattering old twin-engine crate like this one.

Brand had stolen it, of course. The Apache was parked at the Summit airport, having just been fueled. The hulk of the previous Air Force One lay crumpled in the meadow on the opposite side of the field. In the distance they'd heard the wailing of sirens. The stupefied line attendant had just given them a blank stare when Brand informed him that the Apache was being requisitioned for a national security mission.

Libby peered through the crazed Plexiglas window of the Apache's cabin. Forested green hills were slipping beneath them. Brand was keeping them at low altitude, only a few hundred feet above the terrain. They were somewhere over southern Pennsylvania. Taking off from Summit, banking away from the field, they'd spotted the dark silhouettes of helicopters approaching from the south. They'd gotten away just in time. Or so she hoped. At any moment she expected to see the dark shapes converging on them again.

Libby glanced around again at the tattered interior of the Apache. This was not the Air Force One she was used to. The brown vinyl upholstery was faded. Rips in the fabric were covered with duct tape. The black-painted instrument panel was chipped and dented, bright metal showing through, like something from an old war movie. The two piston engines growled in a synchronous baritone.

Brand's face, as usual, revealed nothing. He was focused on flying the airplane. His hands moved over the controls like those of a surgeon, tweaking the power setting, fine-tuning the propeller controls, making tiny adjustments to the airplane's heading.

In the back sat Jill Maitlin and Vic Kreier, the only Secret Service agent they had room for in the Apache. For armament they had Kreier's compact submachine gun and semi-automatic as well as Brand's 9mm Beretta.

Kreier had been assigned over Mike Grossman's objections. Grossman insisted that it was *his* job to accompany the President, but Jill Maitlin overruled him. She declared that Grossman should be the first one to confront the conspirator forces when they arrived at Air Force One. Grossman could buy them time.

Jill was wearing a sour expression while she scribbled notes into a composition book. Libby knew that Jill hated airplanes, and she especially hated cramped little flivvers like this one. It had taken a direct order—something Libby loathed doing—to get Jill to climb into the Apache with her and Brand.

"How much longer?" Libby asked Brand. It occurred to her that it was the same question she used to ask her father when they took road trips.

"Not long," said Brand. Same answer she'd gotten from her father.

She had to shake her head at the bizarreness of this situation. She was the President. In any other scenario she'd be expected to exercise executive authority. Get a situational briefing. Decide a course of action. For this brief sliver of time, she was free of all that. No decisions to make. No authority to exercise. Instead, she was being hauled over the boondocks in a vibrating rattletrap to a fate unknown.

Since fleeing Summit, an idea had been inserting itself into her consciousness. A solution to her problems. To the country's problems. The idea was still forming, indistinct but taking shape in his mind.

She blurted it out. "We could disappear."

Brand kept his eyes straight ahead. "Where?"

"Somewhere they won't find us." And then she realized what she had said. *Us.* Did she mean that? What did Brand think? "What I mean is, let them think I'm dead and—"

"I know what you mean." Brand looked at her. "You want to leave office."

"It's not what *I* want. It's what *they* want. The country, the voters, those people who've been trying to kill me."

"They weren't elected to run the country. You were."

"It was my mistake to run. It was their mistake to elect me." As she spoke, she glanced over her shoulder. She saw the expression on Jill Maitlin's face. Jill's ballpoint was suspended in mid-air. She was staring at Libby with an expression of pure revulsion.

Brand said, "So you don't want the job anymore. What *do* you want?"

"To be free. Is that asking so much? To not be responsible for running a country that wants me gone." She knew her voice sounded tremulous. Not the way a chief executive was supposed to sound. She didn't care.

Brand said nothing for a moment. He tweaked the engine mixtures. "How do you propose to do this?"

"Let them declare me dead. Isn't that better than letting them actually kill me?"

"And then what? Leave the country? Change your appearance? You're not exactly unrecognizable, you know."

"I haven't gotten that far yet. I'm still thinking."

"This is insane," snapped Jill from the back seat. She leaned forward, her face a few inches from Libby's. "Remember who you are, for Christ's sake. You're the President of the United States. Stop talking like a nitwit kid running away from home."

Libby reddened. A scolding by Jill Maitlin cut her to the core. Jill was right, as usual. She was indulging in fantasies. With that thought Libby's shoulders slumped. She felt a weariness settle over her.

Brand seemed not to notice. He adjusted the range on the panel-mounted navigation display. He peered out through the windscreen. "Heads up," he announced. "Air Force One will be landing soon."

<>

"Got 'em," announced Keppler. He looked up from his console. "The only general aviation traffic in the air. No squawk, no transmission. Has to be them."

"Where are they headed?" asked Ripley.

"Looks like Gettysburg. Washington Center is tracking them on en route radar, and the AWACS bird reports the same thing."

Ripley was standing behind Keppler. He scratched his head. "Why Gettysburg? What's there?"

"Who the hell knows? The good news is that it's not far from Washington."

Or from Delaware, thought Ripley. It meant Berg's force was close behind. It would be a matter of minutes.

Again Ripley wondered about the F-15 that had been escorting Air Force One. Why didn't he shoot it down after it took off again at Dover? The F-15 pilot was a light colonel named Apte. He must have gone rogue. There was an unconfirmed report that he had shot down his own flight lead after they'd intercepted Air Force One over the ocean. If it was true, then this guy Apte was headed for a lifetime stay at Leavenworth. Or worse.

No matter. With Paulsen on the ground, the hunt was coming to its inevitable conclusion. She had run out of assets. There was no one left to save her.

<>

The sky looked empty. Too empty, Brand thought. They had observed no other small airplanes since they'd left Summit. Normally they'd see early morning general aviation traffic buzzing through this air space, inbound to Washington or headed north.

And the air traffic control frequencies were silent. Brand had left the aircraft's transpondor off so they wouldn't present a telltale blip on air traffic control radars. He wasn't transmitting on the VHF communications radio, just listening. The eerie silence reminded him of the air traffic lock down after 9/11. Maybe they'd closed the air space because of the Presidential emergency.

Which meant they had to land quickly. Get out of the air before their low-flying, non-transmitting puddle-jumper caught the attention of the sky watchers.

The Gulfstream that Batchelder and Switzer had commandeered would soon be arriving at Easton. It had been Gritti's idea, sending the conspirators off on a false trail. As soon as they realized the deception, the search would be on.

"Is that it?" asked Libby.

"That's it. See the town? That's the national park to the left. The airport's on the other side."

She peered through the Plexiglas windscreen. She squinted, not seeing it at first. Then she spotted it. "It doesn't look like much of an airport."

"We don't need much of an airport. We want to land, attract no attention, get a car, get you to the station."

Libby nodded, but her face reflected her uncertainty. "I don't like this, Pete. What if we get stopped? What if we can't make it to the television station? What if they don't let us—"

"One step at a time. We land, get away from the airport, then we'll worry about what happens at the station."

Libby closed her eyes and nodded her agreement. She looked frightened, Brand thought. She had a right to be. The danger level would ratchet off the scale as soon as they were on the ground.

Stealing the airplane had been Brand's idea. The destination was Libby's. Gettysburg had a regional airport. It was far enough from Washington that it was probably not yet within the net of the conspiracy's security forces. More important, the town had a small affiliate television station. The station director, Dom Cirilli, had been a supporter of Libby's senatorial campaign. Libby thought Cirilli could facilitate a live feed to national television.

Maybe. If Cirilli was there. If they could communicate with him. If the facility was still on the air. If there were no more surprises.

Since discovering that none of their cell phones worked, Brand knew they were dealing with a sophisticated enemy. Their reach extended from the military through the homeland security apparatus to even the cellular networks. What else? Did the conspirators control the broadcast media? Network television?

They were about to find out.

The single runway angled from southwest to northeast. Brand skirted the south edge of the sprawling Gettysburg battlefield and lined up on a two-mile final for runway zero-six. He was slowing, extending the landing flaps, when a voice crackled over the VHF radio. "Twin-engine aircraft on approach to Gettysburg, this is Gettysburg Unicom. Identify yourself."

So much for sneaking into Gettysburg. Brand hesitated with his finger on the transmit button. Reply or remain silent? Tell them this was Air Force One?

No. Stay silent.

He lowered the landing gear.

"Twin on final at Gettysburg, be advised that the airport is closed."

Closed? Why would they close the airport? Brand knew. For the same reason they hadn't seen any other airplanes. The Feds had shut down the air space.

The end of the runway was coming up under the nose. It occurred to Brand that landing on a closed runway was a serious violation. He almost laughed. Another violation. Morganti would love it.

The Apache passed over a stubbled pasture. The threshold of the runway with the big number 6 came up under the nose. It was a typical small regional airport. Single paved runway, three-thousand-some feet. Fixed-base operation buildings off to the left at the far end. General aviation airplanes parked on the ramp.

After flying the Boeing 747, handling the Apache was like stepping from an eighteen-wheeler to a Volkswagen. The controls felt twitchy. Brand reminded himself not to level off sixty feet above the runway, something heavy transport pilots sometimes did in little airplanes. There was almost no wind, only a light breeze from the northeast.

Brand eased the throttles back. The two Lycoming engines popped and sputtered. Brand kept pressure on the yoke, holding the nose off, letting the Apache's energy dissipate, feeling for the runway. *Clunk.* The main wheels landed, followed by the nose wheel. Not a great landing, he thought, but not embarrassing.

He saw the airport terminal ahead, to the left. The concrete apron held half a dozen small airplanes. In the adjoining parking lot were several parked cars. If it became necessary, Brand would expand the list of stolen machines to include an automobile.

Then he saw them. Flashing blue lights. They were mounted atop a white sedan with some kind of official-looking markings. The sedan was leading a procession of cars onto the airport.

The Apache had slowed to a fast taxi, almost to the end of the runway. Too late to shove the throttles up and takeoff again. As the lead sedan with the blue lights sped onto the apron, Brand got a good look at the marking on the side: *Sheriff.*

<>

Ben Waller unsnapped the leather strap over the holstered .357. He wouldn't draw the piece, at least not yet. He'd let the deputies cover him while he made the initial assessment. That was Waller's method and it had served him well all these years. The young bucks liked to joke that Waller's old Smith & Wesson was a relic from the dinosaur age. They were right, considering that most of the badasses today carried semi-automatics. Waller didn't care. He was a dinosaur himself. Six terms as the elected sheriff of Adams County, twenty-three years before that as a patrolman or deputy in three other Pennsylvania counties. Waller and the .357 were prehistoric.

The Homeland Security alert had come an hour ago, just as Waller had gotten to the office. It was a no-shit, pull-all-the-stops red alert. A national emergency, the President missing, and a terrorist action, possibly in a small aircraft. Hot enough to prompt Waller to call in off-duty deputies. You never knew.

Then came the call from the regional airport tower. A suspicious airplane, not responding to instructions, inbound to Gettysburg. On his way to the airport Waller had called in three more cars from the north side of the county. He'd arrived with a force of nine plus a back up of half a dozen more who'd be there within ten minutes. All from the sheriff's office. No outside help.

There was going to be hell to pay no matter how this played out. According to a state judge's ruling last year, county sheriffs were supposed to defer to the Pennsylvania State Police for such operations. And because this was a possible terrorist action, he was obliged to call in Homeland Security. The county sheriff's job these days didn't amount to much more than guarding schools and serving subpoenas.

Screw the state police. And screw Homeland Security, whom Waller regarded as parasites who pissed away taxpayer dollars making old ladies take off their shoes at airports. Ben Waller was in the twilight of a long career. He was going to finish up by handling this matter the right way. His way.

Waller's driver was a new kid named Bradford. He had buzz-cut red hair and a tattoo on his forearm that, as best as Waller could tell, depicted a dead lizard. Bradford was perpetually scared shitless of Waller, which was the way Waller liked it. The kid kept his eyes locked straight ahead and responded to the sheriff's orders with mechanical head nods and terse yessirs.

Bradford wheeled the Crown Vic onto the apron, trailed by the other three patrol cars. Someone from the airport tower had had the presence of mind to open the chained gate to the ramp. The procession of patrol cars, blue lights flashing, arrived just in time to see the twin-engine airplane turning off the runway.

Waller's first priority was to make sure the guy didn't takeoff again. He'd seen this before, back in the heavy druggie days. Claptrap planes like this one alighting on roads and turn rows in rural Pennsylvania every night to dump their stashes. When the pilots realized they were busted, they'd cob it, try to get the hell out of there. The outcome was usually ugly.

"Cut him off," Waller told Bradford. "When he gets headed toward the terminal, pull up to block him." Waller barked into his shoulder-mounted mike to the other cars. "Cars one and two take either side, number three cover the tail." They had the guy pinned. When the pilot knew he was grounded, he'd give up. Or come out shooting.

Waller watched the airplane slow to taxi speed, then continue creeping ahead toward the terminal. It was an old bird, some kind of beat up twin-engine crate. Same kind Waller used to bust in the old days. Those guys were seldom violent, at least not when you had them cornered. Most were just trying to make some quick bucks. They'd almost always settle for a little jail time over getting shot.

But those were druggies, not terrorists. These guys were trying to take down the President.

The old twin was nearly to the terminal. As Bradford pulled up to block its path, the airplane's engines abruptly shut down. The propellers clunked to a halt.

Then nothing. No one moved.

Waller waited. He let the other three cars take their positions around the airplane. Through the shaded Plexiglas he could see silhouettes inside the cabin. At least four occupants. Their only egress was out the right side door. If they came out shooting, he had them covered from every angle. The thought flitted across Waller's mind that maybe he *should* have called in the State Police. If this thing went south, he'd be hung out to dry.

Too late. This was his show. Maybe his last show.

"Out of the vehicles, keep them covered," Waller said into his mike. He saw doors opening on the patrol cars, deputies taking position, weapons in view. Until this moment Waller had been comfortable with the firepower they'd brought. Besides pistols, they had two tactical shotguns. Barnwell, the senior deputy crouched behind the car at the Piper's tail, was hauling the LWRC M6A3 submachine gun. One of four SMGs the department's budget allowed. Now Waller wished they had more.

"They're coming out," said Bradford. The handle on the right-side passenger door was moving. The door cracked open, then swung outward. Waller tensed. If a firestorm was going to light off, it would be now.

A leg emerged from the doorway. Then another. The legs were encased in blue slacks. They belonged to a slender, auburn-haired woman. She was stepping out onto the wing walk. She was wearing sunglasses and a jumpsuit with some kind of logo embroidered on the breast. For a long moment the woman stood on the wing of the Piper gazing around at the blue flashing lights. The officers stayed crouched behind the Crown Vics, weapons drawn.

Waller squinted at the woman. She didn't look like a terrorist. She looked familiar. Damned familiar.

As the woman stepped toward the rear of the wing, a man appeared in the doorway. The pilot, Waller figured. He didn't look like a terrorist either. He was wearing a blue jacket with markings, some kind of military outfit. Waller told himself not to relax. Terrorists were clever. This could be the set up before someone blew them all to smithereens.

The two people in the back seat of the Piper hadn't moved yet. The woman stepped onto the tarmac, and the man followed. The two stood behind the Piper's wing, looking around at the dispersed patrol cars.

Waller opened his door and stepped out, keeping the vehicle

between him and the airplane. His right hand hovered over the still-holstered .357 mag. "Hold it right there," he called. "I'm Sheriff Ben Waller."

The woman exchanged glances with the man beside her, who gave her a nod. She removed her sunglasses and looked directly at Waller. In that instant Waller knew why the woman looked familiar.

"Good morning, Sheriff," she said. "I'm Libby Paulsen and I need your help."

CHAPTER TWENTY-FOUR

O nly in rare moments had Sheriff Ben Waller been speechless. This was one of those moments. Waller stared at the woman while his brain tried to process what he was seeing. *The President of the United States. She needs my help.*

In a daze, Waller took the woman's outstretched hand, held it a moment while she turned the full force of her smile on him. "Uhhh, Ma'am, on behalf of the Adams County Sheriff's Department, it's my honor to welcome you to Gettysburg."

"It's my great pleasure to meet you, Sheriff." The President introduced her traveling companions—an Air Force officer who, as he guessed, was her pilot. A lanky woman who was some sort of advisor appeared from the cabin, followed by a serious-faced young man named Kreier who was her sole Secret Service and who was carrying an automatic weapon. Waller listened attentively while President Paulsen told him that *someone* had tried—and almost succeeded—in destroying Air Force One. That they had barely escaped a trap awaiting them in Delaware. That she was in extreme danger from some still undetermined conspiracy.

Ben Waller felt as if he were dreaming.

"May I ask, ma'am, why you decided to come to Gettysburg?"

"I need to get to the television affiliate station here."

"KGYB?" asked Waller. "Channel 32. Do you know someone over there?"

"Dom Cirilli," said the President. "We're old friends."

Waller nodded. "I know Cirilli."

"Sounds as if you don't like him."

Waller rubbed his goatee. "He's into politics."

"Is that bad?"

"Only when he supports my opponent in the county election.

Like he's done the past four times."

She smiled. "Let me take care of Mr. Cirilli. He may be ready to change his affiliation."

Waller smiled back. "You made the right decision coming here, Madame President. I'm gonna get you to that station. You have my word that *no one* will get close enough to threaten you."

Waller saw her shoulders relax. Libby Paulsen closed her eyes for a moment. She murmured again, "Thank you."

As Waller steered his passengers to the cars, Deputy Sheriff Ray Barnwell eased up beside him. The deputy was wearing a dubious expression. Barnwell had been in the job nearly ten years and was the only one allowed to run his mouth around Waller.

"Are you sure about this, Ben? Don't you think we oughta call in the Pesties?"

"Screw the Pesties. Those clowns will take charge and send us off to write parking tickets." "Pesties" was the in-house term for the Pennsylvania State Police. Over several years of budget slashes, the Pesties had taken over more and more of the duties formerly reserved for local sheriffs. Waller had seen his department shrink from a peak of sixty-two uniformed deputies to its present forty-eight. More cutbacks were coming. Waller knew the time was near, next election cycle probably, when he'd be turning his badge over to someone younger and less cynical. Someone like Barnwell.

Before that, Ben Waller was going to go down in history. He'd be the sheriff who saved the President.

"We don't need them," said Waller. "By the time we get to the television station, we'll have the entire deputy force backing us up."

Barnwell's face showed that he didn't believe it. But the deputy knew when to shut up. He nodded and headed back to his patrol car.

<>

It was a tight fit. At Libby's insistence, the four of them were jammed into the back seat of Sheriff Waller's car. She didn't want them to split up. Libby sat sandwiched between Brand and Jill, with Kreier scrunched against the left door. Kreier had the MP5K positioned across his lap while his head maintained a steady sweep from left to right and back again, peering through the tinted glass of the Crown Vic. Waller sat in the front with his driver, Bradford.

They were number three in the procession. "Shooters would figure that the number one is running interference," Waller explained. "They'd guess that number two would be carrying their target. Here in the number three slot, we have the most escape options."

"Shooters?" asked Libby. "In Gettysburg?"

"Not likely, ma'am. But we gotta be ready. These guys could show up anytime."

Libby just nodded. The Sheriff was right. These guys—whoever they were—had already shown up in the middle of the ocean, off the U. S. coast, in at least two Air Force bases, and in a country airport in Delaware. Why not Gettysburg?

Sheriff Waller was a talker. While the procession wound along the two lane road toward town, Waller gave them a non-stop commentary. The town had swollen in size since he was a kid. "No suburbs in those days, just the town, pretty much like it has been for a century or more." Waller pointed to the right. "Eisenhower's farm is down that road. Big old place, now a historical site next to the battlefield. I got to shake Ike's hand once. He'd just left the White House and come back to live here in Gettysburg."

The undulating greens of a spacious golf course swept by on the right side. To the left passed a succession of strip malls, a gas station. They rolled past a complex of suburban developments. Three more Sheriff's Department cars, identical Crown Vics, pulled in behind them as they passed an intersection. Entering the outskirts of town, they picked up an additional two who were waiting in a strip mall. "Two more are already headed for the station," said Waller. "Thirty some deputies all together. Ought to be enough."

Libby said nothing. Enough for what? She felt needles of fear prickling at her again. Did anyone really believe that three dozen sheriff's deputies were going to hold off the full force of the United States military? She glanced over at Brand. He seemed detached from the sheriff's chatter. Brand was wearing that expression she had learned to recognize—eyes half closed, arms folded across his torso, mind focused on something far away. Did he think that Waller's little band of deputies was going to protect them?

Technically, Brand's duties had ended. He was the Presidential Pilot. There was nothing left for him to fly. No reason for him to be with her. No reason except one. The same reason she had secretly appointed Brand to the job.

Waller was still talking. Asking her something. Who did she think was behind the coup attempt? Before she could answer, Brand blinked, seeming to come out of his doze. "One thing we know for sure," he said. "The military is involved. Fighters have tried to shoot us down. And we know they have agents at Andrews and at Dover and most likely the Pentagon."

"Agents?" This caused the sheriff to frown. "What kind of agents? Civilian or military?"

"Probably civilian, according to a report we received. Guys in blue uniforms."

Waller shook his head knowingly. "Galeforce."

"Galeforce?" asked Libby. "That sounds familiar. What do they do?"

Brand answered. "Civilian security company. They provide services for DOD and State, mostly in the Middle East, all the hot spots."

"We've heard stories," said Waller. "Galeforce is like a private army. Supposed to be hush hush, but my information is that they have a huge presence in the DC area."

Waller's cell phone was chirping. "Sheriff Waller," he said, then listened for several seconds. "You heard right," he said. "It's me, and I wasn't yanking your chain. This is for real. You want to talk to her? Hang on." Waller covered the cell phone with one hand. "It's Mr. Cirilli. He says he has to speak with you."

Libby took the phone. "Dom, this is Libby Paulsen."

A couple of seconds passed, then Libby heard Cirilli's voice. "Yeah, it really sounds like you, Libby—excuse me, Madame President. I had to know for sure. This is crazy. We're hearing from the network office in New York that you'd been killed or captured by terrorists."

"There's a conspiracy of some sort, Dom. I'll tell you all about it soon enough. Right now we need your help. We need a feed to the network so I can go public with—"

Libby heard the phone go dead. No voice, no carrier tone. She stared at it for a moment, then handed it back to Waller. "The call was dropped. Can you get him back on the line?"

Waller tried. He punched more keys, then he glowered at the phone. "No signal. That's weird. We'll try again in a few minutes. We're almost there. Don't worry."

Libby tried not to worry. It didn't work. She couldn't stop the wave of fear that was sweeping over her like a cold wind. *Almost there.* The story of her life.

<>

They drove through a plaza. On the far side Libby could see an open area with a two-story modern structure in the middle. A transmission tower maybe two hundred feet tall stood behind the building. The roadside sign at the looping entrance to the building read *KGYB CHANNEL 32: CONNECTING GETTYSBURG TO THE WORLD*.

Libby felt her pulse quicken. It would all come to a head in this building. The nightmare that began over the Atlantic and brought her to this town in Pennsylvania would play out here. Her image would be flashed around the country, proof that she was alive and still in command. Proof that the cabal that tried to kill her was exposed and defeated.

Unless they were already here.

Two more Sheriff's Department cars were waiting at the entrance to the semicircular driveway. "Parker and Kuhn," said Waller, peering at the scene ahead. "Plus however many guys they were able to round up on short notice. That ought to bring our head count to—" Waller's face froze. "Oh, shit."

Libby leaned forward to peer through the windshield. At first she saw nothing unusual. Just the pair of patrol cars, the station, the girded tower. She heard Waller say, "Move it, Bradford. Haul ass for the front door of the station."

Then she spotted them. Black objects, three of them in trail, swooping down to the open meadow that adjoined the television station. They were growing in size, close enough to be recognizable.

Helicopters. Dark blue-gray paint schemes. No markings. The first one was just touching down.

<>

It was almost a dead heat.

With Waller barking orders in his ear, Bradford accelerated the Crown Vic past the two parked patrol cars, over the curb of the driveway, across the grass and through a plat of wild flowers. He brought the car to a skidding stop at the base of the steps leading into the station.

"Go! Go!" Waller was yelling. "Get inside."

Brand had the door open on the right side. He spilled out of the car, yanking Libby behind him. Jill Maitlin clambered from the car behind them. Kreier burst out the left side door, the MP5K dangling from its strap around his neck. In a hunched-over run he went around the back of the Crown Vic and positioned himself behind the right back fender.

Waller was already crouched behind the right front fender, barking orders into his shoulder-mounted microphone. Over the top of the car he could see the men from the first helicopter. They wore dark-camo fatigues. Each was carrying an automatic weapon, dog-trotting in a column across the grass directly toward him.

They were a hundred yards away. Another helo was alighting behind them, and the third in its descent.

The other cars in the procession came roaring up behind Waller, responding to his orders. Two wheeled onto the grass, blocking the path of the advancing column. Two more screeched up behind Waller's car. The deputies piled out and took up stations behind the vehicles.

Waller glanced behind him. The President and the gangly woman staffer were already inside. Brand, the pilot, had come back outside. He was carrying a pistol.

Waller sent the two cars that had been waiting for them around to cover the back side of the building. Then he turned his full attention to the dark-clad figures trotting toward him. He didn't like the way this was shaping up. Every one of them was carrying some kind of assault weapon. Waller and his deputies were armed with their little semiautomatic popguns. All except Barnwell, who was crouched beside Waller. Barnwell had the LWRC M6A3 submachine gun. If they were lucky, someone had the presence of mind to have grabbed the other three M6A3s from the office armory. Even so, they were seriously outgunned.

Waller said to Barnwell, "Call the Pesties. Tell 'em we need back up *now*."

"I thought you said you didn't want them taking over."

"Never mind what I said. Just fucking do it."

"Yes, sir."

Fifty yards. Close enough. Waller reached inside his car and pulled the megaphone from its clip on the sidewall.

"Hold it right there," he barked into the megaphone. His voice sounded tinny, distorted by the *whop whop* of the helicopter blades. "This area has been secured by the Adams County Sheriff Department. I'm ordering you to leave immediately."

The man at the head of the column stopped, then signaled for those behind him to hold up. He was a tall man, well over six feet. He wore sunglasses, a fatigue cap, and the same dark blue camo outfit as the rest of them. His submachine gun hung over his shoulder, the barrel canted across his waist to the left.

A professional, Waller thought. Not good.

The man in the blue camos scanned the scene around the station building. Then he looked directly at Waller. "Get back in your cars and leave. This has nothing to do with you. This is a homeland security matter." He had a strong, clear voice. A voice of authority. A man accustomed to being obeyed.

Waller didn't answer. Thirty-two years, he thought. That's how long he'd been in this business if you counted the rookie year in Pittsburgh and the four-year hitch in the Army as a military cop. He had seen it all. Drunks, dopers, bank robbers, spouse killers, arsonists, nut cases, deviates of all description. Until today he thought he would wrap up his three-decade career with some kind of community feel-good gesture—a kids' summer program or a courtesy-on-the-highway initiative. While the citizens still had a warm and fuzzy image of Ben Waller, he'd declare his retirement and turn the job over to Barnwell, who would be a shoo-in for election this fall. Waller and his wife would already be somewhere on the road on the long-planned RV tour of North America.

At least that had been the plan.

Waller glanced at Barnwell. "Well? Are the Pesties coming?"

"Nobody's coming. Our goddamn phones are dead. Every one of them."

"Shit. Use the radio in the car. Move."

The tall guy in the blue camos with the MP5 dangling over his shoulder was peering at Waller. So were the couple dozen other armed troops standing behind him. So were Waller's deputies. All waiting to see what Waller was going to do. The smart thing, of course, was to acknowledge reality. These guys had unlimited force behind them. Waller should order his deputies back into the cars and bug out. The Adams County Sheriff's Department had no business involving itself in national security dust ups.

Barnwell crawled back out the right door of Waller's car. "Ben, the radio is dead too. Nothing but static. The sumbitches have got it jammed somehow."

The third helicopter was on the ground. More blue-camoed troops were spilling out and advancing across the grassy meadow. More history in the making, thought Waller. Gettysburg was going to be famous for *two* battles, a century and a half apart.

"You've got thirty seconds to leave," said the man in blue camos. "Then we're coming in."

Waller didn't respond. An image was stuck in his mind. Her eyes. The way her eyes fixed on him after she stepped down from that beat up old airplane. The way she looked at him and said, *I'm Libby Paulsen, and I need your help.*

Ben Waller hated politics. When asked, he always declared himself an independent even though he had the lawman's instinctive bias against liberal politicians. Never would he have been a supporter of a politician like Libby Paulsen. Until today.

Sheriff Ben Waller had made a commitment. He had accepted the assignment to defend the President of the United States. Period. Which meant the RV tour of North America was on hold. Maybe forever.

"Nobody's coming in," blared Waller's voice over the megaphone. "Don't come any closer. This building is secured, and we're not going anywhere."

The man just stared at him. Then he made a hand gesture— some signal that Waller didn't recognize— and the blue-camoed troops began fanning out.

God help us, thought Ben Waller as he slid the old .357 out of its holster.

CHAPTER TWENTY-FIVE

"What are we waiting for?" Rolf Berg said into the Bluetooth mike. He was kneeling behind a hummock a hundred yards from the station. He could see the patrol cars dispersed to each side of the building. The sheriff's deputies appeared to have taken defensive positions around the perimeter. They were amateurs. "We're ready to make the assault."

"No," came Ripley's voice over the encrypted connection. "The general says to hold your position. We don't want to be accused of massacring an entire Sheriff's department."

Berg clenched his teeth, trying to contain his anger. He hadn't hunted Paulsen from Dover to Summit to Gettysburg just to let some hillbilly sheriff block the final phase of the operation. What the hell was McDivott worried about? After trying to gun down Air Force One, taking out a vice president and a joint chiefs chairman as well as several Secret Service agents, what difference did hosing a few dozen Pennsylvania cops make?

"So what are we supposed to do?" said Berg. "Wait until the whole world finds out that Paulsen is holed up here?"

"The world won't find out. Not before she's terminated. The station transmission tower is already shut down, and so are all the cell and landline connections. No one inside that station has communications with the outside. The only link from Gettysburg belongs to us, and you're talking on it."

"So when are we going to terminate her?" Berg already knew the answer.

"You'll find out. We'll give you the order to stand clear."

Stand clear? What did that mean? Why the hell was he getting orders from Ripley? As the director of Galeforce, Berg ranked just a few rungs beneath McDivott in Capella. Without Galeforce, this operation wouldn't be happening. Ripley was a flunkey, never mind the two stars, who had managed to establish himself as McDivott's lieutenant. Now Berg had to go through Ripley to communicate with McDivott. It was bullshit.

Since the operation began, an image had been taking shape in Rolf Berg's mind. He could see the treasonous President cowering before him. Begging for her life. He would put the traitor away with a single round from the P-229. No hesitation, no remorse. A single pull of the trigger and he would be restoring honor and freedom to his country.

And not just Paulsen. There were others. This local yokel sheriff who had inserted himself into the equation. Another who'd be almost as gratifying was the too-clever blue-suiter who flew Air Force One. The one who had somehow kept the President from resting forever on the bottom of the Atlantic. The same one who eluded them at Dover, at Summit, and who was now holed up with her in Gettysburg. Shooting him would be nothing more to Berg than putting down a coyote who was stealing chickens. Doing the world a favor.

Then Berg thought of something else. Something Atwater had told him and McDivott and a few others one night at the Briar Club. Something about photographs of Paulsen and her pet pilot getting it on aboard a boat. It was before she was President, back when she was still in Congress, but it explained a lot about her choice for Presidential Pilot. Atwater wouldn't say where he got them, only that they would be ammunition when the time came to eradicate whatever sentimental attachment the country might have to the late President Paulsen.

Officers in the Spec Ops community were always surprised to learn that Rolf Berg was a prude, at least in matters of morality. Despite the coarse language and intimidating manner, Berg was a deeply religious man whose views had been shaped by his fundamentalist upbringing in West Virginia. To Berg, the image of the commander-in-chief in coitus with her aerial chauffeur was sufficient reason to terminate her. And the chauffeur.

He had discovered that McDivott, also a religious man, had the same view. God hated traitors, but He had a special punishment for traitors who were also adulterers.

"I have snipers," Berg said in his mike.

"So?" said Ripley.

"Do I have clearance to use them if I see an opportunity?"

"Stand by." Berg knew what that meant. Ripley had to check with McDivott.

Half a minute later Ripley was back. "Affirmative. If you see an opportunity, take it."

<>

"Madame President, it's wonderful to see you. I can't tell you what an honor this is."

They were in the outer reception room of the KGYB studio. Libby took Dom Cirilli's hands as he kissed her cheek. "I wish it were under different circumstances, Dom."

"I got here just a few minutes ahead of you." Cirilli peered for a moment at Brand, Jill Maitlin, and Kreier, who had stormed into his studio behind Libby. Kreier was crouched next to the window, his hand clutching the grip of an assault weapon. 'What's going on?" said Cirilli. "The sheriff's cars, helicopters, those soldiers out there . . ."

"Something bad, Dom. We'll tell you what's happened, but first we have to get a live television feed. Just as quickly as you can do it. It's critical that I go on national television."

Cirilli shook his head. "I'm afraid that's impossible."

Libby stared at him. Beneath the mane of slicked-back hair, Cirilli's dark Mediterranean eyes looked somber. And frightened. Libby said, "You don't understand. We *have* to go on live television. Immediately." She almost added, *Before those people storm this place and kill all of us.*

"We're shut off," said Cirilli. "I don't know how they did it. The transmission tower is inert. Dead as a stone, no signal to or from. Likewise all the phone lines. Nothing works. Whoever's doing this has enormous resources."

A feeling of despondency settled over Libby. Seconds before she had been sure they had a chance. They *would* prevail. Now the hope was sputtering from her like the last embers of a fire. Libby was aware of someone squeezing her arm. She turned to look into Brand's face. His eyes had that distant gaze, as if he were peering into a distant landscape.

"Where are the engineers?" said Brand.

"Engineers?" said Cirilli. "Oh, you mean Hagen and Schneider. Hagen's our engineer, sort of, and Schneider's the camera operator and technician. We're a small station. We shut down at ten and don't go on the air until eight in the morning. During the night is when those two do the IT work and set up for the day crew. Hagen isn't going to be much help."

"Let's talk to him."

Cirilli looked doubtful. He shrugged and said, "Follow me."

<>

Hagen smelled of cigarette smoke and perspiration. He was fiftyish, thirty pounds overweight, dark bags under his eyes. His technician, Schneider, was a skinny kid in his twenties with a spiked haircut. Hagen was perched on a battered roll around office chair which he scooted past an array of screens, mixers, and control panels for sound and video. A six-foot window provided a view of the adjoining studio, which was now empty. Above the window was a screen with a sign beneath it that read *NETWORK LIVE*. The screen was blank. So were all the monitors and displays on Hagen's console.

"Someone pulled the plug on us," said Hagen. As he spoke, he kept his eyes fixed on the dead network screen. "Tower's kaput. Phone lines down. No cell. No fiber optics. Not a single goddamn electron flowing in or out of this place."

Brand asked, "How long have you worked here?"

"Fifteen or so years. Maybe sixteen." Hagen spoke without making eye contact.

"That was before the tower went up, right?"

Hagen shrugged. "Yeah, pretty much."

"What did you do before the tower?"

"Fiber optics. And before that, copper. Same as the phone company used. Low bandwidth, not good for real time feed from the network. The tower changed all that. Until now. Now it's toast."

"What would it take to establish another connection?"

"A miracle," said Hagen. "And my union says that miracles are not part of my job description. Now if you'll excuse me, my shift is over. Since no one pays overtime any more—" he shot a glance at Cirilli, "—there's nothing more I can do here." Hagen heaved himself from the rollaround chair.

"In case you haven't noticed," said Brand, "this place is surrounded by armed troops. At any time they're going to storm this building. Or destroy it. And I guarantee they're not going to let you walk away from here."

Hagen gave Brand a wary look. "Hey, look pal, whatever kind of mess you people have gotten yourselves into, I want no part of it. I didn't sign up to get dragged into—"

Hagen's eyes fixed on Libby, who had just entered the room. She strode up to Hagen and Schneider. "Gentlemen, I'm Libby Paulsen. May I ask your names?"

Hagen was dumbstruck. Schneider looked as if he'd been zapped with a cattle prod. After several seconds, Hagen blurted, "Uh, it's Melvin." Then he added, "Melvin Hagen, Ma'am."

"Jimmy Schneider," said the technician. Schneider's eyes looked like oversized marbles.

"Gentlemen, I can tell that you're good Americans. The kind who are willing to step forward and do the right thing." Libby's voice had an intimate sound, almost maternal. "Your fellow

Americans are counting on you to help save their country. As your President, I'm counting on you."

Hagen stood transfixed. He was staring at the woman before him as if she'd arrived from another galaxy. Brand did his best to keep his expression neutral. For the second time this morning he was witnessing a phenomenon. The Libby Paulsen effect. It was magic. The transformation of Melvin Hagen was taking place before his eyes.

The engineer ran a hand through the strands of oily hair plastered to his scalp. He shifted his weight from one foot to another, never taking his eyes off the woman in front of him. The sour expression on Hagen's face morphed into a look of rapture. "Yes, ma'am. I'll see what I can do."

<>

"Three hundred yards," said Jim Ripley.

McDivott was pacing the carpet in the back of his Briar Club office. He stopped to peer at the satellite image on the screen. "Is that all? Are you sure?"

"Yes, if the Jazzum hits precisely on its target coordinates. Rube Carpenter, the munitions officer at Langley, assures me that the missile has a one meter circle of error probability. With this warhead, three hundred yards would be the full radius of the blast envelope." "Jazzum" was the working name for the JASSM—Joint Air to Surface Standoff Missile. The Jazzum was an aircraft-launched cruise missile with a nearly undetectable radar signature and a customizable warhead that could vaporize a soft target the size of the Gettysburg television station.

McDivott traced a circle with his finger around the building in the center of the satellite image. "That means Gettysburg is going to get some collateral damage."

"Carpenter doesn't think so. Maybe some casualties from broken windows and debris. Acceptable, given the reason for using the Jazzum."

Ripley could guess the *real* reason for using the Jazzum. He knew that Vance McDivott, like Capella's founder, Curtis LeMay, preferred blowing his enemies up from the air over simply shooting them on the ground. The rationale was that they had a verified report, backed by infra-red surveillance cameras, that the President and all her helpers were dead. The terrorists—the Iranians, who would be conveniently placed after the fact—had wired the station with explosives. Using the Jazzum cruise missile would save lives by removing the need to storm the place.

The story was full of holes, but it would provide a window of time during which they controlled the evidence. McDivott didn't seem worried. He was the same cool McDivott, firing questions, delivering orders as if he were running a trading desk. If he was feeling the pressure of time running out, it didn't show.

"What about Gavin?" said McDivott. "Is he okay with the order?"

Ripley considered before answering. Maj. Gen. Buzz Gavin, who commanded the air wing tasked with deploying the JASSM, was a Capella member. But Gavin had a reputation for disputing orders he didn't like. Gavin had demanded to know the nature of the target. Ripley would tell him only that it was a high value target, critical to national security.

"Gavin said he'd authorize the weapon load out, but he says that the missile launch order has to come directly from you."

"That's Gavin," said McDivott. "More worried about covering his ass than executing the mission. How soon can he have the weapon ready to deploy?"

Ripley glanced at his watch. "Fifteen minutes, give or take a couple minutes. As soon as they've loaded the missile, the F-35 will be airborne and standing by for the launch order."

"Get General Gavin on the line." While McDivott was waiting for Ripley to make the connection, he asked, "Has the Galeforce unit pulled back from the building?"

"Pulled back and dug in," Ripley said over his shoulder. "Berg reports that he has the terrorists and they will be positioned as soon as the building has been hit."

McDivott just nodded. Ripley knew what McDivott was doing. Asking questions, already knowing the answers, just to make sure nothing had been missed. That was McDivott's style.

Ripley was secretly pleased that it would be McDivott giving the order to launch the Jazzum. Never before had such a weapon been directed against a U. S. domestic target. Sooner or later, when the dust had settled and the inevitable inquiries began, they'd ask *who* issued the order to vaporize the building in which terrorists had allegedly murdered the President. Ripley was happy to leave that footnote in history to General Vance McDivott.

When McDivott proposed using the Jazzum, no one in the room—Ripley, Atwater, Reckson, or any of the half dozen general grade and flag rank officers—had offered an objection. Even if they had, the sheer intensity of McDivott's personality would have steamrolled them. They all knew that they had gone beyond a point of no return. McDivott was proposing a quick and audacious resolution.

Ripley handed the encrypted phone handset to McDivott. "General Gavin on the line."

McDivott gazed at the device for a moment. He took a deep breath and accepted the phone. "Good morning, General. Vance McDivott here."

Ripley watched, fascinated as always by his boss's magisterial tone. If God ever spoke on a telephone, Ripley believed, He would sound exactly like Vance McDivott.

"Yes, I understand your concerns," McDivott was saying. "We have considered all the ramifications of using the Jazzum in a domestic operation. Given the sensitivity of this mission, I won't divulge the specific nature of the target." McDivott listened for several seconds, then said, "Yes, General, I have discussed this with the Acting President, and he concurs. We are giving you a direct order. You are to deploy the weapon immediately."

CHAPTER TWENTY-SIX

B rand went back out to the reception room. He left Libby and Jill in the control room, which Cirilli said was the safest shelter in the building. The studio and the control room were the only compartments in the station that had no windows. No sense in giving a shooter a target.

Kreier was still kneeling beside the window. Through the window Brand could see the sheriff's deputies deployed around the front of the building. They were crouched behind cars and the row of low trees that lined the entrance to the station.

Kreier said, "The assault force has pulled back. They're out there beyond that little rise, near the helos. They've spread out, probably got us encircled."

"Are they who we think they are?"

"No question. Galeforce contractors. I can tell by the outfits. I know some of the guys who went to work for them. All hardball spec ops types."

"What chance does the sheriff's little band of deputies have against them?"

Kreier just shook his head. "What do you think?"

"Where's the sheriff?"

"Outside. Just in front of the door. We worked out a signal to communicate. Want me to get him in here?"

Brand nodded. "We need to talk."

Kreier rapped a rhythmic sequence on the door with his knuckles. He waited a quarter minute, then yanked the door slightly open. Sheriff Waller scuttled into the room on his hands and knees.

The sheriff rose creakily to his feet. "Hell of a way for a man of my importance to arrive." He looked at Brand. "How much longer is this going to last?"

"Longer than we want," said Brand. "The station's network link has been shut down."

Waller's eyes narrowed. "So how's the President going to make her speech?"

"She's not. Not unless the technician comes up with something."

Waller's eyes shifted to the outside, seeming to assess this new information. "What about those guys out there?"

"You tell me."

"They could make an assault at any time, but they're holding off," said Waller. "Like they're waiting for something."

Brand said nothing. His eyes swung back to the window, but his mind had already slipped into deductive mode. Yes, they were waiting for something. While they were waiting, they had pulled back. Far enough back to give them room. Room for what? Time was against them. They wouldn't wait much longer.

<>

Berg wasn't waiting. "It's time. Bring the Iranians."

Dunleavy, the senior contractor in Berg's HQ unit, nodded and trotted off toward the farthest helicopter.

Berg was seated on a canvas camp chair at his mobile command post just behind the first helicopter. A hummock rose between the post and the television station, obscuring all but the roof of the building. Berg's equipment was arrayed on a tarp—encrypted satellite phone, binoculars, laptop computer, MP5 submachine gun, and the MK11 Mod 0 sniper weapon. Beside the MK11 was a 20 round magazine of 7.62 ammunition.

I have snipers, Berg had told Ripley. It was a true statement. What he hadn't said was that the best and deadliest sniper in Berg's force was its commander. Early in his SEAL career, when Rolf Berg was still a junior petty officer, he had earned a reputation as one of the elite unit's most lethal marksmen. Forty-two kills in Iraq during three separate tours, the last of which he was an officer. Another dozen in Afghanistan as a platoon officer-in-charge. What Rolf Berg discovered was that he was not only extraordinarily suited for long range killing, he *liked* it.

When he was at war with America's enemies, Berg sometimes experienced an overwhelming feeling of exhilaration. There was nothing like it, not booze, not sex, not money. He had the sense that a divine hand was steadying the barrel of his sniper rifle. Berg's relationship with God was private and personal, something he never discussed with anyone. In his secret heart he *knew* that he was the instrument of a higher power. God had dispatched him for the purpose of punishing the forces of evil.

Dunleavy returned with the prisoners. He was pushing the two blindfolded men ahead of him, prodding them with the muzzle of his MP5. Berg looked them over. Even though they wore ragged jeans and work shirts in place of the business suits, the two didn't look much like jihadists. It would have been better if they had unruly mops of hair and something in the way of beards. The pair still looked like the bland Iranian bureaucrats they actually were.

No matter. By the time they had served their purpose, their appearances would make no difference. Berg wanted to get this phase of the operation over with. Any time now—the sooner the better—the standoff at the station building would be resolved. In the coming scenario the two jihadists, who in their former lives had been officials in the Islamic Republic of Iran, would play a critical role.

Berg rose from his camp chair. "Remove the blindfolds."

Dunleavy took off the blindfolds. The Iranians blinked in the glare of the morning sun. Each was wearing a look of befuddlement. The older man, the diplomat named Mahmoud Said, peered at Berg. "I demand an explanation for this outrage," he said. The querulous voice betrayed his fear. "You have no right to treat us in this manner."

"I must apologize," said Berg. "Our security forces mistakenly detained you because of the national emergency. It has been cleared up. You are free to go."

The Iranian looked even more befuddled. "Go? Yes, of course. We want to go. Where?"

"You should proceed to that building over there." Berg pointed across the meadow, in the direction of the television station. "The President's senior advisor is waiting for you."

The Iranians looked at each other. "Yes, yes," said the second man, whose name was Kamil Al-Bashir. Al-Bashir glanced down at the shabby shirt. "What about our clothes? Our luggage?"

"Not to worry," said Berg. "All your belongings will be delivered to you."

The Iranians still looked doubtful. Hesitantly, Said turned and walked toward the meadow. After a few tentative steps he stopped, glancing back to make sure Al-Bashir was following him. He was. The two men headed toward the building in the distance. With each step toward the meadow, their pace quickened until they were nearly trotting. Neither looked back.

Berg thought again about why they were using the Iranians. It was going to be a tough sell, passing these two bumbling ragheads off as terrorists, especially since some of the passengers on Air Force One had already seen them.

McDivott had assured him that it didn't matter. No one inside that station would be alive to explain how the Iranians got from Air Force One to the television station. As far as anyone on Air Force One knew, the Iranians were with Paulsen. They were jihadists. They killed the President, and we killed them. Good riddance.

That was good enough for Berg. He already accepted the certainty that the deaths of Paulsen and her sympathizers would come under the most intense investigation. Berg wasn't worried. This was war. In every war people got killed. Sometimes the wrong people. When this war was won and the dust had settled, Capella would occupy the executive branch of government. Pardons, if necessary, would be granted.

Berg waited until the Iranians had gone twenty yards. He raised the muzzle of the MP5 and fired a three-round burst into the back of Kamil Al-Bashir. He watched Said stop and stare back at him in disbelief. The panicked Iranian whirled and ran, covering nearly ten yards before the next burst from Berg's submachine gun stitched a pattern across the back of his shirt.

Both Iranians lay face down in the swale of the meadow. The bodies weren't visible from where the sheriff's men were deployed around the television station. Berg liked the idea that the country bumpkin sheriff would have heard the muffled chatter of the MP5. He'd be wondering what the hell was happening. He'd find out soon enough.

Berg turned his back on the scene and returned to his improvised command post. He had no pity for the Iranians. Maybe they weren't jihadists, but they were just as bad. They had made a deal with a traitorous President. God's will had been done.

<>

The F-35 Lightning II soared into the morning sky. No radio communications, no radar transpondor codes, no position reports. All communications were by encoded data link. The JASSM cruise missile nestled in the internal weapons bay was equipped with its own data link transceiver.

The pilot's name was Leo Schwab. He was a major in the United States Air Force, a veteran of two tours in Afghanistan, and one of the early selectees for the elite F-35 program. Schwab was on a fast track in the Air Force's hierarchical promotion system.

Or so he had supposed. Here he was twenty miles off the shore of New Jersey, flying the most advanced attack jet in the world. And in its internal bomb bay was the stealthiest weapon in the Air Force's arsenal. From its perch at 41,000 feet, not only was the F-35 invisible to air traffic control radars along the East Coast, the Jazzum would also be virtually undetectable. When Schwab released the missile from inside the belly of the F-35, the Jazzum would be on its own. Its wings would deploy, and its jet engine would propel it up to near-supersonic speed. The Jazzum would fly a programmed course, navigating so precisely that it could fly through a vent hole to impact within inches of its assigned target coordinates.

Stealth was good. It was especially good if you were deploying a missile against a domestic target.

And that was what had Leo Schwab bothered. *What* target?

"You don't want to know, Leo," General Gavin had told him as he was suiting up for the mission. Gavin had personally walked Schwab out to the hangar where the F-35 was being fitted with its weapon load. "Hell, *I* don't want to know. But I have verified the order, and it comes from the very top."

"The commander-in-chief?" said Schwab. He'd seen the reports about Air Force One. "Who is that?"

"The acting President," said Gavin. "Presumably Atwater, the Speaker of the House. My information is that the cabinet is in session with him right now. They're counting on us to execute this mission."

Which didn't make Schwab feel any better. The President—the *real* President—was dead, according to the intel bulletin that Schwab had just been shown. The nation was in a crisis. Schwab knew in his gut that whatever he was about to do with the Jazzum missile *had* to be connected to the Presidential emergency.

Somebody was about to be obliterated. On American soil. And he, the designated obliterator, had no frigging idea *who* the target was. Schwab didn't even know *where* the target was. And that was the eerie part. Once launched, the only instructions the Jazzum would follow were either internal or from a distant ground base. Schwab's single function was to position the F-35 in the right place. When the launch signal came over the data link, he would trigger the sequence to open the weapons bay doors and release the Jazzum. Less than two seconds later the doors would be slammed shut again, restoring the F-35's nearly invisible radar signature. The rest was up to the Jazzum.

Five minutes had elapsed since Schwab reached his loiter

position. Still no launch order on the data link screen. Stretched beneath his nose was the shoreline of New Jersey. From this altitude Schwab could make out the buildings of downtown Philadelphia and, further off his right wing, the hazy gray blur of New York City. Ahead sprawled the flat coastal plain of New Jersey and the greenish hills of Pennsylvania beyond.

Maybe they'd called it off. Maybe the whole drill was nothing more than a worst-case contingency mission. One of those just-in-case-the-shit-hits-the-fan readiness plays the Air Force loved so much.

What Schwab had always liked about being a fighter pilot was that you went one-on-one with your adversary. If you whacked him, it was because you had the edge. You had better skills or better equipment or better luck. He'd never wanted to be one of those button-pushers tasked with controlling a drone or firing a missile at some defenseless target. Or raining tons of bombs on anonymous civilians. He was a warrior, not an executioner.

And so, he thought, was Buzz Gavin. Schwab had known Gavin since Schwab was a first lieutenant and Gavin was his squadron commander. The older man had taken a liking to him, which counted for a lot in the politics of the military. If you had a mentor like Gavin you got pulled along as he rose through the ranks. Schwab respected Gavin. Unlike a lot of general officers Schwab knew who had sucked their way up, Gavin had paid his dues and earned his stars the hard way.

The Jazzum had a range of 230 miles, which meant that the target was somewhere within Schwab's field of view at this altitude. It had to be some kind of domestic structure. They—whoever was ordering this strike—wanted to contain the damage, and they didn't want any traces left, which was why they chose the Jazzum. The Jazzum had selectable warheads, including one that would vaporize everything in a small space while leaving the outer periphery intact. Perfect for whacking bad guys in urban environments. In small buildings. Pinpoint accuracy, low collateral damage.

Seven minutes past the original launch time. Still no data link signal. Schwab was beginning to feel better. It meant that *someone*—whoever the hell was the current commander-in-chief—hadn't made up his mind to—

He saw it. Something glimmering on Schwab's lower cockpit display. A single line of text ran across the screen: *PROCEED TO GALLIPOLI.*

Schwab's pulse rate spiked by twenty points. *GALLIPOLI.* The launch signal. Only he and Gavin were privy to the code. The general had given it to him as he was strapping into the cockpit. The WWI reference was classic Gavin, who was a history buff.

Schwab sucked in a lungful of oxygen through his mask. He reached for the Stores Management System screen. In a quick pattern of strokes he initiated the sequence.

Ready to release. Command sequence complete. All he had to do was squeeze the trigger on the control stick. For a full second Schwab's finger rested over the trigger while unwanted thoughts streamed through his mind.

Then he squeezed.

In the next instant Schwab felt the rumble of the internal weapons doors opening, a lurch as the two-thousand pound missile ejected from its carriage rack, the *whump* of the doors immediately closing again. The entire sequence took less than three seconds.

Schwab banked hard to the right, then back to the left. His eyes scanned the empty sky ahead of him. *Where the hell was it?* He saw nothing, only clouds and brown earth.

There. It was low, the switch blade wings already extended. The Jazzum was pointed downward, the smokeless turbojet engine running and propelling it to the northwest. Schwab tried to keep his eyes on the fast-moving cruise missile but he lost it against the puffy cumulus clouds that dotted the sky below. The Jazzum was on its own. Out of Schwab's control.

Schwab recalled Gavin's words. *You don't want to know.* Gavin was right.

< >

"How're they doing?" Libby had her arms clasped around her, trying to subdue the anxiety that was gnawing at her.

"Hagen says don't bug him," Brand answered. "He says he's an engineer, not a talk show host."

Cirilli and Brand were standing against the far wall of the control room. They were watching Hagen, who lay on his back amid a jungle of cables and variously colored wires. Hagen's white, hairy belly protruded from the bottom of his shirt. Schneider squatted beside him, handing him tools.

"So we won't bug him," said Libby. "Let's wait in the studio next door."

Cirilli accompanied them into the studio. The cavernous room was windowless, three times larger than the control room, with a stage and a raised desk with *KGYB 32* emblazoned on the front panel. A pair of cameras on three-wheel dollies was positioned on either side of the desk.

"In case you haven't noticed," said Cirilli, "Hagen is anti-social. In fact, until you arrived I've never seen him be so cooperative. I'd have fired Hagen years ago except that he's the only one who knows how to keep the place running."

"Can he really restore the live feed?" Libby asked.

Cirilli gave her a furtive head nod. "No. Whatever cables are left over from the nineties, they're severed and dead. Without getting the tower back on line, it's not going to happen."

Libby felt her spirits slipping even deeper into despair. How could her Presidency have come to this? From the White House, the most guarded enclave on the planet, attended by a cadre of handpicked cabinet secretaries and advisors, to this—a windowless room surrounded by armed mercenaries who wanted her dead. Instead of being protected by the most sophisticated security apparatus in the world, she had a county sheriff and his band of deputies.

Which made her wonder. Why hadn't the mercenaries—Galeforce, or whatever they were called—overrun the place and killed her? What were they waiting for?

Libby didn't want to find out. She wanted out. Out of all of this ordeal. There was a way.

"I'm going to make a deal," she said.

Brand and Jill both looked at her quizzically. "A deal?" said Jill. "With whom?"

Libby nodded in the direction of the Galeforce contingent outside. "With them. I'll give them what they want."

"What's that?"

"My resignation."

CHAPTER TWENTY-SEVEN

Brand said nothing. He watched while Jill Maitlin exploded.

"Resignation?" Jill spat the word out. "That's unthinkable. Even if you wanted to, how could you do it from here?"

"We'll have the sheriff deliver the letter to whoever is directing the Galeforce troops out there. They can announce that the President has stepped down and the Speaker of the House has automatically taken my place."

"You're delusional. Do you seriously think that they'll back off then?"

Libby shrugged. "They'll have me out of office. Isn't that what they want?"

"What they want is for you to be dead. Damn it, try to be rational." Jill was stabbing her finger at Libby. "You're throwing away everything we worked for."

"I didn't work for it. It just happened."

"The hell it did." Jill's face was contorted, and her voice had grown shrill. "You think being elected to Congress just happened? You think your Senate seat was just an accident?"

At this Brand felt a jolt run through him. An old memory surged up from deep in his subconscious. An old puzzle with missing pieces. He let his eyes focus off in space. Libby's voice seemed to come from a distant place.

"I remember when I decided to run for the Senate," Libby said. She was looking at Brand. "And why."

"You almost ruined your career." She nodded in Brand's direction. "Because of him."

Brand saw Libby take a deep breath, furrowing her brow. She turned again to Jill. Libby no longer looked tired. She looked angry.

"What do you mean, because of him? Are you saying that you knew about . . ." She hesitated, then said, "About Pete and me?"

"I was your chief of staff. It was my job to know."

Cirilli was looking more and more uncomfortable. "Excuse me," he said, "I'd better go check on Hagen."

Libby waited until the station manager was gone. She turned to Jill. "If you knew about us, then you know that it ended. It ended before I announced for the Senate race."

Jill didn't answer.

"She knows," said Brand. His eyes were no longer focused on space. They were fixed like beams on Jill Maitlin. "She knows because she made it happen."

Jill tilted her chin up. "I have no idea what you're talking about."

"It was you, wasn't it?" Brand kept his gaze riveted on Jill. "You were the one behind the photos."

"That's enough, Colonel Brand. I won't be subjected to your accusations."

"What photos?" Libby demanded.

Brand didn't answer. The pieces of the puzzle had come together. He looked at Libby, remembering.

<>

Someone is boarding the boat.

Brand is in the forward cabin. He hears the sound and lays down his book.

They are already on the forward deck when Brand emerges from the companionway. Too late he thinks about the Smith & Wesson .38 in the locker beneath the bunk. In a marina at Annapolis, a few miles from the U.S. capitol, a gun is more of a liability than an asset. Its only purpose is for protection when he sails to the Bahamas, something he hasn't done in years.

"Who's there?"

No answer. Brand steps over to the cockpit console and flips a switch. A pair of lights mounted on the cockpit combing illuminate the forward deck.

There are three of them, two men and a woman. Each wears a nylon windbreaker, slacks, sneakers. They are standing on the deck, the sail-wrapped boom between them and Brand. Each is neatly groomed. None is holding a weapon.

"Colonel Brand?" says one of the men.

"You've boarded this boat without permission."

"We're here on a private matter," says the other man. "It's about Ms. Paulsen."

Brand's senses surge into full alert. "Who?"

"You heard correctly. Congresswoman Paulsen. You're acquainted with her."

"What do you want?"

"We need to talk to you."

Brand's danger warning ratchets up another notch. His first inclination is to throw them off the boat. But not yet. Something is going on that he has to know about. He points to the padded settee in the aft cockpit. "Over there."

As they step awkwardly across the deck into the well of the yellow-lighted cockpit, Brand looks them over. He doesn't recognize any of them. The woman is thirtyish, bobbed hair, rimless spectacles. Beneath one arm she carries a black leather portfolio. The two men look a few years older. Lawyers, Brand guesses. Or legislative staffers. Each has the soft features and paunches of career capitol-dwellers.

Brand stands in the companionway while they take seats. One of the men nods to the woman. She clears her throat and says, "We'll get to the point, Colonel Brand. We're here to—"

"You haven't told me who you are."

The man nearest Brand says, "It's better if we don't. We're here on behalf of Ms. Paulsen."

"Did she send you?"

Another quick exchange of glances. "Not exactly. This matter is. . . sensitive. Your relationship with Ms. Paulsen has placed her in a very dangerous situation. We've been instructed to inform you that it is in the congresswoman's best interest—and yours—if you terminate the relationship immediately."

Brand doesn't respond right away. His premonition is correct. These three are trouble. "Instructed by whom?"

The second man says, "A political entity—it's not necessary to be specific—that has a direct involvement in Ms. Paulsen's career."

Brand is thinking. A political entity. Her staff? He knows that Libby's people zealously manage every aspect of her legislative life. Too zealously sometimes. The party national committee? It's no secret that they are pushing Libby to run for the Senate. She hasn't yet agreed. She is considering all options, including leaving politics altogether. Brand is staying out of it. For both their sakes it has to be her decision.

As he thinks about it, Brand feels anger welling up in him. Terminate the relationship immediately? How would these intruders presume that he and Libby have a relationship?

"You don't know what you're talking about. It's time you got the hell off my boat."

"We're talking about this," says the woman. She flops her leather portfolio down on the cockpit table and extracts a manila folder. From it she pulls out a stack of 8X10 photographs. She pushes them toward Brand.

For an instant Brand feels the urge to seize the photos—and the three messengers—and throw them over the side. He takes a deep breath, then reaches for the stack of photos. He looks at the one on top. Even before his eyes focus on the glossy image he knows what he'll see.

A smiling, chestnut-haired woman, topless, is standing in the cockpit of a sailboat. The photo is remarkably sharp, showing every detail, including a familiar mole beneath her left breast.

Brand flips to the second photo. Another view of the same woman, still topless, leaning over, kissing a man seated in the cockpit.

He goes through the stack. Each photo is more explicit than the one before. By the sixth photo, the two have become frolicsome lovers. In one view, the woman's bare breasts are pressed against the man's chest as they kiss. The face of each is in sharp focus, clearly recognizable.

The last several views are through the companionway hatch, looking into the forward cabin. Even though the shadowy figures are barely recognizable, it takes little imagination to surmise what they are doing.

Brand sets the photos on the table. By the blurriness of the background and precise focusing of the subjects, he knows the shots are taken at long range with a high-resolution telephoto lens. There is no mistaking the identities of the couple. Nor can there be any guesswork about the ownership of the boat. The photographer has gotten the gold-lettered Andromeda *in almost every shot.*

By the angle of the shots, they have to have come from another boat. Though the details of the shoreline behind Andromeda are indistinct, Brand knows the location. One of the coves on the eastern Chesapeake. He can almost put a time and date to the occasion. It has to be one of three or four weekend afternoons he and Libby spent there aboard Andromeda.

Thinking they were safe.

Brand feels a surge of disgust come over him. How can he have been so careless? He loves Libby Paulsen. It was his duty to protect her. He has failed.

He turns to the three messengers. They are gazing at him with unpitying expressions. In the yellowish light, Brand thinks he can see something close to a smirk on the woman's face.

"Someone went to a lot trouble to obtain these photographs," says Brand. "Why?"

"We explained that already," the woman replies. The two men each nod in agreement. "To protect Ms. Paulsen."

"By spying on her?"

"We all want the same thing for the congresswoman. To save her reputation. And her career."

"Is she aware that someone is saving her career?"

"It's better that she isn't. That's why you have to terminate this affair immediately. And for her sake, she mustn't know why."

Brand waits a moment. He is sure of the answer to his next question. "And if I don't?"

The woman picks up the stack of photos. "These will be on the editor's desk of the Washington Post *the day after tomorrow. And the* New York Times, *and half a dozen other papers. I'll let you imagine the outcome."*

Brand can imagine. The personal life of Congresswoman Libby Paulsen will be grist for the talk shows, tabloids, late night comedy patter. The media ghouls will drag her through endless miles of slime. Libby will be shamed out of public life. Whatever future she and Brand might have had will be forever tainted by scandal.

And he will be to blame.

"Let me get this straight," says Brand. "You're blackmailing us . . . for some political purpose?"

The woman shakes her head as if lecturing a slow-learning student. "Don't be melodramatic. Blackmail is illegal and immoral. What we're doing is not only legal, it protects the congresswoman's reputation. And it protects the constituents whom she serves."

Brand nods. His first impression has been correct. This acid-voiced shrew has to be a lawyer.

Then the woman's tone softens. And so does her expression, which turns almost kindly. "Look, Colonel Brand, I can only imagine how painful this must be for you. Believe me, we're very sorry that this has to be done. No one doubts that you genuinely care for Ms. Paulsen. If you truly love her, you'll do the right thing and break off this affair."

Brand says nothing. The woman slides the photos back into her portfolio. An uncomfortable silence falls over the cockpit of the boat. Somewhere in the streets beyond the marina, a siren is wailing. The sound of a jet rumbles in the sky overhead.

Looking away from the three messengers, Brand gazes off across the marina. Lights atop boat masts twinkle in the darkness. The urban sprawl on each shore of the harbor shimmers in a yellow glow. Incredible, he thinks. How suddenly his happiness—their happiness—can be snatched away. All it takes is an unguarded moment. A few clicks of a camera shutter. An ultimatum.

The woman rises, and the two men jump to their feet behind her. "The decision is yours, Colonel Brand," says the woman. She tucks the portfolio under her arm, then glances at it meaningfully. "We know you'll do the right thing."

Brand doesn't move. He pays no attention as the three messengers step over the combing of the cockpit, up to the boat deck, and fumble their way onto the dock. When the sound of their footsteps has faded away, Brand flicks off the lights. He sits in the darkened cockpit, gazing across the bay, thinking.

CHAPTER TWENTY-EIGHT

"**W**hat are you talking about?" Libby asked again.

"Don't listen to him," said Jill. "He's been trying to wreck your career ever since you began that disastrous affair in Africa."

"I should have figured it out before," said Brand. "It was you. You had the photos taken. You're the one who sent the team to my boat that night."

Jill's expression remained defiant. Libby watched the exchange with mounting frustration. She said to Jill, "What photos? What kind of team did you send to his boat?"

Jill snatched the pack of Dunhills from the satchel draped over her shoulder. She lit one with her Bic, then exhaled an angry puff of smoke. "It was an absolute disaster waiting to happen. You and Brand, having an affair practically in public view. It was just a matter of time before it was going to be found out. You couldn't have been elected to a garbage commission."

"So what did you do?" Libby said. The answer was already coming clear in her mind.

Jill shot another glowering look at Brand. "Like he said. Photos. The two of you on film. Very professional. No mistaking the players or what they were doing on that boat."

Libby's confusion was being replaced by a mounting fury. "You had someone sneak up and . . . take photographs? For what purpose?"

"Blackmail," said Brand. "To pressure us into ending our relationship."

Libby nodded. It was all coming back. That night in Annapolis. The letter. She turned to Brand. "Am I hearing this correctly? Someone came to your boat and presented you with photos of us . . . together? And what were they going to do if you didn't walk away from the relationship?"

Brand looked at Jill. "Let her answer that."

Jill streamed out another cloud of smoke. "It was the only leverage we had." She pointed to Brand. "If he was convinced that we'd turn the photos over to the media, he'd leave the relationship."

"Would you?" Libby said to Jill. "Would you have turned the photos over to the media?"

"What difference does it make? It wasn't necessary. The purpose was to keep you from ruining your career. It worked. Your reputation was spared and you were elected to the Senate. Then the White House. End of story."

"Where are the photos now?"

"In a safe place."

"To be used for future blackmail?"

Jill stabbed the cigarette into a bean bag ash tray on the work table. "Libby, you've always known you could trust me. I'd never betray you."

"You *did* betray me."

"Nonsense. You weren't thinking clearly. What I did was in your best interest."

At this Libby shook her head furiously. Bad memories were streaming across her consciousness. *You've always known you could trust me.* How many times had she heard that? How many people in her life had betrayed her? Her father. Her husband. Jill Maitlin. And—she thought until this moment—Pete Brand.

She turned to Brand. "That letter you wrote. Breaking off our relationship. It was because of the photos?"

Brand nodded.

"You thought you were protecting me?"

Brand said nothing. She saw it in his eyes.

"Damn it!" she said. "How could you be so stupid? You should have told me. They could do whatever they wanted with the photos."

"Sure," said Jill. "And that would have been the end of your career."

"To hell with my career," said Libby. "Some things are more important than a career."

"There you go again," said Jill. "You're being irrational. That's exactly why I had to intervene. For your own good."

Libby looked at Jill Maitlin as if she were seeing her for the first time. Libby had never deceived herself about Jill Maitlin. Jill provided the inner steel that Libby believed was lacking in herself. Jill provided wisdom when Libby needed it. Jill was her speechwriter, counselor, confidante. Jill was also manipulative, ruthless, even devious, but Libby knew that. She had believed that she could control Jill. She was wrong.

"You're fired," Libby said.

"Don't be absurd. I'm the only one who can get you through this."

"I trusted you. You betrayed that trust. We can never work together—"

Libby stopped in mid-sentence. In the corner of her eye she saw Cirilli rushing back from the control room. "Hagen says to get ready," said Cirilli. "He's got something. Some kind of feed to the network."

<>

The Jazzum leveled at 1,200 feet. A stream of tiny corrections, each measured in hundredths of degrees of course change, spewed from the missile's brain. The Jazzum had selected this altitude because the noise of its tiny turbojet engine was undetectable from the ground while its shape and color made it almost indistinguishable against the sky. A suitable compromise. Built into the Jazzum's airframe was the latest generation of radar-absorbent materials, rendering it virtually invisible on air traffic control scopes.

An alert was buzzing in the Jazzum's brain. Danger ahead. An object had appeared in the forward-looking infrared sensor. Calculating the object's speed, signature, and flight path, the Jazzum sorted the probabilities and identified the threat. A large soaring bird, most likely an osprey. The Jazzum reacted. A quick ten degree course correction, just enough to evade the circling bird, all the while reassessing the surrounding environment. Seconds later, clear of the osprey, the Jazzum was back on its programmed track.

The Jazzum hated birds. Especially large ones. Birds were stupid, which made them dangerous.

Coming up beneath the Jazzum's nose was the border of Delaware. Ahead stretched a short section of flatland New Jersey. The Jazzum would cut across the northwest corner of Maryland before crossing into the hilly region of southern Pennsylvania.

State lines meant nothing. Borders were meaningless concepts. Though the Jazzum's brain possessed thousands of times the computing power of its masters, the Jazzum had no interest in human abstractions. Boundaries, politics, war—all meaningless. The Jazzum felt no emotion, no delusions, indulged no fantasies. The Jazzum had only one obsession. Execute the mission.

<>

Four hundred miles away, the man standing at the situation display kept his eyes on the blinking yellow triangle. A continuous ribbon of data was flowing across the upper band of the screen. All the missile's performance indicators were within parameters. From this console the man could transmit coded data link signals to the missile.

On another band of the screen blinked a steadily decreasing number. It was the predicted time to impact. The number had just blinked downward through *09:49.*

The man's concentration on the screen was total. Only on the second attempt did the voice behind him register. "General," his chief of staff was saying. "General, there's something happening that you should know about."

<>

Libby looked around the room. They were watching her. Cirilli, Brand, Schneider, all looking at her, wondering what she was going to do. All except Jill Maitlin, who had stomped out of the studio.

Hagen was standing in the doorway to the control room, his belly tugging at the buttons on his sweat-stained shirt. "We're on aux power, and I've cobbled together the old coaxial connection we first used with the network. We've got a live feed, sort of. It comes and goes. As long as they keep their end lit up, we've got a shot. But we gotta hurry."

Libby stared at him.

"He means that we don't know how long the feed will last," said Cirilli. "The network is ready, but, well, we don't know when they might shut us down. We gotta move fast."

Libby didn't move.

"We'll use the rolling mini-cam," Hagen said, "with you sitting at the desk over there. Not a studio quality set up, but we gotta move quick with what we've got."

Libby felt paralyzed. An unreasoning fear had taken hold of her. What was she going to say to a country that thought she was dead? That *wanted* her dead? This was all wrong.

Brand took her arm. In a low voice he said, "You can do this. You're going to take back your country. Do it."

"I can't. No one will believe me."

"Yes, they will. I've seen you in action. Remember that hostile rebel commander in Africa? The one you charmed into letting us go?"

"He was hostile because you stole his truck."

"You talked the Iranians into signing a peace accord."

"A lot of good that did. Now my own military wants to kill me because of it."

"I saw you make an ally out of that airport manager in Greenland. You converted Joe Morganti from an enemy into your disciple. You sweet-talked that county sheriff into protecting you with his entire force. You've just charmed the socks off that station technician."

"It's an act. I'm a phony."

"Not in the eyes of the people you're speaking to. They see a leader."

"They see an illusion. I should be an actress, not a President."

"No, you should be a *real* President."

"What's that supposed to mean?"

"It means that if you speak from the heart, you're not acting. You're the President. A real President. Lead and the country will follow."

Libby clasped her arms around herself again. *A real President? What was a real President supposed to say at a time like this?* She'd never been good at extemporaneous speeches. For that matter, she'd rarely made a speech that hadn't been written for her.

The fear was gripping her tighter. "I can't do it."

"You have to."

"I need Jill."

"No, you don't."

"Jill knows what I have to say."

"Not any more. You fired her."

"That was then. This is now. Do as I ask. Go get her."

Brand was giving her that narrow-eyed look she had come to recognize. "Libby, you can do this without—"

"Colonel Brand, your commander-in-chief has just given you an order." She leaned close to his ear. In a soft voice that only he could hear, she said, "Damn it, Pete, do you love me or not?"

Brand nodded. "Yes," he whispered back, "I love you. Very much."

"Then please do as I ask." She squeezed his hand. "Hurry."

"Yes, ma'am. I'm on my way."

<>

Berg squinted through the scope of the MK-11 rifle. The spotter beside him, a sniper named Brooke, was peering through his own

M49 spotting scope, passing on to Berg the range and estimated wind corrections. The two men were perched in the hatch of the CH-53 helicopter. Both were screened by a camo curtain.

Berg had the MK-11 mounted on the Harris swivel bipod. In the distance, just beyond the hummock in the open field, was the KGYB building. From his elevated position in the hatch of the helicopter Berg had a view of the eastern wall of the building. He saw a verandah with a window that shimmered in the morning sun. He could also see the outlines of the sheriff's deputies dug in around the perimeter of the building. Amateurs. Berg almost wished he had the order to take them all down instead of waiting for the missile to do it for them. When it was over and the station was a smoking ruin, he would have to make sure that the bodies, including those of the recently deceased terrorists, were suitably arranged.

The range was slightly over 400 yards. Almost no wind. A piece of cake compared to some of the shots he had pulled off in Fallujah and later in Helmand Province. He could have let Brooke or one of the specialists take the shot while he manned the spotter scope. That wasn't Rolf Berg's style. This was his show. He wanted the satisfaction of knowing that he had performed the ultimate act of patriotism.

The problem was the glare. The sun was reflecting off the window of the station. Even with the vision-enhancing optics of the spotter scope, the window looked like a shimmering mirror.

"Comes and goes," said Brooke as he clicked through the settings on the M49. "This goddamn reflection. I pick up something through the window, then I lose it."

Berg said nothing. He was seeing the same thing through the barrel-mounted scope on the MK-11. He'd learned long ago that the sniper's worst enemy was his own impatience. Even under pressure, you made yourself wait. Still your mind, wait, wait some more. The shot would present itself.

CHAPTER TWENTY-NINE

"**G**o to hell," said Jill Maitlin.

It was precisely what Brand expected her to say. He had found her in the anteroom on the east side of the building. Jill was standing with her back to the window, puffing on a Dunhill.

"Sorry," said Brand. "That's not an option. The President needs you."

"What for? She's got you, right?"

"For some reason I'm unable to understand, she thinks you can help her."

"Only one of many things you're unable to understand."

Brand glanced around the room. Kreier was kneeling by the tall window, the submachine gun resting on his thigh. Sheriff Waller was peering outside, pretending to be oblivious to the conversation in the room. Brand didn't like the room, particularly the window. They were too exposed.

He said, "Look, Ms. Maitlin, this isn't about you and me. We both want the President to get through this. If you can help her, then please do it."

"Why should I?"

"Because you're a good American. Because you want the best for the country. How about this? Because you want the best for the President."

She gave him a withering look. "Oh, please. Spare me all that weepy sentimental crap."

"You worked hard to put Libby in office. Was that just a sham?"

Jill ignored him. She turned to face the window. "What about the photos?"

<>

"You're on, Madame President." Cirilli's voice had an urgent tone. "They're ready for you."

Libby's heart pounded. She was seated at the desk on the raised platform. Across the front of the desk was the station logo and the letters KGYB. Cirilli had fitted her with the nearly-invisible ear bud. Her microphone was clipped to the front lapel of her jump suit.

Several feet from her desk was the rolling camera with Schneider positioned behind it. On the wall in front of her was the monitor. The screen had magically come to life. Libby could see someone in a New York studio talking to the camera. Across the bottom of the screen streamed a banner. BREAKING NEWS . . . INCOMING REPORT THAT PRESIDENT PAULSEN MAY BE ALIVE . . . PRESIDENT TO ADDRESS THE NATION . . .

Impossible, she thought. What was she going to say? How did she look? She'd had no more than forty-five seconds to dab on lipstick and run a comb through her hair. She knew she looked haggard. Where was Jill? This wasn't right.

"Madame President," came a voice over her earbud. "This is Howard Marks at the Eastern Broadcasting Corporation. We have a very tentative link to the studio there in Gettysburg. Can you declare for me that you're not under duress, that you are free to speak without being coerced?"

Libby cleared her throat. "I'm free to speak, Mr. Marks." She surprised herself with the assurance in her voice. "I am not under duress. No one is coercing me, at least at the moment." She wondered how he could possibly know whether or not she was telling the truth. Did it matter?

"Excellent, Madame President. We're going to go with it. We'll be on the air in . . . thirty seconds. Are you ready?"

Libby closed her eyes for a moment. No, she wasn't ready. How could she possibly be ready for something like this? An extemporaneous speech? *You're over your head again.* She wanted to run the hell away. Let this nightmare be over.

"Yes," she heard herself say. "I'm ready."

Where was Jill? Where was Brand? In less than half a minute she had to deliver the most important address of her life. No teleprompter, no speechwriter, no rehearsal.

She couldn't do it alone.

What was it Brand had said? *This is what you do best. You reassure people.*

And what had she replied? *It's an act. I'm a phony.*

When you speak from the heart, it's not an act, Brand said. *You're the President.*

Libby put on her reading glasses. She began scribbling notes on the pad in front of her. Then she removed the glasses. To hell with glasses. She could still exercise a little vanity. She squinted as she continued scribbling.

"Ten seconds," the voice in the earbud said.

Libby took a deep breath. She held it several seconds, exhaled, placed her hands on the desk in front of her. The voice in the earbud was counting, " . . . four . . . three . . . two . . . one . . . we're live."

God help me. Libby looked into the camera. On the monitor above, she could see the announcer, a news anchor named Brian Smedley. "Ladies and gentlemen," Smedley was saying, "the President of the United States."

Then she saw her own image. Actually, despite the frizzed hair and the lines beneath her eyes, she looked almost Presidential. Vastly more assured than she felt. She saw Schneider observing her from behind his rolling camera. In her peripheral vision she saw Cirilli just outside the view of the camera. He was watching her anxiously. Hagen was still standing in the door of the control room. He wore a worried look.

Libby began speaking. It was a strange effect, hearing her voice in the earbud as she spoke to the camera. Viewing herself remotely while she gave a speech.

Good morning, my fellow Americans. I'm speaking to you from a place of historical importance to our nation, Gettysburg, Pennsylvania. It is my duty to report to you a series of events that have gravely endangered our country's security.

First, I must inform you that successive attempts have been made to remove me from office. A concerted effort has been carried out by members of the armed forces to bring down Air Force One, which would have resulted in the loss of life of everyone on board. Only through the skill and courage of the Presidential Pilot and his crew did we succeed in making an emergency landing early this morning here in the United States. The parties responsible for these heinous acts are still unidentified. It is clear, however, that these actions can only have been initiated by high-ranking officers in the armed forces and the Defense Department.

<>

As the angle of the sun increased in tiny increments, the blur on the window changed. Berg glimpsed something inside. Something swimming into view through the glass. Shapes, profiles.

"Got something," said Brooke. "A woman. Somebody next to her, talking."

Berg squinted. The less powerful scope on the rifle wasn't revealing as much as Brooke's equipment. *A woman.* Almost too good to be true. Berg forced himself to wait. His finger curled lightly around the trigger. He wouldn't take an impulse shot, but he wasn't going to let an opportunity get away.

Then he saw it. A woman's profile. *Could it be her?* At least a fifty percent certainty. Berg forced the tip of his tongue behind his teeth, took a long slow inhalation, then held it.   Crosshairs superimposed over his target . . . *wait . . . wait . . . be sure. . . apply pressure . . .*

<>

"The photos?" said Brand. "What about the photos?"

Jill was standing in front of the window. "They still exist.

Someone will use them sooner or later."

"Who will use them?"

She stabbed out the Dunhill in the ashtray on the window ledge. "Someone who wants to disgrace Libby Paulsen and remove her from office."

Brand's mind was racing through the possibilities. A single image kept coming to the surface.

"Atwater," said Brand. "You used to work for him."

Jill nodded.

"Why did you do it?"

"We wanted the same thing. Or so I thought. I thought Fred Atwater was on our side. Same party. We wanted to save Libby's career."

For an instant Brand wanted to lash out at her. The memory of the night on his boat came rushing back to him. The three nameless emissaries with the lurid photographs. The ultimatum. Jill Maitlin and her former boss, Atwater, playing God. *We wanted to save Libby's career . . .*

"You made a mistake."

Jill nodded again. "Yes, I suppose I did."

"It doesn't matter," Brand said. "Nothing matters unless the President says what she needs to say on live television. If not . . ."

Brand didn't finish. Something wasn't right. He glanced out the window. He saw nothing new, but his inner alarm was sending an urgent alert. He grabbed Jill's arm, yanking her toward him, but he knew intuitively that he was too late.

The window behind Jill Maitlin condensed into a single white orb. Jill was no longer there. Kreier and Waller weren't there. The room filled with blazing light.

<>

Libby heard it. A *whump* from the adjoining room. The noise was accompanied by the crash of breaking glass. Libby glanced up and saw her own startled image in the monitor. After several seconds' hesitation, she looked into the camera again and resumed speaking.

Even at this moment, the threat to me and my staff has not ended. As I speak, this television studio is encircled by armed agents of the civilian contractor company known as Galeforce. Until just a few minutes ago, all our communications with the outside world had been severed.

I assure you that all reports that may have been released about my being captured by terrorists, or being coerced by foreign agents are patently false. Such stories are being disseminated by the same parties that have tried to remove me from office.

To confront this ongoing emergency, I am issuing the following directives: I am ordering the immediate suspension of all contracts with Galeforce Security International, whose agents have been implicated in this hostile action. Officers and personnel of that company are hereby ordered to surrender their weapons and will be denied access to all U.S. government facilities and equipment.

Further, I am removing from office the acting chairman of the Joints Chiefs of Staff, General Vance McDivott. As the new chairman of the Joint Chiefs, I am appointing Gen. August Gritti, who is currently serving as my National Security Advisor.

<>

"Wow," said Chief Master Sergeant Lowanda Manning. She turned to Gus Gritti. "Now that you're the chairman, sir, how about getting us out of this place?"

Gritti took his eyes off the television screen long enough to grin at the sergeant. Somehow Manning had managed to retain her sense of humor. She and Gritti, along with the other occupants from the wrecked Air Force One, had been helicoptered to Dover Air Force Base and then detained in this locked conference room. No phones, no explanations, no way out. Armed Galeforce contractors guarded the door from outside. The room had a coffee pot, a single long conference table with chairs, a lavatory.

And a television. They had just watched the President announcing Gritti's promotion to the top military post.

"Sure thing, Sergeant," said Gritti. "You can inform those assholes out there that the new Chairman of the Joint Chiefs says they're fired."

Which, Gritti promised himself, would happen in spades. Getting fired wasn't even close to the deluge of pain that Gritti intended to pour on the perpetrators of this operation. Assuming, of course, he ever got out of here alive.

Gritti returned his attention to the television. Somehow the President had gotten away from that little airport in Delaware, made it to Gettysburg, and was now on television. She looked good. Tougher and more confident than the Libby Paulsen that Gritti had come to know.

Can this be real? Gritti wasn't sure. After the events of the past several hours, he no longer trusted his perceptions. What had seemed like a bad dream felt more like a hallucination.

Gritti slid his chair closer to the television. He wanted to hear every word, just in case it *was* real.

<>

My fellow citizens, I promise you this. A special commission will be appointed to investigate this monstrous attempt to overthrow your government. You can be assured that the perpetrators and participants will be identified and brought to justice.

Regarding the matter of succession to the Presidency as defined in our Constitution, I intend to announce within the next two days my nomination of the new Vice President and I will be requesting an expeditious confirmation by both houses of Congress . . .

<>

"Does anyone know how to get through to McDivott?" said the duty officer, a Navy captain.

None of the watch officers in the J-3 duty room at the Pentagon looked up. The two Army brigadier generals, a Marine colonel, and a pair of Air Force two-stars remained fixed on the flickering image in the television monitor.

"You have to go through Ripley," said one of the Air Force officers. He didn't take his eyes off the screen.

"I tried. He's not picking up. SecDef's going batshit. He says he has to talk to McDivott."

The Air Force major general glanced up at the captain. "Tell the SecDef to forget about talking to McDivott." He pointed to the woman's image in the screen. "He'd better talk to her."

<>

Fred Atwater gazed around the Situation Room. No one was paying any attention to him. All of them—Secretary of State Bowles, Treasury Secretary Cohen, Attorney General Vitale, Interior Secretary Foley, Homeland Security chief Policastro—were staring like robots at the wall-mounted television monitor. Missing was Chad Wilson, the Secretary of Defense, who was in the main hall yelling about why the fuck no one from the Joint Chiefs was talking to him.

Fred Atwater had been Acting President of the United States for something around seven hours, since a majority of the Cabinet confirmed him as the constitutional successor to Paulsen and Bethune. The specific protocol for the elevation of the Speaker of the House to Chief Executive had never been tested. Atwater figured that it would require a ruling by the Supreme Court before a successor's official status—President or *acting* President— became clear.

Just as murky would be his nomination of Vance McDivott as Vice President. In troubled times like these, Atwater had no doubt that the three arms of government would unite around him as the new President.

Or so he had thought. Watching the television, Atwater sensed his plan of occupying the White House for the next two-and-a-half years—no, the next *six-and-a-half* years—veering off the rails. The face on the screen looked damned real. The voice sounded uncannily like the one he had heard—and hated—ever since she and Bethune hijacked the party's nomination and made it into office. Now, instead of being just as dead as Bethune, here she was on television talking about conspiracies and generals and the people's right to express disagreement.

Atwater rose from the table. No one in the room looked up. Each pair of eyes remained fixed on the face in the monitor. Atwater walked out into the passageway between the conference room and the main hall and pulled out his encrypted cell phone. No one except the watch room duty officer at the end of the hall was in sight. Atwater punched the three-key combo that would put him through to the Capella command post.

CHAPTER THIRTY

McDivott became gradually aware of someone speaking to him from behind. It was Ripley. His voice sounded strained. "General, it's Speaker Atwater on the line. He says it's urgent."

McDivott swiveled in his chair. He made no effort to take the phone from Ripley's outstretched hand. "What does he want?"

"He won't say. Only that he has to speak with you immediately."

McDivott ignored the phone. Whatever the former acting President had to say was irrelevant. Fred Atwater was irrelevant. McDivott turned back to the console and the television screen. "Explain to me how this can be happening."

"It can't be," Ripley said. "Every link from that television station was cut. There was no possible way they could connect with the outside."

"Somebody just did the impossible. Why didn't Berg's people take them down when they had the chance?"

"Because you ordered them to hold off. They were waiting for the Jazzum."

"So they held off. And what happened? The site was supposed to be destroyed by the missile."

"The missile is still en route," said Ripley, glancing at his watch. "I'm giving the order to abort."

McDivott continued staring at the face in the screen. The face that was never supposed to be seen in public again. The usurper who wanted to bring America to its knees. The Paulsen woman represented everything he abhorred about socialists and their leftist agenda. If she were not removed, she would do irreparable damage to the United States.

"No," said McDivott.

Ripley looked at him in alarm. "Vance, we have to stop this. We can't go any further. Not with the whole world watching—"

"What happens next is God's will," said McDivott. He continued staring at the screen. "Let the missile do its job."

McDivott glanced up and saw Ripley staring at him. He'd seen that look before. It was the expression of a clerk, not a warrior. Warriors like Vance McDivott gave orders. Clerks like Ripley implemented them. The final battles were won by the warriors, not the clerks.

He turned his attention back to the television. The woman was still talking.

I am aware that my administration's efforts to reach a stable and lasting peace with the governments of Iran and North Korea have provoked intense controversy. I recognize the right of members of Congress and the media and the general public to express their dissent. I hereby promise that we will thoroughly review each of the new treaties which have been proposed. We will conduct public forums in which all aspects of the proposed treaties will be debated and examined. Only then, after thorough consideration and with the consent of Congress, will I take executive action.

<>

The Jazzum detected no interference ahead. No birds, no aircraft, no precipitation. Beneath the missile's nose swept the rolling green hills of southern Pennsylvania. The final act of the Jazzum's brief career was about to begin.

The Jazzum was climbing toward a tiny window two thousand feet in the sky east of Gettysburg. From this point in space, the missile would pivot downward at an angle of seventy-two degrees. The Jazzum knew the layout of the target—a building on the outskirts of the town. The structure had an irregular shape with the largest room in the center. Embedded in the Jazzum's operating memory were the coordinates of the room as well as an analysis of the roof material and thickness. The Jazzum had already calculated the detonation time of its warhead after penetrating the roof structure. The blast pattern would deploy down and outward with the approximate effect of a boot stomping an ant hill.

The reason for destroying the building was of no concern to the Jazzum. Just another human abstraction. The Jazzum's only concern was precision.

One minute.

The Jazzum entered target acquisition mode. Its control movements took on an enhanced, almost twitchy behavior, fine-tuning the missile's flight path to a programmed accuracy of .75 meters. Upward, through the invisible window in the sky, the Jazzum soared.

Then the plunge downward.

<>

And I respect the right—the duty, even—of our military leadership to speak their view and to express their disagreement with the proposed treaties. But our system of government, as expressed in our Constitution, clearly defines the military-civilian relationship.

<>

The face in the television screen was unmistakable. And troubling. What she was saying was even more troubling. The man standing at the console listened for another fifteen seconds. He asked, "Are you sure this is live?"

"Yes, sir," said the aide, an Air Force captain. "From Gettysburg, Pennsylvania."

The man nodded. Gettysburg was about four hundred miles away. The right distance. He turned back to the console. The datalink read-out was counting down. *55. 50. 45 . . .*

He thought about his conversation with McDivott. *We have considered all the ramifications of using the Jazzum in a domestic situation . . .*

The woman was still talking. Something about military leaders who had betrayed the trust placed in him. That the rule of law had been subverted. The man remembered McDivott's parting words. *Given the sensitivity of this mission, I won't divulge the specific nature of the target . . .*

A ripple of anger swept over Maj. Gen. Buzz Gavin. Twenty-eight years of honorable service. A drawer full of commendations for valor in combat. Gavin loved his country, which was why he had become a member of the organization known as Capella. But not for this.

Gavin turned his attention back to the datalink screen. The read-out was still counting down. *30 . . . 25 . . . 20 . . .*

His hand reached for the red guarded switch on the console.

<>

We may have differences about national policy, and we may disagree about the deployment of our military. But once the commander-in-chief has reached a decision and that decision has been ratified by Congress, it is the duty of the military leadership to respect that—

The explosion sounded like a thunderclap. The noise rattled the building, resonating through the walls, causing the pencil to hop around on the desk in front of Libby. She stopped speaking. The sound had been picked up on her microphone, then blasted back through her earbud. She knew that everyone watching was as startled as she was.

"What the hell?" she heard Cirilli blurt, also loudly enough to carry over the mike.

Seconds later came the noise of debris hitting the roof. It sounded like a hailstorm. Libby could hear the clatter of objects clanging off the tops of parked automobiles outside.

What next? she thought. This was turning into a Wagnerian opera. First the ominous sound from the adjoining room. Then thunder, followed by things raining down from heaven. Where was Jill? Where was Pete?

The camera was still on her. She saw her image in the monitor, flashing on and off. She looked frightened and speechless. Not the calming image of a President addressing her troubled countrymen.

This is what you do best, Brand had said. *You reassure people.*

The screen was still jiggling. Libby took a deep breath and looked directly into the camera.

<>

McDivott leaned forward in his chair. The sound of the explosion had been clearly audible. The image in the television was flashing on and off. McDivott knew what would happen next. The woman's face would abruptly vanish, replaced by a blank screen. Or a snow burst of random pixels. The camera feed would switch back to the network. Perplexed announcers would speculate about what happened until someone finally determined that neither the woman or the station from which she was speaking any longer existed.

McDivott kept his eyes on the screen. Nothing was changing. He waited. The image was still there. The flashing stopped. The woman was speaking again.

<>

Once my decision has been ratified by Congress, our differences must end. It is the duty of the military to respect that decision. That's the way our system of government works.

As President, I have always held the leadership of our armed forces in the highest regard. They are superbly qualified officers who have dedicated their lives to protecting our country. Almost without exception, they are loyal Americans who respect the role of the military in our civilian-led system of government. If it is determined that any of our military leaders have betrayed the trust placed in them, it is my duty to remove those disloyal members from our armed forces. And I will.

My fellow Americans, at this hour of crisis I ask for your unwavering support. We must reject this horrendous attempt to overthrow our system of government. With your help we will preserve the executive branch of our republic. Together we must turn back this vicious assault on our values. As your President, I promise you that I will fight to my last breath to fulfill my duty to you and to our great nation.

Thank you, and may God bless America.

<>

"General, you have calls waiting."

McDivott glanced over his shoulder. Ripley was holding the phone out to him again. "Speaker Atwater again," said Ripley, "and the Secretary of Defense, Senator Stroud, Mr. Reckson, half a dozen others."

McDivott shook his head. "Tell them I'll get back to them."

"Sir, I really think you should—"

"No, Jim. No calls. I'm working on something. I need to be alone."

Ripley started to protest, then caught himself. For a long moment he studied McDivott. "Very well, sir. I'll be in the duty room."

McDivott watched Ripley leave. He wondered what Ripley would do. Disappear? No, not Ripley. Clerk that he was, Jim Ripley still had a sense of honor. What would the other insiders do? They were good men, patriots who had cast their lot with Capella. Now their fate was uncertain. Whatever happened to them would be the responsibility of Vance McDivott.

McDivott tilted back in the office chair and gazed around the windowless room that had served as his command post. On his desk were framed photographs of his wife, a blonde socialite with a fetching smile, and his daughter, a pretty nineteen-year-old sophomore at Cornell. McDivott looked up at the face of Curtis LeMay. The old warhorse gazed back at him with what McDivott took to be an expression of approval. The look a warrior gave a bloodied comrade when their battle was nearing a finish. LeMay understood.

McDivott's eyes swept over the console that contained the encrypted communications links to every major command. He stared for a moment at the situation display where he had followed the hunt for Air Force One. Then he looked again at the flickering television monitor. A network announcer was on the screen. He was parsing the President's speech, talking about cabals, coups, removal of generals. McDivott heard his name being mentioned.

McDivott stopped listening. It no longer mattered. Since taking his oath at the Air Force Academy as a newly commissioned officer, he had been faithful to his principles. Patriotism, duty, faith in God—those were Vance McDivott's core values. He had demonstrated courage in the face of enemy fire. He had been prepared to sacrifice his life for his country.

And he still was.

McDivott pulled the ring of keys from inside the briefcase at his desk. He found the one that unlocked the bottom drawer of the desk. The Beretta was still in its holster, well oiled, ready for use. He hadn't carried it with him since his last combat tour. When was that? Afghanistan, he remembered. Over four years ago.

McDivott picked up the weapon, hefted it, checked the magazine. It was full. He slid the action back, pumped a nine mm. round into the chamber. He was in no hurry. For another two minutes he sat quietly, reflecting on the events that had brought him to this juncture. He had no regrets. He had fought the good fight. He had nothing to fear. It was the way of the warrior.

With that thought McDivott raised the Beretta to his temple.

<>

It was over.

Libby didn't move. The face of the announcer, Brian Smedley, was in the monitor.

Another voice came over her earbud. "Wow. That was . . . quite a speech, Madame President. The best I've ever heard you give." It was the network producer again. What was his name?

After a second it came to her.

"Thank you, Mr. Marks," said Libby. "Let's hope it had the intended result."

"Our phones haven't stopped ringing since the moment you went on the air. This is a historic moment."

Libby didn't feel like talking to Marks. She removed the earbud and the clip-on microphone. She gazed around the studio. Cirilli was looking at her as if noticing something he'd never seen before. He began clapping and the applause was joined by Hagen and Schneider. Libby smiled and gave them a bow of her head.

She felt oddly relaxed. It *was* a good speech. She knew it. Somehow she had risen above her fear, her feeling of inadequacy. Where had that come from? Was it just another act?

No. She was finished with acting. Be a *real* President, Brand had said. And so she had been. No speechwriter, no teleprompter, no staff. Without Jill Maitlin she had delivered the most important speech of her Presidency. *When you speak from the heart, it's not an act.* That's what she would do from now on. No more pretending. That included her relationship with Brand. Where would that go? She didn't know, but she knew where her heart was taking her. If the country didn't like it, let them impeach her.

She saw Sheriff Waller come through the door to the anteroom. He was holding what looked like a portable radio. "That's it," said the sheriff. "They're leaving."

Libby didn't understand. "Leaving? Who's leaving?"

"The Galeforce bunch. All of them. They're climbing into the helicopters. Two are gone already." Waller held up the radio. "Our radios are working again, and I've just been informed that the Pesties are on the way."

"Pesties?"

"Penn state police." Waller shook his head. "Right on cue. We handle the crisis, then the Pesties show up to take the credit."

"What was that explosion that shook the building?"

"Something—we don't have a clue what it was—blew up right

above the station. Scared the crap out of everyone. The pieces hit our cars and wounded one of my deputies."

"And that . . . other noise?"

Waller looked uncomfortable. He removed the broad-brimmed hat and ran his hand through his mane of graying hair. "Ma'am, something else happened," he said. "Something we didn't expect."

CHAPTER THIRTY-ONE

Two weeks later.

The Rose Garden is filled to capacity. Rows of folding chairs cover the neatly trimmed lawn. The reporters are poised, waiting for the President to finish the formal remarks before they can jump in with questions. Jennifer Rollins, newly installed in her job as White House Press Secretary, has already served notice that anyone who doesn't wait their turn will get hammered. Transgressors will find themselves barred from future press conferences.

It was Libby's choice to hold the press conference out here. For over a century the Rose Garden has been the warm weather venue for presidential announcements and ceremonies. Along the West Colonnade the tulips are in full bloom. Flowering magnolias punctuate each corner of the garden. The recently planted daffodils fill the beds on the north and south borders of the rectangular lawn. Libby loves the openness, the flood of colors, and especially the tempering effect the lush garden has on audiences. She will need all the tempering she can get today.

Libby turns her gaze back to the battery of television cameras and continues her remarks. "That we have emerged from the events of two weeks ago serves as testimony to the inherent strength of our system of government. As Americans have always done in times of crisis, we have become a more united people. If anything good has come from this terrible event, it is the knowledge that loyal and dedicated Americans are prepared to step up and defend our country."

Her plan is to keep the remarks short. Let the reporters ferret out the salient facts during the question and answer session. She is comfortable with that format, unlike earlier in her Presidency when she lived in fear of open press conferences. When she dreaded reporters and their gotcha questions. Particularly the Washington press corps, who have been notoriously vicious to the Paulsen administration.

She's over that. No longer does she feel intimidated by this crowd. Brand had it right. They weren't elected to run the country. You were.

She continues. "As you know, there have been numerous replacements and new appointments in our military and civilian branches. Some of these replacements are a result of the recent events. Some are simply routine appointments of persons I think are best suited to serve this administration. We've given explanations for some of the replacements, and beyond that I would request that you not draw inferences."

It is a futile request, of course. Drawing inferences is what the press lives for. Once they've scented blood, nothing will deter the hounds from the chase. By last count, ten of those present today have contracts for books on what they're calling "the cabal" and the "failed coup."

"So with these appointments," Libby says, "and with the realignment of our recent treaties with Iran and North Korea, this administration is embarking on a bold new path. I am grateful to the leaders of both parties for the prompt ratification of these amended treaties and for their timely confirmation of our new Vice President. This should send the clearest possible signal to our people—and to the rest of the world—that the United States is mending its wounds and has a brilliant future ahead. Thank you for your attention, ladies and gentlemen. I will now take questions."

Hands are popping up as if they were spring-loaded. Libby gives the nod to Walter Korick, whose forty-some years at the *Washington Post* give him seniority in the White House press corps.

Korick rises creakily to his feet. "Madame President, there is still a great deal of speculation about why you nominated Senator Karl Ozinsky for Vice President, even though Senator Ozinsky is not from your party. Especially since Speaker Fred Atwater was already the acting President during your . . . umm, absence from office. Wouldn't it have been a more logical—and unifying—gesture to name Mr. Atwater as your successor?"

Good, thinks Libby. Get that one over with. "Thank you, Walter, for the excellent question. But I want to correct something. By appointing a new Vice President, I was not, as you suggest, naming my successor. Though this may come as a disappointment to some of you, I have no intention of giving up this job."

A wave of laughter sweeps over the audience. Even old Korick is chuckling.

Libby goes on. "I fulfilled a constitutional responsibility by nominating Senator Ozinsky, who I happen to think would make a fine President." She pauses, then adds, "But not for several more years."

She has to wait again for the laughter to subside. The next question comes from Alice Townsend, veteran columnist for the *New York Times*. "Madame President, when you say 'several more years,' are you signaling that you intend to run for another term?"

Libby smiles. "No, Alice. I'm signaling that I intend to serve as President for as long as the American people want me to serve."

Libby sees the buzz flow through the audience. Townsend is nodding her head approvingly. Amazing, thinks Libby, what a crisis can do for your ratings. Three weeks ago, when her poll numbers were diving toward single digits, the notion of an extended Paulsen Presidency seemed unthinkable. Yesterday's Gallup showed Libby's numbers soaring through seventy percent. Even the stock market has voted its approval. After a short plunge following the failed coup attempt, the Dow has shot up over three hundred points.

Another reporter, Joe Gilstrap from the *Los Angeles Times*, takes his turn. "Madame President, you didn't really answer the question about Speaker Atwater. There are rumors that the Speaker might have been affiliated with the cabal that attempted to remove you from office. Was that a consideration in your decision not to nominate him as Vice President?"

Libby regards him for moment. Gilstrap has been one of her nastiest antagonists in the press. He is also one of the investigative reporters racing to get a book out. "Absolutely not," says Libby. "I am aware of the rumors and I can assure you that they have no validity whatsoever. I hold Speaker Atwater in the highest regard and know him to be an honorable statesman. I wish him continued success as a leader in the House of Representatives."

As she speaks, Libby catches the barely discernible nod from her newly appointed National Security Advisor. Jill Maitlin towers by a head over most of the staff and cabinet members standing off to the side. Jill's right arm is still in the sling. The bullet that ripped the flesh between her neck and shoulder had narrowly missed an artery. She will always wear an interesting scar as a memento of Gettysburg.

It was Jill Maitlin's idea to confront Atwater about the damaging photos of Libby and Pete Brand. If the Speaker had any interest in escaping trial as a co-conspirator with the members of Vance McDivott's cabal, he would surrender the photos and deny that they ever existed. Atwater had required fewer than five seconds to declare his agreement. Though he swore there were no other copies of the photos, Libby doesn't really believe him. In the final analysis, it doesn't matter. She no longer worries about what the media makes of her private life.

There are more questions, most pertaining to the conspiracy to remove Libby Paulsen from office. "As you know," Libby says, "the joint Congressional investigation panel has begun its work and it would be inappropriate for me to speculate on their findings. In a news conference tomorrow, the Attorney General will update you on the indictments he has sought. Some you already know about.

They are senior military officers as well as a number of civilians associated with the security contracting company called Galeforce. Several of these individuals, including General Ripley of the Joint Chiefs staff, have already turned themselves in, while a few others, like Mr. Berg, the former director of Galeforce, and Mr. Schlater, the former Deputy Director of our Secret Service, have not yet surrendered. I have no doubt that they will soon be in custody."

"Madame President," says Milly Watrous, Washington bureau chief for *Fox News*, "can you give us some details about your upcoming trip to the Middle East? It's been only two weeks since the disastrous trip when Air Force One was attacked. The public is wondering why you would want to fly again aboard another of the same aircraft."

Libby turns to the men and women on either side of her at the podium. They are the honorees to whom Libby has presented medals in the private ceremony thirty minutes ago in the East Room. Libby smiles at the slender man in the Air Force uniform with the colonel's eagles on his shoulders. "If you're asking whether I'm concerned about my safety," said Libby, "the answer is no. I have no worries whatsoever. One of the things I have learned is that Air Force One is flown by the most competent and professional crew in the world. Our Presidential Pilot has distinguished himself not only as a highly competent pilot but a courageous and professional officer. My staff and I look forward to flying many thousands of miles aboard Air Force One."

More reporters' hands are in the air, but Libby is still looking at the honorees lined up at the podium. For a long moment she holds eye contact with the woman in Air Force service dress uniform standing closest to her. Maj. Samantha Fornier, leaning on crutches and wearing her newly presented Air Force Cross, has surprised Libby with her attitude. Nothing, Sam Fornier declared, absolutely nothing would prevent her from regaining full use of her legs. She has mountains to climb, trails to hike, marathons to run. To hell with crutches. Libby believes her.

Standing with Sam Fornier is a beaming Ben Waller, resplendent in his five-starred sheriff's uniform and his newly received Presidential Medal of Freedom. Beside him is Secret Service agent Vic Kreier, also wearing the Medal of Freedom, as is Melvin Hagen, looking disheveled as ever in his coat and tie. Standing at the end are the newly promoted Presidential Pilot, Col. Lou Batchelder, and Chief Master Sergeant Roy Switzer. Air Force Crosses dangle from both men's jackets.

Looking more solemn is the group standing in a row to Libby's left. The petite, dark-haired widow of Gen. Jack Cassidy is clutching the Air Force Cross that Libby has presented. Cassidy's two daughters stand on either side of their mother, unable to hold back their tears. The families of the four Secret Service agents gunned down in the doorway of Air Force One are gathered in a small cluster, holding their medals. The large extended family of Col. Joe Morganti—children, siblings, half a dozen nieces and nephews—stand in a protective huddle around Morganti's widow.

Libby turns back to the reporters. A man in the third row, Merle Simmons from *NBC News*, is waving his hand. "Your turn, Mr. Simmons," Libby says.

"Madame President," says Simmons, "there has been no mention of the former Presidential Pilot, Colonel Peter Brand. Can you comment on that?"

Libby doesn't answer right away. She clasps her hand tighter around the hard object in her right hand. The cross has a smooth satin finish. Against her palm she can feel the center of the cross, a gold eagle encircled by a laurel wreath. Libby believes that she is drawing strength from the medal.

She looks at Simmons. "As you know, the death of Colonel Brand has saddened all of us. He will be missed. . ." Libby pauses.

Don't let them see you cry. Brand told her that once. And she hasn't. Not since the service three days ago at Arlington where, beneath a glorious blue sky, standing beside the flag-draped casket while the bugler sounded Taps, Libby whispered her goodbye to

Pete Brand. And her tears had flowed for all to see.

Libby clears her throat and continues. "He will be missed by all of us who knew him. Colonel Brand was one of the honorees at the private ceremony we conducted earlier in the East Room. Because he left no immediate relatives to receive his Air Force Cross, it was appropriate that I, as President, accept the medal on his behalf." Libby squeezes the medal tighter in her fist.

The reporter isn't finished. "Madame President, as you know, there has been speculation in some quarters that you and Colonel Brand may have been . . . particularly close. Would you care to address that subject?"

Simmons is a cobra, Libby thinks. But she has learned about cobras. She no longer fears them. She looks directly at the reporter. "I'm aware of the speculation, Mr. Simmons. For the record, I would not be standing here if it were not for the bravery and skill of Colonel Brand. Nor would several other people with me today, including the new National Security Advisor." Libby glances to her right. Jill Maitlin gives her a nod and look of understanding.

Libby continues. "On more than one occasion I trusted Colonel Brand with my life, and that trust was not misplaced. So, yes, Mr. Simmons, in that context it is correct to say that Colonel Brand and I had a special bond."

The reporter is nodding his head. Libby sees several others scribbling notes. She has no doubt that her remarks will fuel more speculation. The gossip columnists and tabloid writers will run with it. Let them. The personal lives of Presidents are fair game, and there is no reason Libby Paulsen should be excepted. It goes with the job. *When you speak from the heart, it's not an act.* Well, she had spoken from the heart. And it wasn't an act.

Libby knows her grieving isn't over. In her rare moments of aloneness, she will find herself dwelling on what might have been. On the future they might have had. She spoke the truth to Simmons. She and Pete Brand had a special bond. They always will.

Libby will take one more question. She nods to Bernard Weaver, columnist for the *Boston Globe*. Weaver stands and says, "Madame President, as you know, certain members of Congress as well as media spokespersons are urging you to exercise leniency for the conspirators as a way of mending the nation's wounds. How do you feel about that?"

Libby fixes her gaze on Weaver. Like every other reporter here, he knows exactly how she feels. "As I have already made clear," Libby says, "the conspiracy known as Capella has committed heinous and treasonable crimes against this nation. As commander-in-chief I would be derelict in my duty if I did not insure that these perpetrators are prosecuted to the fullest extent of military and civil law."

Libby knows that her voice has taken a hard, almost combative tone. It reflects her feeling about those who plotted against the government. Her combativeness has been noticed by columnists, including Bernard Weaver, who have lately been referring to her as the "Iron Lady." She wonders whether they notice the irony. They are the same columnists who, a few weeks ago, were describing Libby Paulsen as weak-willed and vacillating.

Today Weaver sounds respectful. "Madame President, will there be any consideration of clemency for those in the chain of command who claim they were only following the orders of their senior officers?"

Libby nods. "We will never condone or pardon high crimes on the premise that the criminals were acting in the line of duty. Or in the name of patriotism. Or that they were simply following orders. As Americans we must hold ourselves to a higher standard. And yes, Mr. Weaver, I am aware that some members of the military and government agencies may have executed orders without knowledge of the intended consequences. As each of these cases is adjudicated, I will consider clemency where it is appropriate."

Which is all she intends to say on the subject. Clemency comes too close to forgiveness, something she will extend sparingly. Just as she has forgiven Jill Maitlin, she may in time forgive others. Some she will never forgive.

For several seconds there is no response from the audience. Then comes a ripple of applause, swelling in volume. One after another the members of the audience are rising to their feet. The sprawling lawn of the Rose Garden is filled with standing, applauding reporters. Libby looks at them in astonishment. Who would have imagined? Who would have thought the hard-bitten Washington press corps would give anyone, especially Libby Paulsen, a standing ovation?

The applause continues for a full minute. When the audience is again seated, Libby turns to speak directly to the television cameras. "My fellow Americans, a year and a half has passed since I was sworn in as your President. Today I reaffirm for you the oath I took when I entered office. You have my solemn promise that I will, to the best of my ability, continue to preserve, protect, and defend the Constitution of the United States. So help me God."

For a long moment she stands with her chin tilted up. She gazes out at her audience. This time there is no applause, no cheering, just respectful silence. Clasping Brand's medal tightly in her hand, President Libby Paulsen turns from the podium and strides back into the White House.

ACKNOWLEDGMENTS

For this book I am indebted to the formidable Block literary team. Friend, novelist, fellow aviator, and master story engineer Tom Block has my thanks for his invaluable technical and editorial assistance. Separate thanks and a big hug to Sharon Block for her eagle-eyed proof reading and forthright critique of the work in progress.

Cover photo credit: MarchCattle/Shutterstock.com

ROBERT GANDT is a former naval officer, international airline captain, and an award-winning military and aviation writer. He is the author of more than a dozen books, including the novels *The Killing Sky* and *Black Star Rising* and the definitive work on modern naval aviation, *Bogeys and Bandits*. His screen credits include the television series *Pensacola: Wings of Gold*. His acclaimed account of the Battle for Okinawa, *The Twilight Warriors* (Broadway Books, 2010) was the winner of the Samuel Eliot Morison Award for Naval Literature. He and his wife, Anne, live in the Spruce Creek Fly-In, an aviation community in Daytona Beach, Florida. Visit his website at www.gandt.com

Made in the USA
Charleston, SC
06 July 2014